Praise for the novels of Debra Webb

"A hot hand with action, suspense and last, but not least, a steamy relationship."
—*New York Times* bestselling author Linda Howard

"Debra Webb's name says it all."
—*New York Times* bestselling author Karen Rose

"Compelling main characters and chilling villains elevate Debra Webb's Faces of Evil series to the realm of high-intensity thrillers that readers won't be able to resist."
—*New York Times* bestselling author CJ Lyons

"A well-crafted, and engrossing thriller. Debra Webb has crafted a fine, twisting thriller to be savored and enjoyed."
—*New York Times* bestselling author Heather Graham on *Traceless*

"A steamy, provocative novel with deep, deadly secrets guaranteed to be worthy of your time."
—*Fresh Fiction* on *Traceless*

"Debra Webb's best work yet. The gritty, edge-of-your-seat, white-knuckled thriller is peopled with tough, credible characters and a brilliant plot that will keep you guessing until the very end."
—*New York Times* bestselling author Cindy Gerard on *Obsession*

"Interspersed with fine-tuned suspense...the cliffhanger conclusion will leave readers eagerly anticipating future installments."
—*Publishers Weekly* on *Obsession*

"Webb reaches into our deepest nightmares and pulls out a horrifying scenario. She delivers the ultimate villain."
—*RT Book Reviews* on *Dying to Play*

Also by Debra Webb

MIRA Books

Shades of Death

The Blackest Crimson
No Darker Place

Harlequin Intrigue

Faces of Evil

Dark Whispers
Still Waters

Look for Debra Webb's next novel

A DEEPER GRAVE

available soon from MIRA Books.

For additional books by Debra Webb,
visit her website at www.debrawebb.com.

DEBRA WEBB

NO DARKER PLACE

MIRA

MIRA

Recycling programs for this product may not exist in your area.

ISBN-13: 978-0-7783-1983-2

No Darker Place

Copyright © 2017 by Debra Webb

Every day is a gift. Every moment of life should be appreciated and never taken for granted. But life can be hard sometimes. Sometimes it can take us to very dark places. During those times having someone to hold your hand, to simply stand beside you is an incredible blessing. This book is dedicated to my amazing husband. During more than four decades of marriage we have enjoyed many wonderful times and a few not so wonderful. Not once has he wavered. He has gone to every dark place with me and held my hand, giving me strength in the most difficult of times. Nonie, I will always love you.

NO
DARKER
PLACE

Acknowledgments

When I was a little girl my grandmother would tell me the most intriguing ghost stories. I'm convinced she is the reason I love creating stories filled with mystery and suspense today. Mary Talkington Proctor, my grandmother, was small in stature and big in heart. She washed clothes by hand, cooked on a woodstove and always spoke her mind. Though she never lived or visited more than a few miles beyond her birthplace, her imagination wandered far and wide. I will always miss her and cherish the memories we made together.

Born and raised in small town Alabama, I love writing stories set here. When I chose Montgomery for the Shades of Death series the first of many research trips was scheduled. My dear friend Lisa Day played the part of chauffeur and assistant. Despite the occasional foray into dubious territory, we had an amazing time. Lisa is the kind of friend every woman should have—reliable, honest and simply awesome.

There are many people I want to thank. Officer Frederick J. Brewer for rescuing us that very first night in Montgomery when we had a flat tire. Thanks to Terry at Firestone for getting us squared away the next morning. A big thanks to Chief Bryan and Captain Atchison of the Montgomery Sheriff's Office; and a special thanks to Lieutenant Barnes and Lieutenant Dean of the Montgomery Police Department.

As always I can't imagine taking this journey without the amazing Marijane Diodati, who is relentless and incredible and I adore her. A big shout-out to my fantastic Street Team—truly good friends and the absolute best cheerleaders. A very special thanks to Denise Zaza for always believing in me.

Finally, please know that any errors or additions to the facts are mine and mine alone. Authors sometimes take creative license when writing a story. For instance, a coroner's office and an FBI field office might be added to the setting. Certainly any inspiration for characters is always taken from the very best of those I encounter and the very worst my twisted mind can conjure! Happy reading!

Over and over she cursed herself for the path she chose to take.

The pain a reminder of those devastated for her sake.

One

"What other dungeon is so dark as one's own heart!"

—Nathaniel Hawthorne

Vaughn Road, Montgomery, Alabama
Friday, August 26, 10:30 a.m.

Detective Bobbie Gentry wiped the sweat from her brow with the back of her hand. Despite the early hour she was melting right here on the sidewalk like a forgotten ice-cream cone. The weather forecast called for a high of 101 today—the same kind of record-breaking temps the capital city had been experiencing for fifteen grueling days in a row.

The line of thunderstorms that had swept through about the same time her phone rang that morning hadn't helped one bit. Steam rose from the simmering asphalt, disappearing into the underbellies of the blue-and-white Montgomery PD cruisers lining the sidewalk. The meteorologist who'd insisted milder temps were on the way had seriously overestimated the cool front accompanying this morning's storm. The rain had done nothing but ramp up the suffocating humidity.

She'd been a cop for ten years, a detective for seven of those, and she'd learned the hard way that relentless heat made people crazy. Like the father of four currently holed up in the modest ranch-style home across the street.

Carl Evans had no criminal record whatsoever—not even a parking ticket. According to his wife, the checkup he'd had three months ago showed him to be in good health. Their middle daughter had been diagnosed with a form of childhood leukemia a year ago, and they'd gone through a serious financial crisis a couple of months back, but both issues were under control now. The husband had no problems at work as far as his wife knew.

And yet he'd arrived home at two this morning with no explanation for where he'd been and with no desire to discuss his uncharacteristic behavior. At seven, he'd climbed out of bed, promptly corralled all four of his children into one bedroom and told his wife to call the police.

Bobbie's radio crackled. "No go. I'm coming out," vibrated across the airwaves.

"Son of a bitch," she muttered as crisis negotiator Sergeant Paul York exited the house and double-timed it to her side of the police barrier. York was a small, wiry man of five-eight or so, the same height as her. His less intimidating size and kind, calming presence made him damned good at his job as a facilitator of nonviolent resolutions. Those same traits, however, belied his unquestionable ability to take charge of a situation and physically contain the threat when the need arose.

"What happened?" she demanded, bracing her hands on her hips. She was not going to have a hostage die on her watch. The fear she refused to allow a foothold kept reminding her that these hostages were children.

This wouldn't be the first time you allowed a child to die.

Not going to happen today.

"He won't talk to me." York tugged at his black tie, his gray shirt still crisp despite the rising humidity and immeasurable frustration. "His wife refuses to leave the house as long as the kids are in there."

"Who can blame her?" Bobbie exhaled a blast of exasperation. Before York had arrived on the scene, she'd spoken to Mrs. Evans by phone. Anna Evans insisted she had no idea what had set off her husband. To her knowledge, he had never owned a weapon, much less used one. He was a CPA at Latimer, Latimer and Burton, for Christ's sake. He'd worked there since he graduated from Vanderbilt two decades ago. His wife was completely stunned by his actions.

"Did he give you any idea what he wants?" Bobbie needed something here. Evans surely had a goal he hoped to attain or a statement to make. How the hell could a purportedly humble CPA cause this damned much trouble?

"He wouldn't say a word." York's lips flattened as he shook his head. "Not a single word."

SWAT Commander Zeke Miller held up his hands as if he'd experienced an epiphany. "We're wasting time. He could kill those children while we're standing out here with our thumbs up our asses. It's time *we* went in."

Bobbie rolled her eyes. What was he thinking? The polar opposite of York, Miller was a big, muscular guy with an ego to match. His reputation for playing hard and fast was well-known, but this was her crime scene, and she wasn't going the guns-blazing route. At least not yet.

"And get those kids killed for sure?" Bobbie argued, ignoring the fear gnawing at the edge of her bravado. "Evans has them standing around him in a huddle. Your guys can't get a clear shot at him. A flash bang could freak him out and prompt a shooting spree. And you want to go charging in there?" She folded her arms over her chest and lifted her chin, daring him to challenge her assessment. "Is it just me, or is there something seriously wrong with that scenario?"

Miller glowered at her, but neither he nor York had a ready response for her assessment. There was no easy way to do this, and everyone present understood that unfortunate fact.

"Where the hell is Newton?" Miller demanded. "We need a senior detective on the scene. Are you even cleared for a situation like this, Gentry?"

Despite the fury his words ignited, Bobbie smiled.

This chauvinistic hothead was not going to get the better of her when four children's lives depended on her staying calm and collected. "My partner's daughter is getting married this weekend, so he's not here. You've got me, and I'm as fit for duty as you, Miller. Deal with it."

His arrogant sneer warned he wasn't going to let it go so easily.

"We got movement at the front door!" a uniform shouted.

Renewed adrenaline rushing through her veins, Bobbie turned toward the house as the front door slowly opened. *Please let it be the children coming out.* As much as she wanted everyone present to believe she was as strong as she once was and that she had everything under control…doubt nagged at her. What if she failed? What if someone died— again—because of her mistakes?

No looking back. Focus, Bobbie.

Barefoot and wearing a white terry-cloth robe, Anna Evans stepped cautiously onto the narrow porch, her hands raised high and her red hair tousled as if she hadn't combed it since climbing out of bed. Her face was as white as the robe she wore. She was immediately surrounded by Montgomery PD uniforms and ushered across the street.

"One less potential victim," Bobbie muttered. What the devil was this guy doing? He'd made no demands. He refused to interact with the negotiator. Any time a perp took a hostage and waved around a weapon, he wanted something.

The distant ache in her skull that had started the minute she'd received the call expanded into a dull throb. She resisted the urge to yank free the clasp holding her long brown hair off her shoulders so she could massage the pain away. No need to illustrate to all present that her headaches were still around. The whole department already watched her every move to see if she would crack under the stress. No matter that she had been back to work for four weeks without falling down on the job, she was still the detective who had shattered like delicate, handblown glass thrown against a wall seven months ago. The whole damned world knew that a couple of surgeons and shrinks, as well as a good half of the year, had been required to put her back together again.

Stay sharp, Bobbie. No letting the past intrude.

Once behind the police barricade, the uniforms released Anna Evans, and she almost collapsed on the pavement before they could catch hold of her again.

"We need a medic," Bobbie shouted. She moved toward the woman. "Are you injured, Mrs. Evans?"

She shook her head, her eyes red and swollen from hours of crying. "Are you Detective Gentry?"

"Yes, ma'am. We spoke on the phone a little while ago." The woman appeared unharmed and reasonably composed for a terrified mother. *Let this be a good sign.*

Anna Evans drew in a shuddering breath. "He says he'll let the children go if you—" her pleading gaze latched on to Bobbie's "—come inside and talk to him."

"I can do that." The sooner those kids were out of harm's—

"The hell you say!" Miller roared. "That's all we need is another hostage in there!"

"Hold up, Miller." York turned to Bobbie. "We can do this," he offered in the modulated tone negotiators were trained to use. "I'll go in with you."

While Miller launched another protest, Anna Evans hugged her arms around her trembling body and moved her head adamantly from side to side. "He said you have to come alone, Detective Gentry. Unarmed and alone."

"Not going to happen, Bobbie," York stated, his voice hard now. "You're—"

Bobbie held up a hand for both men to shut up. "Did he say anything else, Mrs. Evans?"

Fresh tears welled in her puffy eyes. She shook her head. "Just that he…he would let the children go. Please." She wrung her hands together in front of her as if she intended to pray. "Don't let my babies get hurt."

Bobbie removed her service weapon from its holster at her waist and passed it to York. "I'm going in."

"I'm calling Chief Peterson," Miller warned. "The rest of the department might believe that you being his college buddy's daughter and all gives you free rein in this town, but I don't. You'll play this by the rules exactly like the rest of us."

His accusation made Bobbie want to unleash the volatile emotions simmering just beneath the surface of her carefully schooled facade. Montgomery was the second-largest city in the state, but the department was like a small village. There were few secrets. Eventually everyone got the lowdown on everyone else—especially as it related to the chain of command or any perceived special favors. She'd understood from day one that the time would come when someone would have the balls to say those words to her face.

Bobbie snatched her cell from her belt and offered it to him. "Go ahead, Miller. Call the chief. He's in my favorites list under Uncle Teddy."

"Enough of that nonsense," York growled, his fierce gaze focused on Miller.

Since Miller didn't take her up on her offer, Bobbie snapped her phone back onto her belt. "I'm going in."

"Think about what you're doing, Bobbie," York called after her. Next to him, Miller made good on his threat and put through the call on his own cell.

Bobbie didn't look back. She headed across the street. If any hope whatsoever existed that Evans would let those children go, she was willing to take the risk. A twinge of pain twisted in her right leg and started to keep time with the throb in her head. She ignored it. She would do some extra stretches tonight before her run.

Assuming she was still alive. As long as she got those kids out of there little else mattered.

*If you get yourself killed, who's going to get
him then?*

She hushed the nagging voice as she hustled up
the sidewalk. At the end of the block, television
cameras and the eagle eyes of reporters would be
straining to see what Montgomery's most damaged
detective was doing next. Let them gawk. She didn't
care what they wrote about her.

Shouldering the weight of York, Miller and the
rest watching, she opened the front door and slipped
into the living room. The interior was as quiet as
a tomb. One would never know that half a dozen
MPD cruisers, a SWAT van and crisis negotiation
vehicle, along with a horde of reporters, were on the
street. Not to mention two ambulances prepared to
provide medical care if the shit hit the fan.

As she crossed the living room and entered the
hall, she called out to the man responsible for all
the excitement this sweltering summer morning.
"Mr. Evans, it's Detective Gentry."

She paused at the door to the first bedroom on
the left. Oddly, the man had chosen a bedroom at
the front of the house, giving SWAT a reasonably
clean view between the slats of the partially open
blinds. Had he planned on committing suicide by
cop and chickened out at the last minute?

*Never take a gun in your hand unless you've got
the guts to use it.* The words of wisdom her father
had shared so often after she announced her intent
to follow in his career-cop footsteps echoed inside
her. If they were all lucky, Evans lacked the courage

to use the weapon he'd waved around at his wife. Shielding himself with the children was certainly the act of a coward.

"I'm here to talk, like you asked," she reminded him when Evans failed to respond. She wiped her sweating palms against her trousers and braced for his move.

The doorknob turned, and Bobbie held very still, her breath stalling just shy of her lungs. The steel of the backup piece strapped to her ankle suddenly felt hot as blazes and far too heavy.

A small face peered up at her from the narrow crack made by the barely open door. Bobbie's heart fractured as memories of another child she couldn't bear to think about attempted to intrude. Seeing this little boy's face sent a jolt of urgency through her. What was this guy doing? How could he risk the lives of his own children?

Like you have room to talk.

"Come in," Evans called, "and I'll send the children out."

The little boy drew the door open wider, and she stepped into the bedroom. She confirmed the four children—three girls and one boy, all still dressed in their pajamas, trembling and red-faced from crying—appeared to be uninjured. Her tension eased marginally. The walls of the room were a soft pink. The twin beds were unmade, cartoon character bedcovers hanging this way and that. Dolls and a plastic tea set littered the floor. In the center of the room, between the two beds, the children stood in that ominous circle around their father. She easily spotted the daughter with the health issue; she was thinner and paler than the others. After numerous rounds of cancer treatments, she'd lost her hair, but it was growing back now and was almost as long as her little brother's. *Poor kid.* Evans should be ashamed of himself for putting her through this kind of bullshit.

Booting aside her anger for the moment, Bobbie lifted the sides of her jacket from her torso. "I'm unarmed just like you requested, Mr. Evans."

The small boy, three or four years old maybe, who'd opened the door stood next to the huddle, staring at Bobbie. She purposely kept her attention away from him. Those memories of another little boy, not much younger, kept whispering through her mind.

Can't look. Can't look.

When Evans said nothing, she gently prompted, "It's time to make good on your promise and let the children go, Mr. Evans." It would go a long way in turning this crappy day around if the guy stuck by his word. She might even be able to breathe again, and maybe the world would stop expecting her to fail every time the pressure was on.

Ten endless seconds passed before he spoke. "First, close the blinds," he ordered.

Bobbie walked to the window and did as he asked. Miller would go ballistic and the no-more-negotiations clock would start ticking louder. She hoped like hell Evans understood he was on borrowed time.

"What now?" Careful to keep her hands up, Bobbie readied to tackle Evans. So far she hadn't spotted his weapon.

"Go outside and wait with your mother," he said to the children.

The older girl reached for the small boy's hand and herded the others out the door. When the sound of the front door slamming behind them echoed through the house, Bobbie felt as if an elephant had been lifted off her chest. Sensing the shift in her tension, Evans lifted the .38 clutched in his right hand and aimed it at her.

Take it slow. Get him talking. "How can I help you, Mr. Evans? We all want to see a favorable resolution to this situation. Your wife and children need you."

Carl Evans was a tall, thin man. He sat cross-legged on the floor in his T-shirt and boxers. His face was pasty from the long hours at the office; his shoulders sagged from slumping over a desk. As if he felt the weight of her assessment, he sank back against the bed behind him. What had taken this forty-three-year-old number cruncher down this ugly path?

He shook his head. "It's too late for happily-ever-afters, Detective."

"It's never too late, Mr.—"

"Just listen," he cut her off. "I don't have much time. What I did was...*wrong.*"

No shit. "Tell me what happened, and maybe I can help."

"You need to listen!" He jerked at the loud sound of his own voice reverberating in the small room.

Bobbie's tension cranked up a few more notches. "Okay. Okay. I'm listening."

"It was necessary." He shook his head, tears slipping down his cheeks. "I didn't stop to consider how it would end."

The muzzle of the weapon angled downward as he spoke, his attention shifting inward. All she had to do was keep him talking, and when his aim strayed far enough, she would make a move. Less than four feet separated them. *Keep talking, pal.*

"I did what I had to do," he said, his voice resolute even as his hands shook. "I would do it again. Anything to save my little girl." He fell silent for another moment. "I didn't think you would be hurt—not really, I mean. I had no idea…"

Bobbie's attention swung from the muzzle to the man's face. "Me?"

His lips quivered. "I was desperate. The treatments for my daughter had taken everything. My credit options were maxed out. The house is already triple mortgaged. I couldn't pay for the new treatments, and my family was going to be homeless." His head moved from side to side with a weariness and resignation that were palpable. "The insurance company claimed the new treatments—the ones that might save her life—are experimental, so they won't pay. I would have done anything." He searched her face as if looking for understanding, his eyes glimmering with emotion. "I had no choice."

"You love your children. No one can fault you for that, Mr. Evans." She felt badly for the family, especially for the kid, but the man wasn't making a whole lot of sense. What did this have to do with her? "What can I do to help?"

He scrubbed his face with his free hand. A sob tore loose from his throat. "I need my family to know it was for them. Tell my wife I checked the life insurance policies. She and the kids will be okay."

Oh hell. "I'll make sure they know," Bobbie promised. "But, Mr. Evans, whatever trouble you're in, you don't have to do this. Your family needs you. *I* can help you."

His shoulders stiffened, and he steadied his aim at her. Anticipation coiled in her muscles.

"You can't help me. *You* are the reason he came looking for me."

Suddenly there was not enough air in the room. "Who came looking for you, Mr. Evans?"

"He's coming for you, Detective Gentry."

A chill as cold as ice settled in her belly. "Who's coming?"

His gaze, clouded with defeat, locked on hers. "He was right. Your eyes are the palest blue I've ever seen."

A shudder quaked through her before she could grab back control. *How could he know that?* Her mouth went so dry she could scarcely form the words. "I don't understand, Mr. Evans." Her heart rammed harder and harder against her sternum. "Who're you talking about?"

"He said he has to finish your story."

The words rocked her with the strength of hurricane-force winds. He couldn't mean...

"This is the end of my story." Evans jammed the .38 into his mouth.

Bobbie lunged for the weapon. She needed him alive.

The bullet exploded from its chamber, charging through his skull. Blood and brain matter sprayed the pink-and-white cartoon character comforter and matching sheets.

She dropped to her knees. "Jesus Christ."

Deep breath. Bobbie shook her head. Torn between desolation and elation. Seven long months she had waited, and finally *he* was here.

But why like this? Her chest ached with the agony brought against the Evans family.

Why drag anyone else into her private hell? To shock her? Fury hardened her against the softer emotions.

Blood trickled from Evans's mouth and nose. *Poor bastard.* Bobbie closed her eyes and tried to banish the image from her retinas.

The front door banging against the wall announced SWAT's entrance into the house. Bobbie got to her feet. It made her sick that a man had died, leaving behind a wife and children, to serve the whims of the psychopath who had already destroyed too many lives.

She drew in a deep breath as determination roared through her. Now it seemed he was back, and it was her turn to destroy his life. He just didn't know that part yet. Anticipation joined the determination.

Come and get me, you son of a bitch.

Montgomery Police Department
320 North Ripley Street, 6:45 p.m.

"The chief is ready to see you now."

Bobbie stood. She'd flipped through every magazine in the lobby during her twenty-seven-minute wait. Apparently Chief of Police Theodore Peterson wasn't concerned that she had other things to do, like hound the lab to see if they had gleaned anything from Evans's computer. Or maybe conduct the interview with the one unavailable colleague who would be returning from business in Birmingham in about half an hour.

"Thank you, Stella." Bobbie flashed a smile and headed for the door to the top cop's inner sanctum.

Her time was being wasted because the SWAT commander had tattled on her for making him look bad. *Arrogant bastard.* Miller had probably blown the whole incident out of proportion. She had Miller's number. He didn't like having women—especially a younger woman—order him around. If her partner had been the one going into that house, no one would have said a word. Some things never changed.

"Bobbie!" The chief tossed a report aside as she walked in. "Close the door and have a seat."

"Yes, sir." She did as he asked, settling in one of the two chairs in front of his desk. She worked hard to appear relaxed, but inside about a half a dozen emotions were battling for her attention. The Storyteller had sent her a message. He was back. *Finally.* For months she had worried that he'd slipped beyond her grasp. The idea of him escaping was unbearable. She could not allow that to happen.

"We need to talk."

Bobbie snapped her attention back to the chief. Theodore Peterson was a towering hulk of a man. He'd been a lineman for the Crimson Tide with her father under Coach Paul "Bear" Bryant. Forty years later, he'd lightened his playing physique by a few pounds and his hair had gone from blond to gray. Still, Theodore—Teddy to his family and closest friends—was an intimidating figure and a genuinely handsome man. As chief of police he was respected by friends and enemies alike. Even those who disagreed with him couldn't argue with his outstanding record of keeping the citizens of Montgomery safe and happy at the same time. Not an easy feat.

He removed his reading glasses and studied her for a moment. Tension trickled through Bobbie. She had known this man her whole life. The deep frown lines he wore told her he was far from pleased at the moment.

"I'm having trouble with this one, Bobbie."

"I'm not following, Chief." *Don't let him see what he can't possibly know.* Other than relaying the message to his wife, she hadn't told anyone what Evans said to her. The Storyteller's message was meant for her alone.

"According to your statement, Mr. Evans asked you to convey his regrets to his family."

"Yes, sir. He did."

"Had you and Mr. Evans met before?"

Bobbie shook her head. "Not to my knowledge. I did speak with his wife when I first arrived on the scene. She probably mentioned my name, which would explain why he asked for me."

The chief grunted a noncommittal response. Dread started a slow churn in her belly.

"Clearly Mr. Evans suffered some sort of breakdown," she added for good measure.

"Clearly," the chief agreed. He picked up the paper he'd moments ago put aside. "Based on this report from the lab, I have reason to believe any detective on the scene would have had to round you up for Mr. Evans."

Well damn. She'd been pacing the floor waiting for news from the lab. She'd hoped to see it before anyone else for exactly the reason the chief no doubt now understood. Carl Evans's actions hadn't been any more random than his request for her presence had been. "Is that the report on Mr. Evans's computer?"

The chief nodded. "Evans's first cousin is a nurse. You might remember her, Gwen Adams?"

Surprise registered before Bobbie could suppress the reaction. "Of course I remember her." Frustration threatened to resurrect the headache she'd suffered earlier. Or maybe it was just hearing the name. Gwen Adams was the private nurse who had taken care of Bobbie all those months as she recovered. What did Gwen have to do with any of this? Bobbie hadn't seen her in four or five weeks, not since the day before the orthopedist signed off on her release to return to work. "Has she been interviewed?"

"We're trying to locate her now. She's not answering her cell or home phone. Since she didn't show up for her shift at the hospital today, we've issued a BOLO."

A new thread of tension wove its way through Bobbie. Choosing her words carefully, she shrugged as if she didn't see how Gwen's absence and Evans's suicide connected. Frankly, she didn't...*yet*. "How is she involved? Is she helping with the little girl who has leukemia?" Valid questions.

"According to Evans's wife, Adams has been immensely helpful during their daughter's illness." He waved the paper. "But that doesn't explain the troubling aspect of this report."

Bobbie consciously relaxed her shoulders once more, and then her facial muscles. Whatever Forensics found on that computer, her only reactions could be surprise and disbelief. She hoped the chief was about to give her something she could use rather than more questions. Deep inside a new fear trickled its way into her bones. *Don't let Gwen be in trouble.*

"Evans's most recent internet search history showed he had been reading everything he could find on *you*, Bobbie."

Bobbie pretended to mull over the news, and then she turned her hands up in a so-what gesture. "Who hasn't? I've been the local freak show for a while now. Returning to the job put my name back in the news. Gwen probably mentioned me."

"Your medical records—specifically the ones from this year," the chief went on, his tone reflecting his unhappiness with her indifferent attitude, "were on his computer. We believe those records were provided to him by Adams."

Damn. Bobbie blinked and hummed a sound she hoped suggested confusion rather than the slow, icy climb of uncertainty up her backbone. "Maybe Evans intended to sell info about me to some reporter or one of those publishers who's been pestering me about a book deal." She lifted one shoulder in a stilted attempt at a shrug. "I can't see Gwen being involved in something like that."

The chief nodded. "Those were my first thoughts, considering around the same time he transferred the files to one of those personal cloud storage services, a one-hundred-thousand-dollar deposit was made into his bank account."

Bobbie gave another wooden shrug. "Well, there you have it. The man had a sick child, and he needed money. Is there any way to tell who bought the files?"

Her blood pounded in her ears. *It was him!* Any

doubts she had were gone now. One way or another she would make him pay for what he had done to her…for all the lives he had destroyed. She would not rest until he was dead.

Again the chief studied her for several seconds before responding. "Mrs. Evans mentioned something her husband said this morning that we believe sheds a little light on the other party involved—the buyer."

Anna Evans had been too devastated at the scene to give a statement. Whatever the chief had learned, he couldn't possibly know what Evans said to Bobbie before blowing his brains out.

"Before getting up this morning Evans tossed and turned, according to his wife. He kept muttering the same phrase over and over. *He wants to finish her story.*"

Bobbie flinched. *Damn it.* She clenched her jaw against the anticipation, fury and determination twisting inside her. *Do not let him see.*

"That's it?" the chief demanded, making no attempt to hide his outrage. "No shock? No anger or fear? Just a little tic?"

"The whole country was privy to what happened to me," she fired back. "Carl Evans as well as everyone else in Montgomery had it shoved down their throats day in and day out for months." *Deep breath, Bobbie.* One by one she quieted the emotions pressing against her chest. And then, more calmly, she added, "I don't know what you want me to say."

"You might start with what Evans said to you in that house." His gaze narrowed with blatant suspicion. "What he *really* said."

"If you've read my report, you know what he said." She hoped he couldn't see the lie in her eyes. This man had known Bobbie her entire life.

The chief folded his hands atop his desk and sighed loudly. "I promised your father on his deathbed that if you ever needed anything, I would make sure you were taken care of." Bobbie opened her mouth to protest his use of the father card, but his sharp glare had her snapping it shut once more. "Eight months ago Gaylon Perry almost killed you. If he's back…"

The air evacuated her lungs. Just hearing his name spoken aloud set off a chain reaction of voices, sounds and images that rushed rapid-fire through her mind before she could block them. Not a day—not an hour—passed without some thought of the monster sweeping through her brain. The memory of him was imprinted on her very DNA. The way her mind worked had changed because of him. She ate, slept and breathed differently because he was with her every minute of every damned day. And still the sound of his name was like having her entire body dunked in ice-cold water. It stole her breath and shocked her system.

With effort, she steadied herself. "Surely you know if I had any insights about the Storyteller, I'd be the first to share them. We'd have the FBI in here pronto." She produced an unconcerned expression. "Besides, he hasn't taken a victim since my escape. The feds think he's dead. You know and I know that if he was still alive, he would have taken one by now."

She had damned sure tried to kill the son of a bitch. But she knew he wasn't dead. Deep inside, she could still feel him. He was out there…waiting for the right opportunity. He wanted to finish what he'd started. *Come on, asshole.*

"I hope that's true, Bobbie." The chief leaned back in his chair. "As for the FBI, I've already made the call."

Which meant she didn't have a lot of time. Urgency hummed in her veins. "Well, then, I guess we'll know soon enough whether it's really him. Anything else?"

"You don't feel the need to amend your report in any way?" he pressed.

Telling him won't help. "No, sir." She stood. "I should get over to the lab and pick up a copy of that report." Once the feds confirmed a connection to the Storyteller, she wouldn't be allowed anywhere near the investigation.

"I'd like you to take a few days off, Detective."

"What?" She should have seen that one coming. "This is my case, Chief. Maybe Gwen reminded Evans about what the Storyteller did to me, and that gave him the idea to try using it to make the money he needed. Plenty of people have offered to buy my story. Maybe he sold the info to some rag. Desperate people do desperate things. Until we have proof the Storyteller is involved—"

"Apparently," he cut her off, "you've forgotten what Gwen Adams looks like."

He opened a folder and displayed a snapshot of the nurse who had worked closely with Bobbie for six long months. Gwen's long dark hair spilled over her shoulders. She was tall and thin, with pale skin that refused to tan. Bobbie's heart dropped. Like her, Gwen matched the profile of the Storyteller's preferred victim.

No. No. No. She would not believe the worst yet.

Bobbie shook her head. She'd felt confident the Storyteller wouldn't risk taking another victim—unless it was her. "You can't be sure Gwen isn't in hiding. *If* she's involved, she did break the law." No matter that her intentions might have been noble. Bobbie's head was really throbbing now. The knowledge of what the Storyteller would do to Gwen if he had taken her twisted in her gut like a wad of fishhooks.

The chief rose from his chair. "No buts, Detective. Until we locate Adams and uncover exactly who Evans was working with, you are on paid administrative leave. Now go home. I don't want to see you here again until we understand what we're dealing with."

"What about—"

"Until I say otherwise," he cut her off, "I want to know where you are and what you're doing every minute. I'm assigning a surveillance detail. Don't give them any grief."

Bobbie stowed the rant she wanted to launch and squared her shoulders. "Yes, sir."

Holding back the anger and frustration, she walked out. How could she find the Storyteller if she was on admin leave? Maybe she didn't have to find him. If what Evans said was right, he was already here. All she had to do was make sure he had the opportunity to come a little closer.

A damned surveillance detail would complicate that goal.

As she bounded out of the building, she reassured herself that the cunning psychopath would find a way. After all, he was here to finish her story.

It was what the bastard did between this second and then that scared the hell out of her.

Where the hell are you, Gwen?

Two

Bobbie paced the sidewalk outside Central, one of the city's most celebrated restaurants that overlooked the Alley, an equally prominent downtown entertainment district. When she'd called, Newt had urged her to come inside, but she couldn't. She shouldn't even be here.

This is what desperate people do, Bobbie. Just like poor Carl Evans.

She peered through the expanse of windows and scanned the crowd inside. Smiling guests were huddled in clusters of conversation. Chatter and laughter spilled out onto the sidewalk every time the door opened. The popular dining spot was a preferred venue for elegant social gatherings from campaign fund-raisers to wedding rehearsal dinners. Newt was here for the latter. His daughter's future in-laws had chosen Central for the rehearsal dinner. Almost a decade ago Bobbie's in-laws had done the same.

If only she had known then what she knew now.

"Another life." Bobbie exiled the memories as she leaned against the old brick building that more than a century ago had been a warehouse. The location so close to the freight depot and waterfront made for prime real estate then and now. Smart entrepreneurs had helped turn Montgomery's historic downtown district into the most happening scene in the city. Tonight was a perfect example. The foot traffic was heavy, even for a Friday night. Unlike her, most people had social plans at the end of the workweek.

Guilt nagged at her. Interrupting Newt's evening was wrong. So damned wrong. She pushed away from the wall with the intention of leaving. Desperate or not, she shouldn't have come here like this. Her partner was too good to her. She had no business taking advantage of him this way. Tonight was a special time for his family.

"Whoa, where you going, girlie?"

Bobbie's chest tightened at the sound of his voice. She stopped and turned to face the man who was more like a father to her than a partner, even if she had tried a dozen ways to distance herself from him these past months. Her family was gone. She refused to hold anyone else that close anymore.

The risk for pain was too great. *Coward.*

However hard she tried, she couldn't quite deny or ignore the deep attachment she felt for the man. The tension clamped around her ribs eased a fraction. The charcoal double-breasted suit Newt wore had probably set him back a full month's pay. The red tie provided a nice contrast to the light gray shirt. He'd had a fresh haircut, maintaining his vintage salt-and-pepper flattop. He looked good. He looked happy. A little more of her tension melted away.

"Is my tie crooked or something?" Howard Newton adjusted the silk accessory.

She hadn't realized she'd been staring for so long until he spoke. "Sorry. I got distracted for a minute." Her lips twitched with the unexpected need to smile. It had been so long since she'd wanted to smile she'd forgotten how. "You look great, Newt. Really great."

Grinning, he strolled over to where she stood. "I try." He pulled her into a hug. "I love it when you smile, even just a little bit." He drew back and searched her face. "It reminds me that the real you is still in there."

She looked away. "This is the real me, partner." Forcing her gaze back to his, she added, "The girl you used to know isn't coming back."

As usual when they hit this particular wall, he changed the subject. "Why don't you come inside and have a drink with me. Have you had dinner?" One eyebrow reared up his forehead. "I'll bet you haven't eaten all day."

He'd win that bet. "I'm sorry." She shook her head. "Really, I shouldn't have interrupted your evening."

He made a scoffing sound. "Trust me—I was ready for a break. They're just drinking and chatting in there now. Besides, if you'll recall, you were invited, but you said you couldn't come." He patted his pockets and grimaced.

Bobbie scowled at him. "I thought you quit smoking for good this time." They had been partners since she'd made detective. He'd quit three times during those seven years.

"I did—I swear," he promised. "I need a stick of gum or a mint."

Bobbie shifted her purse around and dug for the Tic Tacs she carried. "The chief put me on administrative leave."

Her partner accepted the box of mints and shook out a couple. "Yeah, he called me." He popped the mints into his mouth.

The urge to kick something came and went, thankfully without her acting on the impulse. To occupy her hands, she stuffed the box of mints back into her bag, and then clutched the leather straps. "It's my case, Newt. Miller had no right running off at the mouth—"

"Bobbie," he said gently, "we both know this isn't about your pissing contest with Miller. This is about Perry."

She turned away from him, watched the couples and families strolling along the sidewalk. Her surveillance detail idled in a no-parking zone on the opposite side of the street. She wanted to scream. "There's no proof the Storyteller is involved. For all we know, this could be a copycat looking to grab the headlines."

"Who do you think you're talking to, Bobbie Sue?"

Frustration knotted tighter. She should have known better than to take that approach with Newt. Foolishly she'd hoped to keep him and the whole damned department out of her private war. "Go back to your party. I should go home."

"Hold on a minute."

Reluctantly, she turned to him once more. He wore his stern face—the one her father used to wear when she'd gotten into trouble at school. Nothing too serious, just the occasional playground or lunch-room scrape. Even as a kid she was never able to tolerate a bully. Didn't matter how big he or she was, Bobbie refused to accept the role of bystander. She had to get involved, had to stand up for the tormented and the intimidated. More often than not as a teenager, her blackened eyes had nothing to do with makeup trends.

But you couldn't be a hero when it counted most. The fist crushing into her chest prevented a decent breath.

"Peterson and I were there," Newt reminded her, "in that cabin in the woods where that bastard held you."

She stared at the cobblestone sidewalk, unable to look at the hurt in his eyes—the same hurt that coiled like barbed wire inside her, ripping wider the wounds that would never completely heal.

"We took turns sitting next to your bed every day and night for weeks in that hospital," Newt went on, despite the knowledge that she did not want to hear the words. "First waiting for you to wake up, and then for you to be well enough to come home."

Bobbie squeezed her eyes shut. He was also the one who gave her the news that devastated her as nothing else in this world could have.

Jamie's gone, Bobbie. He died three days after you were abducted. I'm so sorry. We kept it out of the news to protect you.

Her baby was dead, and that, too, was her fault. She forced the haunting memories away.

"I'm the one who moved in with you after you tried—"

"You made your point." His words were like salt grinding into those old, festered wounds. Bobbie cleared her throat of the emotion wedged there. Keeping the truth from Newt was the hardest. He deserved better from her. "Maybe the Storyteller has resurfaced."

"I'd say that's a given. Peterson is worried sick." Newt sighed and tugged his tie away from his throat. "And, frankly, so am I."

"You think I'm not." She shook her head. Her partner and the chief wanted to treat her as if she were incapable of handling the pressure, much less any potential threat. If the bastard had Gwen, Bobbie had to do all in her power to find him before it was too late. "No matter how terrifying the idea is, I can't sit on the sidelines. I need to work this case—it's *my* case."

"What you need, girlie," he countered, "is to be extra careful."

She gestured to the cruiser across the street. "I'm reasonably confident careful isn't going to be a problem."

"Just promise me you'll take every precaution until we figure this out."

"We?"

"Owens assigned the case to Bauer and me. Tomorrow, as soon as my daughter and her new husband are carted off to the airport in that two-hundred-dollar-an-hour limo, we're meeting at the office. He'll bring me up to speed."

Ridiculous! She should be on this case, damn it. Newt was *her* partner, not Bauer's. "How's your wife going to take you ditching her as she watches your youngest offspring drive off into the sunset? Don't you think maybe she'll need your shoulder tomorrow evening?"

"Trust me, if this wedding goes off without a glitch, she'll take a couple of Xanax and go to bed for the rest of the weekend."

Bobbie rolled her eyes and heaved a big breath. "This sucks—you know that, right?" She had walked out of that hospital the last time for one reason and one reason only—to get the Storyteller. Peterson was not going to take that away from her. Of all people, her partner should understand.

Newt stared at her for a long moment, visibly torn about what he wanted to say next.

Bobbie scowled at him. "What?"

"There's someone you may want to talk to. He's here. I've seen him. I didn't want to mention it and get you upset."

"Who?" LeDoux, the FBI agent in charge of the Storyteller investigation, couldn't be here already. Even if he was, Bobbie had no desire to ever lay eyes on the man again. He had purposely put her in harm's way last year. No, that was wrong. He'd asked for her; the decision to work on the Storyteller case had been hers.

"While you were in the hospital the...*second* time," Newt explained, "a man visited you. His name is Nick Shade, or at least that's what he goes by. You won't remember him. He was there the last day you were in the coma."

She ignored the whispers that tried to intrude. "Who's Nick Shade?"

Newt shrugged. "I'm not sure anyone really knows. He didn't say a lot about himself. I talked to an old buddy of mine, Dwight Jessup, up at Quantico. Jessup says the feds are familiar with him. They just don't acknowledge him—which is code for they're not giving the guy credit for what he does."

"What does he do?" Newt's story had taken a turn toward totally confusing, and her patience was wearing thin. She felt like a caged tiger. She needed to do something besides this incessant going back and forth, accomplishing nothing at all.

"Some call him a hunter," Newt went on. "Others call him a ghost. Anyway, Jessup said Shade was *unofficially* connected to dozens of arrests. As long as he doesn't get in their way and he's useful, they let him do what he does without interference."

An unsettling feeling stirred deep inside her. "So why was he at the hospital when I was there?"

"He heard you survived the Storyteller, and he wanted to talk to you."

Bobbie laughed, a dry, weary sound. "Did he not notice I was in a coma?"

Newt held her gaze for a moment, his expression suddenly clean of tells. "I can't explain it, but even before I called Jessup, I had this feeling that Shade was okay. I let him sit with you for a few minutes." He held up his hands as if he expected her to rail at him. "Don't worry. I checked him for weapons, and I was watching through the glass the whole time."

"He just wanted to look at me or something?" That was creepy.

Newt shrugged. "Guess so."

"You said he's here—do you mean in Montgomery? Now?"

After surveying the street, her partner nodded. "I've spotted him around. Yeah."

"You think someone hired him?" She couldn't fathom any other reason for the guy's appearance. Still, he couldn't possibly know what Evans had told her, and the lab analysis of the victim's computer had barely made it to the chief. Not one word about the possible Storyteller connection had been released to the media. "Is he like a private investigator?"

Newt shook his head. "Word is he can't be hired."

"You said some call him a hunter. So what does Shade hunt?"

Newt hesitated for five seconds before answering. "Serial killers. The ones no one else can find."

North Montgomery, 10:50 p.m.

Five...more...blocks.

Bobbie charged forward in the darkness, running harder along Fairground Road. The pain had faded two miles back, overpowered by the endorphins that finally kicked in after three grueling miles. Slowing to a jog, she made the turn onto Gardendale Drive. Air sawed in and out of her nose and mouth in an attempt to keep up with the racing organ in her chest. Her muscles felt warm and fluid, as if she could run forever.

She'd pushed to five miles tonight rather than her usual three. The too-familiar twinge in her right leg served as a reminder that hardware held it together. No matter how young and strong the endorphins made her feel, she was still Bobbie Gentry—thirty-two and broken inside. Somewhere deep in the darkness she kept hidden from the world, memories of the woman she used to be dared to stir.

She hadn't been that woman in 246 days.

She is never coming back.

Cursing herself for the lapse in restraint, she banished the echoes of the past as she walked the final block. Two of the three streetlights were out of commission. Didn't matter. She knew the area by heart. The line of unremarkable houses in sad need of routine maintenance. The narrow, unkempt lawns used as parking lots for the multiple families crowded into the compact two-bed, two-bath rentals. Same old, same old. Very little changed in this neighborhood.

Three doors from hers the brindle pit bull named D-Boy surged forward, testing the heavy-duty chain that secured him to the porch post. The dog issued a low, guttural growl before he captured her scent and recognition registered.

"Good boy," she murmured. He whimpered and whipped his tail back and forth. She made a mental note to check his water bowl before going to bed. The single mother of three who lived in the ramshackle two-story left her kids at home alone more often than not. Making sure the chained animal had food and water was even lower on her list of priorities. Some people shouldn't have kids or pets. Then again, Bobbie had no right to judge anyone.

Her legs felt a little rubbery climbing the steps to her front door. She wiped the sweat from her brow with her left arm as she jammed the key into the lock. A long, hot shower was on her agenda, and then she planned to review the lab reports from the Evans case. The chief could take her off the job for a few days, but that wouldn't stop her. She had friends at the lab. Andy Keller, the new tech, had been delighted to email her the report when she'd called. Of course, she hadn't mentioned being off the case.

The MPD cruiser assigned as her surveillance

detail edged up to the curb in front of her house. She didn't know the two uniforms in the car. If she wanted to play nice, she would offer them coffee. Maybe later. It wasn't their fault the chief had gone all overprotective today. Bobbie understood from experience that his need to keep her safe wouldn't be going away anytime soon. The man would do all within his power to keep her out of the line of fire. If not for Lieutenant Owens, her division commander, she might be jockeying a desk. After spending nearly six months in physical rehab and psychiatric counseling in order to be deemed fit for duty once more, the chief had barred her from field duty. Somehow the lieutenant had convinced him the move was a mistake. Bobbie had worked hard to make certain her division commander never regretted backing her up.

Now here they all were back at square one. She hoped Owens could calm down the chief this go around. It was bad enough word of his overreaction would spread through the department like a new strain of summer flu. Guys like Miller would use the chief's resolve to protect Bobbie as proof she received preferential treatment. So not true. If anything, the chief held her to a higher standard. Since there was nothing she could do about it one way or the other, she ignored office politics most of the time.

Confrontations like the one today made following that self-imposed rule difficult.

She opened the front door and stepped inside.

The cool air instantly enveloped her, making her shiver. Before closing the door, she held her breath and listened for a few seconds. The incessant low hum of the air-conditioning unit underscored the silence. The blinds throughout the house were shut tightly, leaving the interior nearly black. She inhaled deeply, sorting through the lived-in house smells for anything new. *Clear.* She shoved the door shut with her foot as she hit the switch for the narrow entry hall's overhead light. With a few flicks of her wrist she secured the two dead bolts.

Room by room, she moved through the house. Bedrooms and closets. *Clear.* Bathroom and kitchen. *Clear.* She turned on the rear floodlights, parted the blind on the back door and scanned the yard. Nothing to get excited about. Grass that needed to be mowed, a rickety picnic table left by previous tenants in bad need of an overhaul. Bobbie exhaled a tired breath as she shut off the floodlights and then checked the dead bolts on the back door. Time for that shower.

She hesitated, toed off her running shoes and dragged the elastic band from her ponytail. For a moment she closed her eyes and indulged in a slow massage of her scalp. The headache was long gone, but she felt the tension in her shoulders and neck gaining a second wind. She stretched her neck and groaned. The shower was going to have to work some serious magic tonight. The prospect of standing under the flow of steaming water until she emptied the water heater had her weary body moving in that direction. After the shower and a cold beer, she intended to check D-Boy's water bowl, and then—

A solid rap on the front door derailed her train of thought. She stalled, the cold of the hardwood floor seeping through her damp socks. Why would anyone drop by at this hour? Couldn't be about a case because she was on leave by order of the chief. Wouldn't be her partner since he was no doubt home by now, getting some rest before the big day tomorrow.

Another round of bangs, this time hard enough to shake loose the peeling paint on her shabby door and have it drift down around her visitor's feet like dingy gray snowflakes. Could be the cops outside, but why not call if they wanted to talk to her? She checked the screen of the cell phone strapped to her upper arm. No missed calls.

Bobbie bypassed the door, her steps silent, and eased to the living room picture window a few feet away. When she'd first moved in, she'd cut out a tiny section of one plastic slat in the cheap blind as a way to see a visitor without becoming an easy target bellied up to the door. The overhead porch light, dimmed by the hundred or so bugs that had found their way inside and died there, stayed on 24/7. The faint glow allowed her to confirm the visitor was male. Her pulse rate bumped up a few beats. Dark hair, too long to be a cop, unless he was undercover. Tall, six feet or so. Thin. Broad shouldered.

He suddenly turned his head and stared directly at her as if he'd felt her scrutiny.

She drew back. *What the hell?* Giving herself a mental shake, she moved toward the door. The living room was dark; he couldn't possibly have seen her. At the door she decided to leave her backup piece in the holster strapped around her ankle for now. Considering there were two uniforms parked in front of her house, she didn't expect she would need to use it. She leaned toward the door.

"Who are you, and what do you want?" No point beating around the bush.

"Nick Shade. We need to talk."

Surprised and more than a little intrigued, she peered through the peephole she'd installed. So this was the guy Newt had told her about. He was younger than she'd expected. "Let's see some ID."

He withdrew his wallet and stuck his driver's license in front of the hole. *Nicholas Shade. Atlanta, Georgia.* She harrumphed. *Thirty-five.* He wasn't much older than her. Did she open the door or not? Newt's Quantico contact hadn't given him anything concrete on Shade other than a generic assessment that he was one of the good guys. Shade might be after nothing more than the inside scoop on the Storyteller in hopes something she knew would be useful to him. He wouldn't be the first to show up at her door. She'd had reporters, publishers and private investigators come knocking. Just because Shade supposedly tracked down serial killers didn't mean he wasn't in it for the money. A man who couldn't be hired had to be making a living somehow.

Even so, why would he appear now? As of the

ten o'clock news Evans's connection to her hadn't been made, but that would change soon enough, and then her street would be littered with reporters once more. Any member of the media familiar with the Storyteller would give just about anything for an exclusive from his only surviving victim. If that was the reason Shade was here, he needed to get in line somewhere besides her front door. This was *her* hunt.

"Call your partner if you have any questions," Shade suggested, taking her delay for uncertainty. "We've met."

"Did my partner send you here?" His showing up only a couple of hours after Newt mentioned him was a little convenient.

"No one sends me anywhere." Shade stared at the peephole as if he sensed her watching him.

Who the hell was this guy? She released the dead bolts and opened the door. "What do we have to talk about?"

Dark eyes assessed her. "May I come in?"

Not a chance. "Whatever you have to say, you can say it right where you stand." She bracketed her hands at her waist and blocked the doorway.

He glanced over his shoulder at the cruiser on the street. "I think you're going to want to hear what I have to say in private."

The tension that had started in her neck rushed through her chest, spreading quickly through her limbs. "Are you carrying?"

"No." He held his arms up and turned all the way around for her to see.

The shirt and jeans hugged his body. He wasn't carrying unless, like her, a small backup piece was strapped to his ankle. "Let's see what kind of socks you wear, Mr. Shade."

He lifted one foot and tugged up the pants leg, and then did the same with the other. Black socks and matching hiking boots, both of which fit too snugly to conceal a weapon. "Satisfied?"

"Fine, but make it fast. I take issue with having *my* time wasted." She stepped back and allowed him inside before closing the door. "What is it you have to say?"

The weight of his gaze settled on her. When he continued to stare without speaking she fought the impulse to fidget. His eyes were more black than brown and impossible to read. He wasn't thin as she'd first believed, more lean. His sleeves were rolled up to his elbows, showing off muscled forearms. The broad shoulders she'd already noted filled out his cotton button-down shirt with no room to spare. His jeans were well-worn, as were his boots. Her attention drifted back up to his face, where those dark eyes watched her steadily. Rather than be put off by her sizing him up, he seemed to expect it. As undeniably handsome as he was, with that square jaw and classic straight nose, there was something distant about him…something untouchable and more than a little unsettling.

She rubbed at her neck. *Enough with the silent*

treatment. Had he intruded on her evening to stare at her or to talk? Maybe he only wanted an up-close look at the anomaly who'd escaped the Storyteller while losing everything else in this world that mattered. Her irritation flared. "I don't know what you want—"

"I need the full details of what happened inside Carl Evans's home."

Bobbie made a halfhearted sound that failed the definition of a laugh by any stretch of the imagination. "If you're looking to verify the manner of death, I'll be happy to set the record straight. He stuck the muzzle of a .38 into his mouth and pulled the trigger. Any other questions, Mr. Shade?"

Something flickered in his eyes, too quickly for her to read. "I'm well aware of how he died, Detective. I'm interested in what he said to you while you were alone together."

Now she understood. Shade was on a digging expedition. "I'm afraid you'll have to wait for the press release the same as the rest of the world. Now, if that's all you wanted…" She gestured to the door.

Rather than leave, he moved a step closer. "You asked me not to waste your time—maybe you can refrain from wasting mine. What did Evans say to you before he pulled the trigger?"

"I'm certain you're aware I can't comment on an ongoing case."

He watched her closely, analyzing her answer, her expression, as well as her body language. "Did the exchange between the two of you have anything to do with his recent interaction with Gaylon Perry?"

Bobbie froze at the mention of *his* name. How could he know what Carl Evans had been doing? "Why would Evans be involved with the Storyteller?"

Shade's penetrating gaze narrowed. "I've been briefed regarding the findings on his computer, Detective."

Impossible. "This conversation is over, Mr. Shade. If you have more questions, you can direct them to the department's community liaison officer."

She reached for the door.

"Carl Evans was a pawn. Perry used him to get information on your recovery. He's active again. Doesn't that concern you in the least?"

Shock moved through her, tracing the fault line in her heart. He could not possibly know any of this for a certainty. He had to be guessing, hoping for a telling reaction. Whoever this guy was, she wanted him out of her house. All she had to do was open the door and send him away. Somehow her body wouldn't take the necessary action.

"Perry used him," Shade went on when she remained still. "And it cost Carl Evans his life. Gwen Adams may be next. Whatever you believe or don't believe, you need to understand this is only one of many steps toward the Storyteller's final goal—finishing what he started with *you.*"

What the hell? Did he read minds, too? Bobbie struggled to quiet the whirlwind of emotions threatening to develop into a raging storm inside her. *Don't let him see.* "Good night, Mr. Shade." *Just open the fucking door.* Her fingers tightened on the knob but refused to turn the damned thing.

"I see what's driving you, Detective Gentry," he warned, his voice dangerously low. "It shows in every move you make. Your need for vengeance is blinding you. You should think long and hard about the danger to yourself and to others before you proceed."

A flood of outrage spun her around to face him once more. "You've done your homework. Good for you. You're damned straight I want him to pay for what he did to me." Her fingers curled into fists. "For what he did to all the others. Come back when you have something original to talk about, Mr. Shade."

"He stole everything from you."

The words were uttered so softly and yet they pierced her like the sharpest knives. She closed her eyes, unable to conceal the pain burning there. *He's seen too much already.*

"He crushed you, shattered your entire world. Knowing he's still out there can't be easy. It would be completely understandable if you wanted nothing more than to lock yourself away and hide in fear."

Bobbie blocked the images his words triggered, summoned her goddamned MIA courage and looked him straight in the eye. "You're mistaken if you think I can give you any answers. Now." She took a breath and squared her shoulders. "I've had a long day. I need it to be over."

When she reached for the door once more, he flattened his wide palm against it, blocking her move. "You're the one who's making a mistake, Detective."

If she managed to hold back the hurricane of emotions another thirty seconds, it would be a miracle. She grasped the doorknob tighter as if it were the anchor that prevented her from spiraling out of control. "Leave or I'll have you hauled away for harassment."

"We both know you're not the slightest bit afraid," he went on, ignoring her edict.

He was so close she could feel the heat of his words against her skin, blocking her ability to do anything except to listen.

"You maintain a public Facebook page without turning off the location services when you post. You go to work, and you come home. You've pushed away all the friends you once had, unless you count your partner and the chief of police. I suspect you only interact with them because you have no choice."

A new rush of anger roared through her. She hated herself for permitting him to see her emotions. She hated him for making her lose control. "You don't know a damned thing about me."

"I know all I need to. You have a home in a tidy, middle-class neighborhood on the east side, yet you rent and reside in a house in one of the worst neighborhoods in the city. You run alone every night well after dark."

"That's right." She lifted her chin in defiance. "I'm more than capable of defending myself if the need arises."

"I'm sure you are." His gaze slid down her body and back up once more, pausing on her lips when they trembled. "You carry a piece strapped to your ankle, a sheathed knife at your back and a mini-stun gun tucked in your bra."

She stiffened. How the hell did he know all that?

As if she'd asked the question aloud, he said, "I've been watching you. At some point during to-night's extended run, you adjusted each of your hidden weapons."

She put up her hands in a wait-a-damned-minute gesture. "First, you have no business following me around. Second, I arm myself because I'm smart, not because I'm afraid."

"I got that last part loud and clear. You're not afraid of anyone, and you're certainly not hiding from the Storyteller. You're baiting him. You want him to find you." He leaned closer still. "Tell me, Detective, what do you think your chances are of surviving him a second time?"

For one fleeting instant she couldn't move, and then she drew back, putting much-needed distance between them. "So you're psychic and a shrink, too, are you?" She told herself to make him leave. She told herself to stop talking and to open the damned door. She apparently couldn't do any of the above.

"What would you know about how it feels to survive the worst a monster can do to you?"

His jaw tightened a little more. "Trust me," he murmured in that dangerous whisper of his, "I know that feeling very well, and I don't need to be a psychic or a shrink to understand that if you wanted to avoid trouble you wouldn't live here. You'd have a monitored security system and a mean-ass dog."

"I don't have time for a dog."

"Time has nothing to do with it." He gave a dry chuckle and dropped his hand from the door. "You can't have a dog because you won't risk allowing another living creature to get close to you. You won't take the chance that someone else—not even a dog—will get caught in the cross fire of what you have to do."

She couldn't contain the tremors any longer; her body shook in spite of her best efforts. She pointed to the door. "I want you to leave now."

He manacled her forearm and stroked the pad of his thumb over the scarred underside of her wrist. "Take my advice, Detective—don't try to do this alone."

She tugged at his hold, and he released her. "Go!"

He reached for the door, grasping the knob with long fingers. "One more thing—try not to get anyone else killed."

A full minute lapsed after he'd gone before she managed to lock the door, her hands shaking. Fury warring with the other emotions he'd resurrected, she marched to the bathroom. She hung a towel over the shower curtain bar and turned on the water. She withdrew the stun gun from her sports bra and placed it on the counter next to the sink, and then the five-inch blade and sheath from her waistband at the small of her back. The fact that he had so easily spotted all three alternately outraged and frustrated her. She ripped the holster holding the .22 from her ankle and placed it next to the other weapons. By the time she'd peeled off her running clothes and socks, steam had started to fill the room, and tears rolled in rivers down her cheeks.

She stood in front of the full-length mirror a previous tenant or maybe the owner had hung on the wall. Her right calf was marred with scars from the surgery. Little distinct bumps where the hardware was positioned still showed. Jagged scars marked her arms, her breasts, her thighs and belly from the torture she had endured. If she leaned closer to the mirror, she could see the thin, barely noticeable line where the Storyteller had kept a nylon rope fastened around her neck. Plastic surgery had taken care of the worst of the scarring there. Vanity had nothing to do with her decision to have that particular elective surgery. Erasing that hideous scar had prevented the inevitable shocked looks and sympathetic questions from anyone she encountered.

She turned to face the mirror over the sink so she could see her back…and the story *he* had begun on her flesh. Flowing strokes of black ink tattooed the words describing her agony onto her skin.

Over and over she cursed herself for the path she chose to take...

She squeezed her eyes shut against the memories, and yet those memories were the very reason she refused to allow the words to be removed. She didn't deserve to have them removed...to be free of what they meant.

Who the hell did Nick Shade think he was? Damn it, she had every right to want vengeance. She climbed into the shower and let the hot water blast over her. Hard as she tried she could not clear her mind of the voices...the images...the pain.

She slid down the wall and wrapped her arms around her knees. For the first time in months she sobbed. She sobbed so hard she couldn't catch her breath. She never cried for herself. It was pointless. A waste of energy. She cried for all the victims and their families. She cried for her son—her sweet, sweet little boy—and her husband. She cried because she had failed to keep them safe.

Shade was right...she wanted to get that bastard. She wanted to make him pay... She wanted to watch him scream in agony for hours on end. And then she wanted to watch his body bleed and seize and twitch until he took his last breath.

She turned her palms up and stared at her scarred wrists.

But Nick Shade didn't know everything.

She couldn't have what she really wanted just yet.

What she really wanted was to stop waking up in the morning to face another day without her baby…without the man she had loved with her entire being…without the life that had been stolen from her. What she wanted was to never again dream of what might have been.

What she wanted above all else…was to die.

But Gaylon Perry had to die first.

Three

"I know what you must be asking yourself right about now," Gaylon said, a smile stretching across his lips as he tightened the noose he'd made around her slender neck. He draped the short remaining length of nylon rope along her chest. "Did I spend all those grueling hours at the gym for this?"

Registered Nurse Gwen Adams shivered, her soft green eyes going wider and her nipples peaking into hard points as his gaze raked over her body. Despite the relentless heat, fear caused her body to shake as if she were stretched out spread eagle on a bed of snow rather than the piss-stained mattress he'd picked up on the street in one of Montgomery's derelict neighborhoods.

His personal taste leaned toward those who hadn't spoiled their bodies with tanning beds and pointless body art. No annoying tan lines or wasted ink to disrupt the satiny, white skin stretched smoothly over toned muscles and interrupted only by rosy nipples and a neatly manicured triangle of silky hair. A perfect canvas. The lovely perfection would make any man want to burrow between her creamy thighs and plow into her pussy right this instant.

But not Gaylon. His ability to restrain his baser desires was far more sophisticated than that of the average male. Besides, it wasn't time to give her what she deserved just yet. Preparations had to be made first. He sighed. *All good things come to those who wait.* His loving mother had ensured that adage was deeply ingrained in him during his formative years, and Gaylon had learned his lessons well.

He'd allowed his baser needs to lead him once, and look at what it had cost him.

Exiling the memory, he reviewed the essential steps he had taken. He'd placed the mattress on the floor well away from the only window that wasn't boarded up. A table and a chair, both of which he would need in the coming days, were picked up at a thrift store. In the corner was a five-gallon bucket he'd purchased at the hardware store for waste. If his guest relieved herself anywhere but in the bucket at the appropriately scheduled piss breaks she would clean it up with her hands and mouth. The unpleasant mistake was rarely repeated. His guests were generally quite obedient.

This morning he'd brought the tools required to finish his work inside and stored them in the other room. The two-room board-and-batten shack had no electricity, and the rusty tin roof leaked. "Off the grid" was an apt description. More important, there were no neighbors. The closest occupied house was more than three miles away. Though ideally he selected a location deeper in the woods to do his work, this abandoned hovel would do quite well.

He tapped his lips with his fingers, suppressing a knowing smile. A remote location was part of his modus operandi, or so those who profiled him said. His MO and signature were carefully detailed in their haughty reports. What a spectacular waste of human resources.

All these years those who attempted to dissect and analyze him had gotten so very much wrong. The chances of the FBI catching him with their fancy profiles had been somewhere in the vicinity of zero before he made his one ruinous error. Anger flared inside him. Prior to seven months ago, no one had known his identity. Not one of his victims had survived to tell. Not one body had revealed the first significant clue about the Storyteller. He'd been far too careful…until he allowed a mere impulse— sheer lust—to best him. The relentless need had grown too insistent and too urgent to deny. He'd acted on that irresistible impulse, and it had swallowed him completely, sucking him into an uncontrollable frenzy. He'd become lost to anything but the blinding need until reality had spit him out onto the floor of that desolate cabin, bleeding like a stuck pig and gasping for air like a fish out of water.

Now his face was plastered all over the internet and in every post office in the country. The anger spread through him like a raging wildfire. Not to worry, that costly error would be rectified as soon as he was finished here. Then he would disappear. A nice tropical island with no extradition treaty. Perhaps he would create a new MO, develop a more intriguing signature, and this time there would be no lapses in judgment...no distractions.

All good things come to those who wait.

Gaylon moved to the side of the mattress. He sat down, and his lovely nurse struggled to draw away, but her restraints prevented her from doing so. "I'm going to remove the gag. If you scream, I'll hurt you like you've never been hurt before. Do you understand?"

She nodded, a fresh wave of tears trickling from her eyes. *Pathetic creature.*

He tugged her panties from her mouth. "There. Now, I want you to tell me the story again."

Moving her head up and down like a shaken bob-blehead doll, she swallowed and then cleared her throat. "Can I have a drink of water?"

"After the story." Irritation furrowed his brow. Every time he removed the gag she wanted something. She'd been here barely twenty-four hours. He hadn't even started preparing her, and all she could do was make requests. She should be pleading for her life—not that pleas for mercy would help. Gwen Adams was going to die.

As aware of her improbable odds of survival as she might be, it was human nature to cling to hope. The foolish instinct made his work far more inter-esting and vastly more entertaining.

"Where..." The word croaked out of her dry

throat. She cleared it some more. "Where would you like me to start?"

"At the beginning. From the moment you saw Detective Gentry in the ER."

"It was just over two weeks after she escaped." Her lips trembled, and she averted her eyes as if she feared her words would anger him. "January 31."

He smiled. "She was in very poor condition."

The nurse nodded, the movement stiff and uncoordinated. "She had spent two weeks in the hospital in Meridian, Mississippi."

Gaylon had held Detective Gentry in an abandoned cabin about twelve miles outside Meridian. Even now, his body hardened at the memory of fucking her...of tasting her blood. He'd never had a cop before. She had been his most challenging and most satisfying prey. If only he'd been able to finish her story. "They had to do surgery while she was in Mississippi," he prompted, not wanting a single detail left out.

"Yes." Adams licked her lips. "The femur was fractured, but the worst was the fibula. It had to be reassembled and stabilized with screws and a rod."

His heart raced as his mind replayed him standing over Gentry and crushing those bones in a fit of rage. He rolled his hand so the woman staring at him with such sheer terror in her eyes would continue the story.

"She had three fractured ribs and one toe that had to be partially removed from the frostbite."

He squeezed his toes together inside his sneakers.

His own injuries had been life threatening. Running through those woods, blood leaking from his chest and his ability to draw in air compromised, had been terrifyingly exhilarating. It was only by utter force of will that he survived long enough to reach help. His mother had always called him determined. Ah, but determination was merely one of his tenacious traits.

"Numerous lacerations were infected and required attention," Adams continued, her voice growing faint with understanding that those very words described the fate awaiting her. "One spot on her left breast required removal. The tissue loss was repaired with a small amount of fat and skin from her buttocks."

She fell silent, her body trembling.

"Then the doctors in Mississippi sent her home," he said, urging her beyond the more mundane details. Why was it that no one knew how to tell a good story anymore? His students had been utter morons. True storytellers were a nearly extinct breed. *Such a pity.*

"She was released, yes." Adams executed another of those awkward nods. "She was back home in Montgomery for barely a day when her partner found her near death."

"Found her where?" Gaylon demanded. She knew better than to leave out the best parts. Her lips trembled with renewed fear. How utterly tedious. "I'm waiting, Nurse Adams."

"In her little boy's bedroom." Adams drew in a

halting breath. "Later, when I was taking care of
her, Bobbie told me about that day. She was supposed to go directly into rehab, but she'd insisted on
spending one night at home first. She said as soon
as she was at home alone she'd gone straight to her
baby's room and slit her wrists. She wanted to die.
She didn't want to go on without her family."

Gaylon savored the words for a moment before
he prompted, "So she lost a lot of blood before she
was found."

"It was a miracle she was alive. She'd lost more
than enough blood for her heart to simply stop beating." Her mouth worked for a moment before more
words came out. "She was in a coma for five days."

"A coma? Why?" He knew the answer already,
but he wanted to hear her repeat the splendid details.
He couldn't have written a more compelling story
himself. Perhaps since it was his work that inspired
her actions he could be considered the director.

"She'd given up." Her voice sounded distant now,
as if she was remembering the day a grief-stricken
patient had shared her most painful thoughts with
a trusted medical professional. "She didn't want to
wake up. But for some reason, on the fifth day, she
opened her eyes and started trying to live again."

"Bravo!" Gaylon clapped enthusiastically, making her jump. "Detective Gentry survived." Providing a second chance for her as well as for him.
He hesitated, pondering the last part. He'd been so
excited when he read the medical files and listened
to Adams tell the story the first time that he hadn't

thought to ask a very important question. "Why do you suppose she changed her mind? Did her family sway her decision?"

Gaylon knew better. Bobbie Gentry didn't have any family. There were her in-laws who blamed her for their son's and grandson's deaths. She had the chief of police, who was a lifelong friend of her father, and she had her partner. Such a sad little detective. She hardly had anyone to care about her since she'd pushed all her friends away. He couldn't wait to dismantle her mentally and physically all over again. Piece by piece, and this time he would destroy her completely. He would watch the life drain from her body as he finished her story.

"Either Chief Peterson or Detective Newton had been with her day and night." The nurse blinked, licked her lips again. "Maybe one of them said something that finally got through to her. I don't know."

"No priest visited her? Maybe it was all those people praying for her," he mocked. He recalled the many requests for prayers in the local news for poor, poor Detective Gentry.

"She never mentioned church while I was working with her." Adams's body was trembling harder now. Fear that her unreliable memory would anger him was no doubt coursing through her veins. "I can't be sure."

Gaylon knew the answer. Bobbie Gentry was like him; she never had time for such trivialities. Her husband, the man who failed to protect his family, had gone to church and taken their child. Bobbie had only attended on special occasions if work didn't get in the way. Her work was her religion, her weapon her cross.

Gaylon understood every part of her. He had become thoroughly obsessed with her during those weeks when she participated in the joint task force with the FBI to find a heinous serial killer who could not be found. He'd wanted to possess her so badly that he'd thrown caution to the wind and taken her like he'd taken no other victim.

All those witless profilers had been running in circles. *He's deviated from his MO! He's never taken victims without waiting the usual year.* What fools! Admittedly, he had acted impulsively last year. With the loss he'd suffered, he had been undeniably weak. But he was beyond that now. Now he would finish what he'd started.

He reached down and stroked Adams's lean rib cage. She shuddered deliciously. His cock stirred. Another hardworking, dedicated woman. Despite being a full-time home health nurse, Gwen still picked up every available shift at the hospital. She was saving up to buy a home. *Poor thing.* He wondered if Chief Peterson had paid her well to take care of Bobbie. Gaylon hoped so; after all, accepting the extra work was going to cost her so very, very much.

"There…there was one other visitor," she said suddenly.

He drew his hand away, giving her a moment's

reprieve. "What visitor? You never mentioned another visitor."

"I just remembered. It was on the last day she was in a coma." Her brow creased in concentration. "Her partner was sitting with her that day. He told me to take a break. When I came back, he was waiting in the corridor outside her room and there was another man inside. I assumed it was a family friend, so I took a few more minutes and went to the bathroom. When I came back, the door was open and this man I'd never seen before was sitting next to her, holding her hand."

"Holding her hand?" Rage coiled hard and fast. "Who was this man?"

"I don't know. Detective Newton started talking to me. I guess the man left while we were talking."

"What did this stranger look like?" Gaylon thought he knew everyone who had come into contact with his detective since he touched her. If there was another man and he got in Gaylon's way, he would die in the same tragic manner as her husband had. Bobbie Gentry belonged to him. Only he could finish her story.

"He had longish dark hair, maybe down on his collar. He was tall. I only got a glimpse of his face, and then his profile." She shook her head, instinctively tugged at the restraints binding her hands above her head. "I don't know. Bobbie's partner must have known him. I never saw him again."

Gaylon had watched Bobbie running tonight. He noticed a man he couldn't place at her door. He'd assumed this was a cop from her department. Perhaps not. "If I bring you a picture, would you recognize him?"

She blinked back a new rush of tears. "I think so. I'll try."

He trailed a finger between her nice breasts. "You're doing very well, Nurse Adams."

A sob tore from her throat. "Please don't hurt me."

"Now, now. You know I'm going to hurt you—the only question is how much."

The sound of whimpering had her twisting her head around to see where it came from. "What was that?" Her worried gaze collided with his. "Is someone else here?"

"That's none of your concern." His cock hardened again as he thought of what he had in the other room and the way it was going to hurt Bobbie. "Now be quiet before I change my mind about how much I need you."

Gaylon stood and walked to the window. He peered beyond the dirty glass. In the distance he could just distinguish the taller of the buildings that was downtown Montgomery.

In her wildest imagination, Bobbie Gentry could not possibly conceive what was coming.

Four

Nick Shade taped another photo of Detective Bobbie Gentry on the wall. He stood back and surveyed the new additions to the timeline he had created. The data he'd collected during this hunt were far more extensive than he usually gathered. The instinct he'd recently started to ignore warned again that he had ventured too close on this one.

What the hell had he been thinking going to her house?

He plowed his hands through his hair. He hadn't been thinking. That was the problem. But had there really been a choice? He scrubbed a hand over his jaw. Gaylon Perry had proven significantly more resourceful than he had anticipated. For such a singularly focused killer, whose carefully choreographed world had been so abruptly turned upside down, Perry had regained his balance and scurried out of reach in the blink of an eye.

Nick could only watch and wait for his return.

Fury tightened his jaw. "I knew you'd come eventually."

Nick studied a photo of the forty-year-old English teacher. His generic brown hair and eyes were less than memorable. His soft jaw and weak chin along with a slim build disguised his physical strength. Classroom videos showed a soft-spoken man who interacted comfortably with his students. Those same students, as well as Perry's colleagues at the high school, considered him to be kind and compassionate. And yet fourteen murders, not counting Gentry's husband, had been attributed to him. The community of Lincoln, Nebraska, was still reeling from the news. Parents were sickened at the idea that their impressionable teenagers had been taught by a sadistic serial killer.

According to the statements Gentry had given, Perry had mentioned other murders. A total of twenty-three. Based on his sophisticated signature, Nick felt confident that number was closer to right than the one previously thought. The Storyteller's first victim, as far as the cops knew, had been dumped in a quiet Louisiana town when Perry was twenty-seven. He had followed that pattern annually until last year. The MO was simplistic, yet it was that very simplicity that had protected Perry for so long. Each year between June 1 and mid-July, he took a victim from one of the southern states, kept her for three to four weeks, torturing her relentlessly before tattooing a sadistic poem on her back and then murdering her. The body was immediately dumped in another state. Each step was carefully planned and executed.

Nick considered the photos of the crime scenes where the bodies were discovered. Perry did more than dump his victims. He posed them in prominent places so they would be found quickly while his poetic masterpieces were still fresh. No one, not the FBI or any other law enforcement agency, had come close to identifying him, much less catching him, until Detective Gentry survived, providing a break in the case.

Even before Nick had known his name, he had understood one thing with complete certainty. As long as he was still breathing, the Storyteller would return to Montgomery for the one that got away.

"What have you been waiting for?" Nick rubbed at the tense muscles in his neck. He'd been in Montgomery watching Gentry for nearly four months—since her release from the rehabilitation center. His gaze narrowed with the only possible conclusion. "You waited for her to go back to work, didn't you, you sick fuck?"

Perry would see having the damaged hero cop resume duty before he murdered her a more dramatic and poignant chapter in his killing history. Nick's gaze settled on the photo he'd snapped of Gentry entering the Criminal Investigation Division last month on her first day back. She'd worn a pair of dark trousers and a matching suit jacket. Muted pink blouse. Rubber-soled loafers. No jewelry. No scarves or other accessories. Her stride had exuded strength and confidence. Watching her from afar, no one would have suspected she had spent long, grueling hours in physical therapy day in and day out for months to regain that strength and confidence. Not to mention the hours of psychiatric counseling. Continuing the counseling was a condition of her return to work. Nick had watched her leave the department psychiatrist's office each week knowing she had played the part everyone wanted to see. She presented the picture of strength and determination except when she thought no one was watching.

Those were the moments he couldn't get out of his head.

He reached out and traced her face. "Why did the FBI ever let you anywhere near this case?"

She was a perfect example of Perry's typical victim. She was tall and thin with long, lush brunette hair that sharply contrasted her pale skin. Her facial features were delicate and finely sculpted. Her eyes were an uncommonly pale blue. Perry wasn't particular when it came to the color of the eyes, but each victim had a uniquely light hue and eyes slightly larger than average.

Gentry's eyes brought to mind a clear blue sky. Nick blinked away the notion. How long had it been since he'd noticed the sky beyond assessing coming weather conditions? He couldn't remember. Research and tracking his prey consumed his nights and his days. One case became another, and then another. Home was wherever his work took him—

the desert or the mountains, under a city overpass or in an abandoned house deep in the woods.

Nick moved to the map of Montgomery County he'd tacked to the wall. Every minute he didn't have eyes on Gentry, he was poring over aerials of the area using Google Earth and driving to remote locations similar to those Perry had utilized before. If Nick was lucky, he would find Perry before he made a play for Gentry.

His phone sounded a warning. Nick reached for it and checked the status of the tracking device he'd planted on Gentry's car. "Can't sleep either, eh?"

He snatched up his keys and headed for the door. Apparently neither of them was going to get any sleep tonight. He wasn't surprised. She went for middle-of-the-night drives several times a week. Detective Gentry went to great lengths to make herself available for the taking. Nick suspected Perry wanted her to suffer a little more before he obliged her and made a move.

"You won't get away this time." However else he had screwed up on this one, Nick would see to it that Perry didn't escape.

The streets of Montgomery were quiet. Most of the bars and clubs would be closed by now. He checked the blinking dot that represented Gentry's progress and took the necessary turns. When he spotted her black Challenger, he shook his head. The police cruiser was right on her tail. He thought of the neighborhood—a neighborhood known for serious drug and gang problems—where she currently resided.

"You like punishing yourself for surviving—don't you, Bobbie?" He didn't have to wonder how she explained that one to her psychiatrist. He'd slipped into the doctor's office and read over his notes more than once. *I need the space to get back to who I am.*

"Liar." She still owned the house she and her husband built before their son was born. She had closed the place up four months ago. The cars she and her husband had driven were still in the garage. A lawn service kept the exterior maintained. Gentry had taken nothing, not even her clothes from the home. She'd bought a new muscle car and moved into the Gardendale house to "find herself."

He shook his head as he watched her taillights in the distance. "I've got you all figured out, Bobbie."

Trouble was, learning her so well had cost him. Too early just yet to tell how much.

She made a left onto Commerce Street. After parking on the Dexter Avenue side of Court Square, she emerged from her car. The cruiser parked a few yards beyond her. Nick eased to the curb half a block away. Gentry walked to the fountain in the center of the square. Montgomery's historic downtown district centered on the 1880s fountain, but the fountain's historic significance and the goddess of youth statue that topped it weren't the reasons she had come.

It was in this cobblestoned square that Perry had

left his last victim before abducting Gentry. Alyssa Powell's body had been posed at this fountain on December 3. Perry's decision to make a second abduction in one year and to leave that victim here had forever changed Gentry's life.

She walked around the fountain, once, twice, and then she surveyed the deserted square. Nick exhaled a heavy breath. She was doing all within her power to draw out the Storyteller, and obviously she no longer cared if anyone knew. The surveillance detail hindered her efforts toward her goal, but that was only temporary. She was a smart, determined lady. When she was ready to ditch the detail, she would make it happen. Nick had to make sure she didn't do the same to him.

The first time he saw her she had given up. Perry had murdered her husband, and her child had died as a result of the abduction. The torture Perry had inflicted left Gentry vulnerable, but it was the loss of her family that had destroyed her, and she simply hadn't possessed the wherewithal to go on.

Nick had just finished a hunt. He'd been physically and mentally exhausted, but the news that a victim had survived the Storyteller was too significant to ignore. The Storyteller had been on his top-ten list already. After seeing Gentry and hearing her story from her partner, Nick had made his decision. The Storyteller would be next. He'd been tracking him since.

Gaylon Perry wasn't the most intelligent serial killer he'd hunted, but he possessed incredible will-power. He allowed himself one theatrical event each year, and then he returned to school in the fall and carefully maintained his seemingly normal persona until summer rolled around again. Last November his mother's death had caused him to act out of character, to make a move beyond his meticulously maintained boundaries. Then a second trigger had prompted a dangerously impulsive move.

That trigger had been Bobbie Gentry.

Since Perry had taken several broad steps outside his established MO, maybe Nick should move his grid search closer into the city. Perry would want to be near her. He would need to see Gentry often. To relish her flagrant actions of invitation. Her every move was like foreplay to the serial killer who had already come so very close to ending her life.

Nick wanted to shake her. She had to know she couldn't do this alone.

As if she'd felt his censure across the night, she climbed back into her Challenger and drove away. Her official shadow rolled behind her. Nick allowed some distance and then he followed. She returned to her house on Gardendale and backed into the driveway. Nick watched until she was inside and the house went dark again before he returned to his motel.

Once he was between the sheets, he closed his eyes and waited for exhaustion to take him. Between now and then one face and one voice would taunt him. He hadn't slept a single night without thinking of Bobbie Gentry since back in February, when he'd held her hand in that hospital room and made that damned promise.

She wouldn't remember and he couldn't forget.

In that sterile room all those months ago he'd watched her sleep, absorbing the pain and desperation emanating from her weak and broken body. He had known then that Perry would come after her again. She would be the key to stopping the sadistic bastard. From that moment Nick had learned all he could about her. He'd searched the home she'd shared with her husband and child; over and over he'd watched the videos they'd made. He knew her every move, her every look, her serious side as well as her playful one. The nuances of her voice and the sound of her laughter. He understood her vulnerabilities, few though they were, and her infinite strength.

The woman he had spoken to tonight was nothing like the one captured in those videos with her family and friends. He thought of the way she had smiled before…the way her eyes lit with happiness in the videos. The light was missing from her eyes now, and he was yet to see her lips form a real smile.

Something about her—something he couldn't quite name—haunted him. Reached a place inside him that no one had touched in a very long time. The longer he remained near her, the more powerful that inexplicable link became.

He never permitted personal involvement to develop during his hunts. His life as well as his sanity depended on maintaining distance. Somehow in the past few months he'd lost the ability to distance himself from Bobbie Gentry.

Something he and Perry had in common.

Five

The hum of her cell phone vibrating woke Bobbie. She reached toward the floor and snatched it up. She squeezed her eyes shut and then opened them again in an effort to force her bleary eyes to focus. She hadn't come to bed until after four. It was... 7:30 a.m. glared at her from the screen of her cell. Groaning, she rubbed her eyes and read the name flashing beneath the time. *The boss.*

Bobbie bolted upright. "Morning—" She cleared her throat. "Ma'am."

"I need you at the office ASAP, Detective."

"I'll be right there."

Owens ended the call and Bobbie stared at the phone. Had the chief forgotten to tell Lieutenant Owens about the admin leave? Doubtful. Something was up.

Bobbie pushed to her feet; her right leg protested. She winced and made a path down the hall to the bathroom. One glance in the mirror confirmed she looked as bad as she felt. Good thing she'd showered after her run last night. She dragged a brush through her hair and wrestled it into a ponytail. She washed her face, rolled on deodorant and took care of other necessary business.

She reached for the door and froze. For the first time since she left the rehab center she found herself without a weapon. Her Taser, her knife and both her handguns were still in her bedroom.

Fear expanded in her chest, sliding over her muscles, creeping along her limbs and lodging in her throat. The Storyteller was alive and he was close, and she was in this damned bathroom with no window for escape and no weapon. Sweat coating her skin, she steadied herself and struggled to suck in air around the swelling fear.

Bobbie flattened her hands against the door and closed her eyes. *Listen. You know his footsteps. You know the sound of his breathing.* She forced herself to quiet. Slowed her respiration. Her heart and pulse rates followed suit. The roar of the blood in her ears hushed. Then she held her breath. The low hum of the air coming from the floor vents...and silence.

Drawing in a gulp of air, Bobbie concentrated on the doorknob. Slowly her hand descended to wrap around it. Braced for battle, she twisted the damned thing and jerked the door open. No one jumped at her. No sound of running footsteps echoed. Nothing but the darkness and the stale air being circulated by the old HVAC system.

"Coward," she cursed herself as she stormed back to her bedroom.

Just another secret she kept from the world. Bobbie Gentry was a coward. Without at least one of her weapons she was nothing but a sniveling scaredy-cat. No matter that she'd taken every defense and hand-to-hand combat class she could find between here and Birmingham, she was still a coward.

The world knew the Storyteller had taken her family, but they didn't understand he'd taken something else from her as well...some vital piece she couldn't name.

Doesn't matter. She peeled off the T-shirt and shorts she slept in and tossed them onto the bed. She didn't need that piece to do what she had to do.

Stepping into a pair of panties, she scanned the floor for her shoes. The black leather loafers lay next to the closet door. She pulled on a sports bra and grabbed a pair of socks. Yanking the plastic from a freshly laundered suit, she surveyed the row of pullover blouses that were basically alike except in color. Scooped neck, short-sleeved, functional. She grabbed a white one. The navy suits and black suits were all the same. Serviceable and comfortable.

Dressed, she threaded a regulation leather belt through the loops on her trousers, and one by one stationed her police-issue Glock, cell phone and badge around her waist. She grabbed the black leather shoulder bag that held the rest of her life, including Tic Tacs, latex gloves, an emergency tampon, sunglasses, wallet and her keys, and stepped into her loafers. She headed for the door. At the living room window she checked the street, noted her surveillance detail at the curb. Only one uniform this morning. He lifted a McDonald's coffee cup to his lips, and her own need for caffeine awakened.

There would be coffee at work. She didn't want to take the time to stop at a drive-through en route. Now that her head was clear of sleep, she realized the call from Owens meant new developments. If her presence had been requested despite being on admin leave, something big had gone down— something related to the Storyteller.

Outside, the young officer flashed her a smile as she loaded into her Challenger. "Nice ride."

"Thanks." She started the engine, grateful for the quiet exhaust system. When she'd bought the Hellcat, she'd immediately taken it to a shop to tone down its roar. She wanted the speed and agility but not the growl of the beast under the hood. With this vehicle, if the need arose, she could outrun basically anything else on the road.

Traffic was light. No kids hurrying along the sidewalk headed for school. Jamie would have started pre-K this fall. The realization sank like a massive rock in her gut. She blinked away the burn in her eyes and forced her attention back on the passing surroundings. D-Boy lifted his head and watched as she rolled past. She'd filled his water bowl and taken him a treat around midnight last night. He was a good dog, but she didn't need one.

Nick Shade's image intruded on her thoughts. He'd been watching her. She'd seen him at the fountain last night. There was a darkness about the man. She lacked enough detail to make a valid assessment beyond the fact that he disturbed her somehow. Just another obstacle and potential distraction she didn't need.

She rolled to a stop at the intersection behind a vintage Camaro as black as the car she drove. The Camaro waited for an opportunity to turn left on Fairground Road. She'd seen it around the neighborhood. Probably belonged to a member of Quintero's thug gang. One of these days the guy was going to get what was coming to him. He ran the illegal activities on this side of town. Everyone knew it, but no one could prove it. He and Bobbie had butted heads more than once.

When five then ten seconds passed with no traffic and no movement from the Camaro, tension slid through her. She reached for the gearshift to move into Reverse, but the passenger-side door of the Camaro opened and a man emerged.

"Speak of the devil." What the hell did he want?

Javier Quintero approached her passenger-side window and leaned down to stare at her. "I need to talk to you, *mami*," he said, the glass muffling his voice.

She powered down the window. "We have nothing to talk about, Javier."

He unlocked the door and got in.

Bobbie rolled her eyes. "I don't have time for this."

"Your friend—" he hitched his head to indicate the cruiser behind her "—is causing my *eses* discomfort."

Like she cared what his homeys suffered. "Get out of my car, Javier."

In her side mirror she watched the officer emerge from the cruiser. She swore as she powered her window down.

"Ma'am, is everything all right?" Officer Delacruz, she read his name tag, already had one hand sitting on the butt of his weapon.

"Everything's fine." She offered one of her fake smiles. "Just chatting with a neighbor. Wait in your car, Delacruz."

The painfully young officer, who shared absolutely nothing but a Hispanic heritage with the gangbanger currently occupying her passenger seat, glanced at Javier before giving her a nod and heading back to his cruiser.

"You see what I mean?" Javier complained. "This is bad for business."

There were a number of things Bobbie could have said just then, but she decided in the interest of time she would give it to him straight. "You know that serial killer who almost killed me?"

Javier nodded. "I remember. He's one sick motherfucker."

On instinct, Bobbie checked her mirrors. "He's back, so the chief put a tail on me."

Javier laughed out loud, showing off his gold-and-silver grill. "Your *jefe* thinks that little boy back there is going to protect you, *mami*?"

"I told you to stop calling me that."

"You tell your chief this is *my* neighborhood,"

Javier said, ignoring her comment. "That fucker comes up in here—"

Enough. Bobbie slid her Glock from her belt and jammed it in his face. "Get out of my car."

His mouth eased into a big grin, stretching the scar on his cheek where someone had sliced his face the last time he was in prison. "Don't tease me, *mami.* I get hard when you play with me like this." He flicked out his tongue and traced the muzzle.

She gritted her teeth. "Get out."

The smile vanished and his brown eyes bored into hers. "Tell your chief that Johnny Law needs an unmarked car. He's fucking with my cash flow and I don't like it."

With that demand he exited her car and climbed back into the Camaro. The driver spun out, tires smoking and squealing. Bobbie shook her head and rolled to the intersection. She hoped Delacruz hadn't pissed his pants.

Criminal Investigation Division, 8:15 a.m.

Bobbie entered the building and waved to the sergeant stationed at the visitor's registration desk. If she was lucky, there would be some fresh coffee somewhere in the building. She rounded the corner and bumped into Bauer.

"It's about time you got here, Gentry. Everyone's waiting for you."

Detective Asher Bauer was average height with a well-muscled build maintained by his obsession with the gym. His need to heft weights was matched only by his determination to keep a year-round tan and a trendsetting club wardrobe. The sandy-blond hair and sleep-deprived gaze completed the party-player look he appeared to fancy. If he was smart, he'd find something for those bloodshot eyes. Since his fiancée died he was determined to spend his off time deep in a bottle of Jack and screwing anyone who would spread her legs. Bobbie wished she could find the right words to make him see alcohol and casual sex weren't the answer.

At least he hasn't slit his wrists the way you did.

Bobbie closed out the thoughts and produced another of her standard fake smiles for the guy. "As soon as I get coffee, I'll go to the LT's office."

Bauer moved his head from side to side. "Go to the conference room. I'll bring your coffee. Peterson's in there, too."

"Black, no sugar," Bobbie reminded him before changing directions and heading for the conference room.

Whatever was going on, the chief's presence confirmed it was a high-profile situation like the Storyteller. *Why else would they have called you?*

Anticipation seared through her veins and her fingers itched to draw her weapon and hold on to it just in case. The door to the conference room was open. Peterson sat at the head of the table, Lieutenant Eudora Owens to his right, Sergeant Lynette Holt next to her. Across from the LT were Montgomery County Sheriff Virgil Young and Special Agent Michael Hadden from the local FBI office.

All looked up when Bobbie entered the room. "I guess I'm the last one to the party." She reached for a chair.

"Not quite, Detective."

Her pulse bumping into a faster rhythm, Bobbie turned to the man standing in the open doorway. *Special Agent Anthony LeDoux.* Resentment, bitterness and no small amount of dislike stirred. She clenched her jaw and tamped down the surge of emotions.

LeDoux was only four years older than her. He had been on the Storyteller case since the eighth victim was left at his front door. At the time he'd been a brand-new profiler and his work had apparently drawn the Storyteller's attention. LaDoux's light brown hair was shorter now than it was last December when she'd first met him, and the wedding band he'd worn back then was missing.

"Why don't we get started?" the chief suggested, impatience radiating in his tone. Peterson didn't care much for LeDoux, either, and he didn't mind showing it.

Bobbie shifted her attention to those gathered at the table. "What's going on?" She didn't ask why she was here, she was just grateful not to be left in the dark.

"Lieutenant Owens will brief us," Peterson said, his somber gaze now resting on the Major Crimes Bureau commander.

Bobbie sat down next to Holt. Bauer showed up and took the seat beside her. Thankfully the cup of coffee he sat in front of Bobbie smelled drinkable, which wasn't always the case around here. Many of the detectives in CID were former military who'd done numerous tours of duty overseas, and their definition of full-flavored coffee was something strong enough to eat a hole in the cup.

"About five this morning the car belonging to Gwen Adams was discovered in the driveway of a vacant home on Highland Avenue," Owens announced. "Her purse and keys were still in the car. No sign of her cell phone. Witnesses say the car has been there since yesterday morning or the night before, but none saw the driver or anyone else in or near the vehicle. It wasn't until this morning when the Realtor came by on his way out of town that anyone realized it shouldn't be there. We've had no hits on our BOLO on Ms. Adams, and her boyfriend, Liam Neely, is missing, as well. Based on the number of calls made between Neely and Carl Evans during the forty or so hours before Evans's suicide, we've listed Neely as a person of interest."

Equal parts pain and anger welled inside Bobbie. If the Storyteller followed his usual MO, he would torture Gwen relentlessly and rape her repeatedly. Bobbie closed her eyes. She had to do something. Gwen had worked so patiently with her during her recovery. She refused to give up even when Bobbie was at her lowest. The chief could keep her on admin leave, but Bobbie had to help find Gwen before it was too late. Before the bastard did those things to her...

Whispers and images attempted to invade her thoughts. Strong-arming those ugly memories aside, she glanced at LeDoux, who was busy flipping through pages of reports. To Owens, she said, "Obviously you've decided her abduction is the work of the Storyteller." Bobbie didn't know why she'd bothered with the statement. Of course it was the Storyteller.

"Actually," LeDoux cut in, "I made that call."

Another wave of tension washed over Bobbie as she met his gaze. "Based on what?" Was there more he wasn't telling her, because he couldn't possibly know what Evans had said to her?

To say she despised LeDoux would be a vast understatement. He had known having her on the task force last December would push the Storyteller's buttons. He'd been desperate to see movement on the case. But then, she couldn't hold him responsible for getting her family killed. She had quickly realized the Storyteller would be drawn to her since she fit the profile of his preferred victim and she'd stayed on the case anyway. Both she and LeDoux had hoped to be the one to bring the infamous serial killer to his knees. Apparently—she glanced at the bare ring finger on his left hand—they had both paid a price.

"Based on my recommendation," Chief Peterson announced.

"Why am I here?" Bobbie asked this question directly of the chief. She could feel Lieutenant Owens glaring at her. Didn't matter. The question was a valid one.

"Because I wanted you here," LeDoux answered.

Bobbie turned back to the agent, his words reverberating inside her. This time she couldn't keep the anger from her voice when she spoke. "I should have recognized the MO."

"That's enough, Detective," Owens warned.

"We believe," LeDoux began, "Gwen Adams is being held somewhere in Montgomery County. Perry will want to stay near you, Bobbie."

She wouldn't give him the satisfaction of an acknowledgment.

"Chief Peterson called me yesterday as soon as the Carl Evans case broke," LeDoux continued, speaking to the room at large. "Considering the transfer of Detective Gentry's medical records and the research Evans had been doing on the internet, it's clear this case is related to the Storyteller investigation."

"With Perry active again in our jurisdiction," Owens picked up from there, "we have to assume he has returned for you, Detective."

All eyes at the table moved in Bobbie's direction. She shrugged. "Why else would he resurface and risk getting caught?"

"Precisely," the chief punctuated. "Which is why I believe it would be in your best interest to go into protective custody."

Bobbie had wondered when that suggestion would come up. She was not running from Perry. The only way to stop him was head-on. The one chance Gwen had of surviving was if they found him quickly enough. Bobbie stood and placed her badge and her service weapon on the table. "I'm done here."

A rap on the open door drew the room's collective attention in that direction. The desk sergeant looked from the chief to Bobbie. "I'm sorry to interrupt, but there's a lady at the desk who refuses to leave without seeing Detective Gentry. She says it's urgent."

Shoving her weapon and her badge back into place, Bobbie was at the door before anyone else at the table moved. The sergeant stepped out of her way, and then hurried to keep up with her. With every step, she hoped a little harder that the woman would be Gwen…that maybe she hadn't been taken by the Storyteller.

"Did she give her name?" Bobbie asked the sergeant.

"She wouldn't tell me anything except that she needed to see you."

By the time they reached the lobby, the rest of those gathered for this morning's trap to force Bobbie into protective custody had caught up.

"I'm Detective Gentry," she said as she approached the woman standing alone near the sign-in desk. Not Gwen. *Damn it.*

The woman was medium height, on the thin side and younger than Bobbie, twenty-nine or thirty. Her blond hair didn't look as if it had been brushed this morning. Her brown eyes were red and swollen from crying. "Detective Bobbie Gentry?" she asked.

Bobbie nodded. "Yes, ma'am. What's your name?"

The woman held on to her purse as if she feared someone might try to take it from her at any moment. "Heather Rice." Her lips trembled. "You have to help me." A sob tore from her throat.

"Why don't we sit down, Heather?" Bobbie ushered her toward the row of chairs nearby. Once they were seated, she said, "Start at the beginning and tell me what happened."

"He said I had to find you and that I couldn't talk to anyone else." Heather glanced at the crowd gathered nearby. "Only you."

Peterson stepped forward. "Ms. Rice, I'm the chief of police. You have nothing to fear here. No matter what anyone told you, you may speak freely."

She held his gaze, tears sliding down her cheeks. "You can't help me." She turned to Bobbie. "He said it had to be you." She loosened her hold on her purse and reached inside.

Every armed cop in the vicinity except Bobbie readied to go for their weapons.

Oblivious to the new tension in the room, the woman withdrew a five-by-seven photo from her purse. She handed it to Bobbie. "He said for me to give this to you, and you would understand what it means."

As Bobbie held the photograph, ice formed in her veins, its chill sinking all the way to her bones. She stared at the sweet little face captured there.

The little boy looked to be about three years old. He had wide gray eyes and scruffy blond hair. An ache pierced the one tender spot left inside her, and it took every ounce of courage she possessed to meet the woman's hopeful gaze. "This is your son?"

Heather nodded. "Joseph. I call him Joey. When I woke up this morning, he was gone from his bed. There was a note with a number for me to call. The man who answered told me if I did anything besides what he told me to do he would…" Her face crumpled. "He said he would kill my baby."

Bobbie handed the photo to Bauer, who was already standing by waiting for it. "Where is Joey's father?"

"He was killed in a car accident two years ago." She grabbed on to Bobbie's arm. "Please, you have to find him. He's all I have left."

Before Bobbie could reassure her, the main entrance door opened and another woman walked in. She glanced around, worry and fear cluttering her face. "I need Detective Bobbie Gentry," she said, her voice wobbling on the words.

Numb, Bobbie stood. "I'm Detective Gentry."

The woman's lips trembled. "My boy is missing. The man who took him said I had to find you."

She thrust a photo toward Bobbie. Her heart sank. Little boy…three to four years of age. Blond hair, gray eyes.

"Please," the woman pleaded, "you have to help me find him."

Six

Bobbie moved through the house a second time, searching for any details she might have missed on the first walk-through. Marilyn Taggart's home was neat and well kept, just as Heather Rice's had been. The Taggart home, a small craftsman bungalow in the Capitol Heights neighborhood, was about half the size of the Rice home, located over in a higher-end East Chase subdivision.

With two crime scenes, Bauer and Owens had taken the Rice home while Bobbie and Sergeant Lynette Holt, her immediate supervisor, had come here. The chief had not been happy that Bobbie was involved, but he had deferred to Lieutenant Owens's wishes and taken her off admin leave for the time being. Evidence techs were already crawling over both residences.

Bobbie stood in the doorway of the little boy's bedroom. His room had been dusted for prints and scanned for any other evidence that might not be readily visible to the naked eye. As sad as it was, most children were abducted or harmed by familiars—people they knew. Far too often that person was a parent. That wasn't the case this time. They knew who had taken these children and they knew why.

More of that agony she'd been fighting off tore at her. If he hurt either of these children…

Focus, Bobbie. Gwen and the children need you to do this right.

The Spider-Man comforter was tousled and the window next to the bed was unlocked and open. Anyone could have removed the old wooden screen and come inside. The window locks no longer worked in the old home. Her pulse rate building in spite of her best efforts, Bobbie forced herself to inventory the details of the room. A small bookcase was lined with stuffed animals and Dr. Seuss books. Cars and Legos and Minions littered the floor. Colorful posters of Disney movies along with his drawings and finger-paint creations filled the walls.

Bobbie's soul ached. The room could be Jamie's room. He had loved Legos and Minions. What little boy didn't love cars? She swallowed, hoping to loosen the tightening muscles of her throat. Suddenly she was grateful she hadn't touched the coffee Bauer had brought to her back at the office.

Keep it together. Finding this son of a bitch is all that matters.

Rice was a stay-at-home mom, surviving comfortably on her deceased husband's Social Security payments and the life insurance he'd left behind. She rarely allowed Joey out of her sight. Taggart, on the other hand, was a working mom. She'd been employed as a secretary for Redmont Brothers Construction since before her son was born.

Aaron—his name was Aaron. He would be four next month. Bobbie took a slow, deep breath. Monday through Friday Aaron spent his days at Learning Tots Daycare. Taggart's estranged husband, Scott, was currently unemployed—an ongoing issue—and MIA. A BOLO had been issued for his sorry ass, though it was highly unlikely he had anything to do with Aaron's abduction. Beyond, she amended, the fact that he hadn't been home to protect his child.

You were home, and you still couldn't protect your child.

Bobbie forced away the voice. Amber Alerts had gone out on both children.

She moved away from the door and returned to the kitchen. Holt was outside with the evidence techs working the backyard. Bobbie picked up the carefully bagged instruction letter left behind for Aaron's mother. The single page had been placed on the boy's pillow. Bauer had confirmed the same scenario at the Rice home. Joey Rice's room had been entered through the window, as well. Rice insisted she had not left the window unlocked, but that wouldn't have stopped the Storyteller. He often entered the homes of his victims repeatedly before taking them. Evidence of his visits had been found in each abduction—even in her own.

Newt had told her about how they'd found the little notes Perry had left behind. Descriptions of an item or a room, small notes like a writer would use as reminders of the details needed in developing a story. *A window that overlooks the park. A drawer filled with intimate silk. A teddy bear with only one eye.* None of which she and James had noticed. She'd been too busy working on the case. Those final three weeks before Christmas Eve last year Bobbie hadn't been home more than three or four hours a night—and sometimes not at all. As the librarian at the university, James had been able to take some extra time off and stay home most of the month of December. *Mommy keeps the monsters away.* James whispered those words to Jamie every night when he tucked him into bed to explain why Mommy wasn't there. Agony swelled inside her. She'd fallen down on the job…

She banished the memories and set her attention back to the here and now. The only notes left in the Rice and Taggart homes were the ones giving instructions to the mothers. The cell phone the two had been instructed to call would turn out to be an untraceable burner. He was too smart to make such an elementary mistake.

Bobbie's gaze settled on the photo posted on the fridge with colorful magnets. Aaron Taggart grinned from ear to ear. Those big gray eyes tugged at her heart. *You can't let these kids down, Bobbie. You gotta do better this time.*

"We're done here."

Bobbie turned to the back door as Holt walked in. Holt was not happy—then again she rarely was. She'd spent the entire year pissed at the world because she was turning forty in October. Her wife was pregnant with their long-awaited first child and they'd just bought a fixer-upper in the Garden district. Holt was overwhelmed.

"You find anything out there?" Bobbie followed her toward the front door.

Holt shook her head. "Not one damned thing. They lifted a few prints, but God only knows if we'll get lucky and find a match that doesn't belong to a member of the family. If it's Perry, it's all irrelevant anyway unless he'd added an accomplice to his repertoire."

"Doubtful," Bobbie commented. "He wouldn't want anyone to share the spotlight."

Holt gave a nod of agreement. "Let's get out of here."

Outside a small crowd had gathered behind the police barricade. Neighbors watched and reporters jockeyed for better camera angles. How much longer would they be able to keep the real story out of the news? Once that happened, Bobbie's face would again be all over the papers, television screens and internet. Something else to look forward to.

No feeling sorry for yourself. Imagine what Gwen is going through this very minute.

Bobbie dropped into the passenger seat of Holt's Crown Vic. "We headed to East Chase?" She would like to have a closer look at the other house.

"We can stop by. No problem. I gotta go by the office first, though." Lynette glanced in Bobbie's direction as she started the engine. "You holding up okay?"

"Sure." Bobbie snapped her seat belt into place. "Any of the neighbors see anything?" Uniforms had been canvassing both neighborhoods. If they'd found any witnesses no one had told Bobbie. She didn't expect Holt or anyone else to keep her fully informed. Owens would walk a fine line between keeping her on the job and making the chief happy.

"Nothing so far at this one. A neighbor at the other scene—" Holt swiped her red bangs out of her eyes "—heard a dog barking and a car door slam during the night, but nothing that's going to help us."

Bobbie exhaled a frustrated breath as they drove away. The possibilities of what the piece of shit had planned for these kids ripped at her insides. If he wanted her, why not come for her? Why hurt an innocent child? *I will kill you this time, you bastard.*

"If Peterson gets a whiff of your fear," Holt said, dragging Bobbie's attention back to her, "Owens won't be able to keep you on the job."

"Who the hell said anything about me being afraid?" Holt might outrank her, but Bobbie had no qualms about giving it to her straight. The only thing Bobbie was afraid of was Gwen or one of those children ending up dead before she could find and exterminate the Storyteller.

Holt shrugged as she made a left turn. "I don't

know, maybe it was the way your hands were shaking back there or the way your face is pasty white."

"I'm afraid for Gwen and those children." No point lying about that part.

"This sicko has come back for you, Gentry," Holt said with a glance in her direction. "If you're not just a little bit afraid for yourself, then you need more counseling."

"I go to counseling every week." Bobbie stared out the window. She told the shrink what he wanted to hear, and then she went about her business. No one except someone who'd had her whole life destroyed by a goddamned serial killer would understand.

After a mile or so of silence, Holt spoke again. "He won't stop until he kills you. You know that, right?"

"Unless I kill him first," Bobbie countered. Killing him first was all that mattered.

"I'm going to pretend I didn't hear that." Holt made the final turn into CID and parked. "Don't let anyone else hear you say that kind of shit, Detective."

"Yes, ma'am." Bobbie doubted there was anyone in the department who didn't recognize she wanted to get the Storyteller. It was human nature. As true at that was, Holt was right. She couldn't go around expressing the desire out loud in front of just anyone.

Holt tugged her cell from her belt as they emerged from the car. She made a couple of affirmative sounds before saying, "We're walking in the door now."

Bobbie reached for the door. "We got something new?"

"Gwen Adams's boyfriend." Holt gestured for Bobbie to go in ahead of her. "He turned himself in. LeDoux is headed here to interview him."

"Any chance I can sit in on that interview?"

Holt paused in the middle of the lobby and eyed her for a long moment.

"I mean—" Bobbie shrugged "—I know LeDoux won't like it…"

"Fuck LeDoux. Tell Bauer I said you're taking that interview."

Bobbie did a mental fist pump and thanked the sergeant. She dropped by her cubicle to check her messages. Nothing new. A couple of calls on cases she'd already closed. She didn't know what she'd expected. Maybe a note from the Storyteller telling her his location and inviting her to join him. He would never be that direct. He enjoyed torturing his prey far too much to go straight to the kill.

Hang in there, Gwen. We will find you. She didn't have to wonder if the nurse would take care of the kids. If she was alive and able, she would. Maybe her boyfriend would give them something to go on. Any lead would be better than the nothing they had right now.

"What the hell's going on, Bobbie?"

She turned at the sound of her partner's voice.

Dressed in an elegant black tux, he stopped at her cubicle, his face tight with worry.

"What're you doing here?" Bobbie glanced at the clock hanging on the wall above the side exit. "Your daughter is getting married in one hour. You'd better haul yourself back over to that church." Had Newt lost his mind? His wife would wring his neck.

"Bauer said two children are missing." Newt tugged at his bow tie and grimaced.

"It's *him*," she said, answering the question she saw in his eyes. "He instructed the mothers to talk to no one except me." Fury ignited anew inside her.

Newt shook his head and muttered a curse. "You holding up okay?"

She wished people would stop asking her if *she* was okay. Two children were missing. Gwen was missing. No, she was not okay. She glanced around to ensure no one was nearby. Most of the detectives were in the field. "We don't have the first lead— does that answer your question?"

He dropped his head. "Sweet Jesus."

"Remember you said you'd seen that Shade character around?"

Newt lifted his head and met her gaze once more, his face furrowed with the same worry writhing inside her. "Yeah. A couple of times. I'm pretty sure he wanted me to see him."

"He came to my house."

Newt's eyebrows shot upward. "When did this happen?"

"Last night." She rubbed at the tension in her

neck. "A couple hours after I talked to you, he showed up at my door."

"What did he want?"

"To talk." Bobbie shouldn't have brought it up. Newt had a wedding to get back to. "He warned me to be careful." She had no intention of telling Newt or anyone else the rest of what Shade said. She knew her partner too well. He would try to protect her and get himself killed. This was her fight.

Newt nodded. "I knew it. He's here for Perry. I suspected as much when he came to see you in the hospital."

Urgent whispers sifted through her mind. "You're confident this guy is on the up-and-up?" If Shade was after the Storyteller, too, she needed to know. She didn't want him getting in her way.

"According to Agent Jessup, he's the real deal." Newt shrugged and added, "If you ask me, the guy's psychic or something. Jessup suggested he knows stuff no one else does."

"So why haven't I heard about him?" She shrugged. "I mean, if he's such a superhero, why isn't his name familiar?"

"He doesn't like the limelight," Newt said. "That's what I made of Jessup's assessment. He hunts serial killers and he's very good at it. If there's more to know, it's above my pay grade."

"Is he a vigilante?" *Doubtful*, she decided. He'd be all over the news if that were the case. Blood and guts always led the headlines. Which was all the more reason she didn't want him getting between her and the Storyteller. She didn't want Perry captured and thrust into the justice system, she wanted him dead.

"The one case I know for a fact he was responsible for closing was the Black Widow investigation over in Atlanta." Newt pinched his lips together in concentration. "The one where the woman was using an online dating community to off older guys who used Viagra and dated younger women."

Bobbie vaguely remembered the case. "I thought some firefighter found her or something."

"They did. She was tied up in her bedroom with all the photos she'd taken of the men she'd murdered."

"Shade set a fire and left her there?" Not that Bobbie felt any sympathy for a woman who'd murdered a dozen men.

"There was no fire. It was a false alarm."

"Gentry!"

Bauer hustled over to her cubicle. He looked Newt up and down. "Don't you have a wedding in like forty-five minutes or something?"

Newt heaved a sigh. "I have to go, but I will be back in a few hours."

Bobbie waved him off. "Go. I don't want to see you again until tomorrow." She knew him too well to believe for a second that he'd stay gone that long.

As Newt hurried away, Bauer motioned for her to follow him. "Come on. LeDoux is about to interview the nurse's boyfriend. Holt said you're supposed to be in there."

"Thanks, Bauer." No one wanted to hear what the lowlife boyfriend had to say more than she did.

Liam Neely was thirty-one years old and hadn't had a steady job since his paper route back in middle school. Six feet, 170 pounds, with thick, slicked-back black hair and deep blue eyes, he was quite a handsome man and undeniably charming—which was how smart women like Gwen Adams wound up supporting his sorry ass.

"Mr. Neely, you've been advised of your rights," LeDoux said, "but before we proceed, are you certain you wish to waive your right to an attorney?"

Bobbie wanted to slap him. The idiot had already stated he didn't want an attorney. Was LeDoux trying to help him change his mind? Bobbie clamped her jaw shut and kept her thoughts to herself.

"I had nothing to do with Gwen's disappearance," Neely said, holding his hands up in the air as if to prove he had nothing to hide.

"Why don't you start from the beginning," LeDoux suggested, "and tell us what you know about Gwen's most recent interaction with Carl Evans and her subsequent disappearance."

"Evans needed money. His kid's real sick, and he was tapped out." He clasped his hands on the table. "About a week ago, he asked Gwen to help him. He wanted a copy of Detective Gentry's medical records." He glanced at Bobbie. "Gwen told him no. She was real upset about it because she wanted to help the kid, but she couldn't do it. She was like that, you know. Ethical and all."

Bobbie tensed at his use of *was.*

"Was?" LeDoux frowned. "You spoke about her in the past tense. Is there something we should know about Gwen's welfare beyond the fact that she's missing?"

"No way, man." Neely held up his hands again. "It's not like that. It's just that, hell, it doesn't take a rocket scientist to figure out she's fucked. Nobody survives the Storyteller."

The silence in the room expanded while Bobbie struggled with the emotions determined to undo her. "Are you sure about that, Mr. Neely?"

Neely glanced at her again. "You know what I mean. Most don't survive."

"Did Gwen ever mention why Carl wanted the records?" LeDoux sipped his coffee and stared expectantly at Neely.

"She didn't tell me nothing except she couldn't help him." He studied his fingers. "I went to Carl myself and asked him what was going on. He said this guy on the internet had contacted him. Said he had the answer to his problems."

"So," LeDoux went on, "if Gwen refused to give him the files, how did Carl Evans end up with the medical records?"

Neely looked from LeDoux to Bobbie and back. "You said if I told you the truth, you wouldn't arrest me."

"That's correct," LeDoux confirmed. "I have no interest in arresting you, Mr. Neely. I only want to find Gwen and two missing children. If you can help me, I would sincerely appreciate it. I'm certain you want your girlfriend to be found alive."

He nodded. "Yeah. I do. Absolutely. I would have come forward sooner but I was afraid you'd think I had something to do with her disappearance and I didn't. I swear to God, I didn't have nothing to do with that part."

"Why don't you tell us what happened after she told Evans no," LeDoux suggested in the casual, I'm-your-friend voice interrogators used with guys like Neely.

Bobbie wanted to reach across the table and shake the idiot. He didn't really care about Gwen. He only cared that he didn't get blamed for anything.

"I felt real bad for the kid, you know." Neely stared at the table now, glancing up only occasionally to prevent anyone seeing the lie in his eyes. "So I went to Carl and told him I would help him."

"Help him how?" LeDoux coaxed.

"Sometimes Gwen works from home. Doing paperwork, catching up, stuff like that. She keeps all her passwords for her online stuff written down in a journal in her desk. I got on her computer and checked her search history. It was easy to find where she accessed the different databases for her patients." He shrugged. "I logged on, located the records Carl needed, downloaded them and forwarded them to him." He shook his head. "I know it was wrong, but it was for the kid. I just wanted to help, that's all."

Fury rushed through Bobbie. What a stupid-ass jerk.

"Did Evans show his gratitude in any way for how you helped him?" LeDoux asked, providing the rope Neely needed to hang himself.

"Only ten thousand," Neely said. "He needed the rest of the hundred grand for the kid. I wouldn't accept more than that."

"What happened when Gwen found out?" LeDoux prompted.

Neely sighed. "She told me to get out and never come back." He scrubbed his hands over his face. "Maybe if I'd been there, that twisted motherfucker wouldn't have gotten his hands on her."

Yeah right. Bobbie struggled not to roll her eyes.

"Have you spoken to her since that time?" LeDoux asked.

The dumbass shook his head. "She wouldn't take my calls."

The door eased open, and Bobbie glanced that way. Bauer motioned for her. Since Neely was doing nothing at this point but whining about how much he loved Gwen and how he wished he'd done this or that differently, Bobbie felt confident she wouldn't miss a thing. To LeDoux she said, "Excuse me." She stood and moved to the door.

"What's up?" she whispered with a glance over her shoulder at the table where Neely had lapsed into tears and dropped his face into his hands. Did the guy really believe that act was going to save him?

"They found Scott Taggart's body."

Bobbie jolted. She had hoped they would find the MIA father, but she hadn't expected him to be dead. "What happened?"

Bauer made a pained face. "Damn, Bobbie, it's not easy to tell you this."

"Just tell me already," she muttered.

"His mother came home from work and found him in her kitchen. Deep stab wound to the gut. He bled out right there on the floor just like…" He shrugged and looked away.

Just like her husband had. "Thanks, Bauer." She glanced back at LeDoux and Neely. "You might want to stay for this."

"You worried this guy will give you a hard time?" Bauer asked, surprised.

"I'm worried I might give him one," she let him know. She couldn't afford even the slightest misstep, or she'd be back on admin leave.

Bauer grinned. "You got it."

Bobbie returned to her seat while Bauer loitered near the door.

"I believe that's all for now." LeDoux stood. "Thank you, Mr. Neely."

Neely looked up. "Am I free to go now?"

LeDoux looked to Bobbie before saying, "You'll have to work that out with Detective Gentry."

Bobbie pushed up from her chair. "Liam Neely, you're under arrest." As Bobbie explained the charge and read Neely his rights, Bauer took him into custody.

"Wait!" Neely shouted. "He said I wouldn't be

arrested." He stared after LeDoux as he exited the interview room.

"Agent LeDoux said *he* wouldn't arrest you," Bobbie clarified.

Whether or not Gwen would have been spared her fate if she'd never become involved with a no-account like Neely was an unknown variable. What Bobbie did know was that the woman who had taken such good care of her deserved far better.

"Why aren't you out there searching for Gwen?" Neely demanded. "Look at all she did for you! She helped you!"

The words hit Bobbie hard even though she'd been thinking the same thing. "We're doing all we can, Mr. Neely." And none of it would save her... The painful understanding bored deep into her bones.

Neely dug in his heels as he and Bauer reached the door. "This is all your fault!"

Bobbie met his accusing glare.

"Shut your face," Bauer ordered.

"You know that, right?" Neely shouted at Bobbie as he was dragged out the door. "None of this would have happened if you'd just died like all the others."

Seven

The last of the coffee he'd drank this morning burned its way up his throat and splatted into the toilet. Asher spit and gagged at the nasty-ass taste. The anger had subsided, and all that was left was the goddamned dull, throbbing pain that never really went away.

His body shook from the receding rage. He wiped his mouth with the back of his hand and got to his feet. A toilet two stalls away flushed. Frustration and humiliation wrapped around him and tightened like a vise as he waited for the other guy to clear out. Two quick pumps of soap accompanied the rush of the water running in the sink, and then the drag of paper towels yanked from the dispenser conveyed that he was almost finished. Finally the door opened, followed by the slow sigh of the hydraulic closer allowing the door to drift back into its frame.

Asher braced his forehead against the cool metal wall of the stall and focused on leveling out his breathing. He couldn't tolerate bastards like

Neely. What kind of no-good son of a bitch treated a woman the way Neely had treated Gwen Adams? Asher would give anything—any damned thing—to have Leyla back while ass wipes like Neely tossed away the woman he supposedly loved like yesterday's trash.

No man should get away with that shit.

Who was he to throw stones? Maybe if Asher had been a little more tuned into Leyla, he wouldn't have lost her so soon. He would have recognized the signs and stopped her from taking her life. If he'd been there for her the way she needed, she could have been stronger.

He shut down the painful thoughts. "Gotta pull it together."

He fisted his trembling fingers and fought to regain control. He had a job to do. People were counting on him. Bobbie needed him to help find that damned serial killer. He owed it to the department to do the job right.

Hard as he tried he couldn't get the shakes under control. He damned sure couldn't go back out there like this.

Just a taste. That was all he needed. Enough to get through the morning and then he'd be good to go. He didn't permit this kind of lapse often. Once in a while wouldn't hurt. He was always in full control of his faculties.

Damn straight. *Always.*

He dug into the interior pocket of his jacket and fingered out the slim flask he carried for emergencies. This morning definitely met the classification of emergency. He downed a couple of shots of smooth whiskey and savored the familiar burn. Even before the Jack Daniel's hit his bloodstream he felt the flood of relief.

Tucking the flask away, he exited the stall. He washed his hands and face and popped an Altoid. As the shaking slowly subsided he drew in a deep breath and squared his shoulders. He was good to go.

Work was all he had now. Fucking it up wasn't an option.

Eight

Bobbie retied the laces of her running shoes. She checked the small holster strapped at her ankle, tucked the stun gun into a better position in her sports bra and gave the knife sheathed at the small of her back a final pat. Shade's words about her checking her weapons ricocheted through her mind. She'd have to make a conscious effort not to check them during her run.

Pulling on her spiral wrist key chain, she headed for the door. She went through her usual routine of checking beyond the window blinds before exiting her house. Once the door was locked, she bounded down the cracked sidewalk. Her surveillance detail readied to roll. The two new officers on duty tonight had obviously been advised of her nightly rituals.

Rather than allow her frustration to compound, she focused on the street and cleared her head of the day's stressors and static. No matter how hard she tried, Neely's voice intruded again. *None of this would have happened if you'd just died like all the others.*

Her jaw tightened, and she pushed into a run. Maybe she should have told him that she'd wished the same thing too many times to count. But she couldn't take the easy way out. She had a different mission. She had to find Gwen and the children. Once the Storyteller was dead...then it wouldn't matter if she lived or died.

D-Boy wagged his tail as she sprinted past his yard. She was already dreading winter for the animal. Maybe she'd call the landlord and see about getting permission to install a large fenced enclosure in the side yard. As long as it didn't cost the landlord, surely the woman who owned D-Boy wouldn't mind. She could buy D-Boy a good-sized doghouse, and then he'd stay warm this winter. She couldn't bear the idea of him freezing on that porch. Winters in Alabama weren't severe, but the weather dropped well below the freezing point too often for an animal to be chained to a porch post with no proper shelter. More often than not when she came home, his chain was tangled to the point that even if he had a decent shelter on the porch he wouldn't be able to reach it. He should be freed from that damned chain.

Farther up the next block a dark car eased to the curb on her side of the street beneath the only working street lamp. The nose of the black Ford sedan pointed in her direction. No one she recognized. Tension rippled through her warming muscles. As she approached the vehicle's position the driver's-side window powered down. Light from the street lamp spilled over Nick Shade's face.

Bobbie slowed to a walk. The surveillance detail moved up next to the vehicle. Bobbie waved them on, but they didn't go far. The cruiser pulled to the curb a few yards beyond her position.

She braced her hands on the roof of the car and stared down at the driver. "If you plan to show up every night like this, you need to come prepared to keep up on foot. Using your car to tag along is an unfair advantage."

He studied her a moment, his dark gaze eventually settling on hers. "There's something I need to show you."

Bobbie laughed, mostly to cover the unexpected tremor prompted by his words. What the hell was wrong with her? "You really should sharpen your pickup skills, Shade. But, just so you know, don't waste your time with me." She straightened, drawing away from his car.

"It's about Perry."

She hesitated for about three seconds, long enough to remind herself that no matter what Newt had heard, she didn't know this guy.

"I'm not armed, Detective. You have nothing to fear from me."

Somehow she doubted the latter was true. She rounded the hood and climbed into the passenger side. "Where we going?"

"The motel I've been staying in since the middle of May."

Not wanting him to see her surprise, Bobbie fiddled with her seat belt rather than look at him as he guided the car onto the street. He'd been here—watching her—for more than three months? Why the hell hadn't he talked to her before Carl Evans blew his damned brains out? Before Gwen Adams and two children were abducted?

She didn't have to ask. The answer was simple. If he was the kind of hunter Newt believed he was, lying in wait for his prey was what he did. A good hunter familiarized himself with his prey's territory and behavioral patterns. Shade was no doubt well aware his prey—the Storyteller—would return to Montgomery for the one that got away.

Whatever Shade was, he was no better than the media vultures who showed up at her door every few weeks and pestered her. Anger rumbled inside her. He had his agenda and nothing else mattered. Did he even care about the victims? Did someone somewhere pay him to track monsters like the Storyteller? Some benevolent benefactor of mankind in general? Or some twisted recluse obsessed with serial murders?

She took a breath and reminded herself that if he could somehow contribute to her goal of finding the Storyteller she didn't give a damn what he was or who sent him—as long as he didn't get in the way.

"We want the same thing, Detective."

She frowned, hating the notion that this guy

seemed as though he could read her mind. Damned sure felt as if he could. "I doubt you know what I want, Mr. Shade."

"You want to stop him. I want the same."

What she wanted was to watch him die, but she kept her mouth shut. Holt was right. She shouldn't mention that to anyone if she wanted to continue working in an even remotely official capacity— and that was the sole way to ensure she was kept in the loop. As long as Owens allowed her to work on the case, she intended to keep her mouth shut and play by the rules, at least when anyone was watching and until she had the right opportunity. When that opportunity presented itself, nothing and no one would stop her from killing the Storyteller by any means possible.

Bobbie watched the street signs as Shade drove. The cruiser's headlights remained in the rearview mirror. He made no attempt to lose them. The dim glow from the dash allowed her to see the rigidity in the line of his jaw. He wasn't as relaxed as he would have her believe. His fingers were clenched on the steering wheel. She inhaled deeply, smelled his skin but nothing else. He wore no aftershave or cologne, only the clean scent of soap or maybe shampoo. His shirt was long-sleeved, but the sleeves were rolled up to his elbows. Like before, he wore jeans. She couldn't see his footwear, but she imagined they were the same boots she had noticed the first time they met.

He made a turn onto South Boulevard, and then

into the half-empty parking lot of the Economy Inn. He backed into a slot in front of a door she would lay odds on as the one leading to his room. He shut off the engine and climbed out of the car. Before she'd opened her door, he was there waiting.

Her surveillance detail parked facing their location. She gave them a wave while Shade unlocked the door to his room. Maybe the two cops would believe this was a booty call and wouldn't report it to Owens or Peterson. She doubted she would ever be that lucky.

Shade opened the door and waited for her to enter before him. The room was the usual single. A bed, along with a table and a chair that sat in front of the one window, and not much else. Next to the sink on the far side of the room were the closet and a door to the bathroom. Under the counter that held the sink was a chest cooler—the kind people used for tailgating parties.

When Shade closed the door and she turned back in that direction she saw the reason he'd brought her here. The entire wall had been cleared of any cheap artwork that came with the room and was now devoted to the Storyteller case.

Startled and at the same time curious, Bobbie wandered to that side of the room. Photos from every single crime scene attributed to the Storyteller were posted. Older crime scene photos that she couldn't readily identify drew her to a column topped with a big question mark.

"I believe those were his first murders, but I have no evidence to support that theory."

The deep, rich sound of his voice stirred something distant and somehow familiar inside her, but it was the suggestion that made her shiver. "These were where?" She tried to identify the official vehicle captured in one of the photos. "France?"

"Yes. In a village just outside Paris." Shade indicated one of the photos as he moved closer, the heat from his body crowding around her, making her feel restless. "Perry and his best friend from high school, Kevin Woodson, spent a summer in Paris after graduation. Though the murders were very different, the victims were remarkably similar to the ones Perry has chosen since. I believe those young women were his first kills. Maybe he and Woodson killed them together. The two had been friends since grade school and were the class nerds voted mostly likely to be forgotten senior year. I've tried to locate Woodson, but he disappeared a couple of years after their return to the States."

Bobbie studied the photos, her pulse beating faster and faster. "Perry..." She swallowed the bitter taste of his name on her tongue. "He may have killed his old friend to keep him quiet. He told me he'd killed three men—" she wished her throat wasn't so damned dry "—including my husband."

"I read the reports."

She swung her attention to him. "How do you have access to official MPD files?" Not to mention FBI files.

"Accessing databases isn't that difficult."

She started to demand a real answer, but right now what she actually wanted was to know more about the Storyteller. "You don't find it surprising he's killed both women and men?"

"Less than one-third of serial killers do, but the answer as to whether he falls into that category or not lies in the motive for murdering the male victims," Nick explained. "If he murdered Woodson, it was likely to ensure his freedom was never in jeopardy. He murdered your husband to accomplish a particular goal. Neither of those kills was for pleasure as his others were."

He murdered James to get to me. Bobbie blinked away the thought. "Do the French authorities know about this?" She looked from the man to the photos on his wall and back. With him so close she could see the fine lines that bracketed his eyes—the ones that came with pain and defeat rather than age.

"After the FBI announced his identity, I started digging, as did LeDoux and his team. I anonymously forwarded the information to the detective in France who worked this case." He indicated the victims listed beneath the question mark. "LeDoux did the same a couple of weeks later."

Shade gestured to the other photos she hadn't seen before, two women with very similar physical characteristics as the victims discovered in France. "I sent the same information to the investigator who worked the case at the university Perry attended in Minnesota. I believe he's responsible for those murders, as well."

"I hope you tip the housekeeper well." She was surprised MPD hadn't gotten a call already about Shade and the collage in his room.

"The manager and I have an arrangement. I clean up after myself and pick up fresh sheets at the office."

Sounded like the man had all his bases covered. Putting a little distance between them, Bobbie examined the other photos and the accompanying details. Her lungs struggled to draw in enough air as she scanned Shade's in-depth accounting of the Storyteller's killing history. He had documented facts even the feds hadn't discovered—at least, if LeDoux knew about some of this he had chosen not to share the information with the MPD.

"This is incredible…" Her breath caught again as she came to the photos of her. Shade had documented her history from college until now. Whispers from those memories she couldn't quite grasp resonated inside her. The newer photos—the ones of her running, going to work, dropping by the supermarket—ignited an emotion she couldn't fully label.

She turned to him, the unfamiliar feeling making her angry. "You have no right to watch me like this." She reached for a photo of her outside her home… the home she had once shared with her family. She ripped it from the wall. "This is private." She trembled with the bombardment of raw sensations. How dare he intrude on that part of her life? That part had nothing to do with this goddamned nightmare.

He tugged the photo from her hand. "This is the part that will get you dead, Detective."

"I don't need you telling me what to do or—" she waved a hand at the intrusive photographs "—watching over me."

He stepped in toe-to-toe with her, sending her tension to a whole new level. "You can't really believe you'll be able to stop him alone."

She refused to argue the point. "I've seen enough. I'll catch a ride back to my place with the uniforms outside."

Long fingers closed around her arm. "He'll use this weakness against you. You can't win with all that emotional baggage strapped to your chest. It's like a ticking bomb, and it will go off."

Another burst of fury charged through her. "What the hell do you know about me other than this?" She flung her free hand at the wall. "You don't know me at all."

He put his face in hers. "I know you're operating on emotion, and that will be your downfall. You want him dead. You don't care when or how as long as it happens. You're playing fast and loose, no plan—just draw him in. Don't think for one second that Perry hasn't noticed. He has and he's using it against you."

Shade was guessing. "Good thing you're not a poker player." She jerked free of his hold, her skin on fire from his touch. "I have a plan."

He moved his head side to side. "You walked into the Evans home against the advice of the negotiator and the SWAT commander. You sat at an intersection and permitted one of the most notorious gang leaders in the city to get into your car. You allowed me—a complete stranger—into your home. Right this second you're standing in a low-rent motel room with that complete stranger. You don't have a plan—you have a death wish."

The truth in his words seared through her soul. "I was armed in each of those instances." Her fingers itched to draw her backup piece and shove it in his face. "I'm armed right now."

"You protect yourself from what's right in front of you, but you don't protect your back."

"What does that mean?" He was grasping at straws in an attempt to distract her.

"Even butterflies and moths use their wings to deceive their predators into believing they're much larger and more dangerous than they really are. You." He moved his head slowly from side to side. "You don't bother. You throw caution to the wind—opening yourself to attack. You're practically begging him to come get you."

"I know the enemy, Shade. It's called setting a trap. Are you familiar with the concept?" She turned to the crime scene photos stacked in ominous rows like a freshly planted killing field. She needed to calm the hell down. The man had done some serious digging; she had to give him that. He had photos of the Storyteller going all the way back to his childhood.

"A monkey recognizes its enemy, as well," he said, his voice too damned soft. "Which is why some of its wiliest predators have developed a way to mimic the distressed cries of baby monkeys. Are you certain you're the one setting the trap here?"

"Damn straight." She wanted to scream. What else could she do but lure the son of a bitch? A woman was missing. Two children were missing... two blond-haired, gray-eyed children. *Like Jamie.* Her heart squeezed. Obviously Shade knew as well as she did what could happen to them. She evicted the too-painful reality and glared at the man standing so damned close. "Who the hell are you?" She shook her head. "Better yet, *what* are you?"

"Who or what I am is irrelevant. All that matters is that I will find Gaylon Perry, and I will stop him. But I can't do what I need to do if you get in the way."

Bobbie laughed. "Really?" She lost her cool completely then and poked him in the chest with her forefinger. "You come into my jurisdiction and tell me not to get in *your* way? Get over yourself, Shade. You're not some comic-book superhero, and I'm no terrified victim running for my life. I'm a cop and a damned good one. I know what I'm doing. What I don't know is who you really are and what the hell you're doing." She gestured at his work. "With all this."

Shade held her glare for what felt like an eternity.

"First, you are a good cop, but your instincts are compromised by emotion." When she would have protested, he held up a hand. "Before you make any more rash decisions, why don't I tell you who Gaylon Perry is?"

"I already know who he is. He's a twisted psychopath and a serial killer." Shade was evading her question. She would not waste time going back and forth with him. If he didn't start giving her some straight answers rather than repeating the same bullshit, she was out of here. Three lives were counting on someone to find the goddamned Storyteller.

"We'll see about that, Detective." He motioned to the chair next to the table. "Have a seat, and I'll tell you what you *don't* know about the serial killer who devastated your life."

Saying no wasn't an option. She never made it to the chair. Her knees held out only long enough to lower herself onto the foot of the bed. As much as she needed any information this stranger could give her...the fact that he was right on at least one count scared her to death.

Emotion had compromised her instincts, which made her an easier target. She had to fix that problem. She was too close to make a mistake now.

She could not get herself killed until the Storyteller was dead.

Nine

She could hear them again.

Gwen Adams tugged at her bindings. She had decided there was more than one child being held in the other room. Either that or the drugs the son of a bitch had given her were making her hallucinate. Fear and anger warred inside her. This was Liam's and Carl's fault. Her heart ached at the thought of sweet, sweet little Tara. Gwen couldn't really hold Carl responsible for his actions. He was only trying to save his precious Tara. Another eruption of anger twisted in her belly. But Liam, he was nothing but a no-good piece of shit.

How had he fooled her for so long? He was the reason she was here. He was the reason she would die.

Terror, ice-cold, snaked through her naked body. Liam had told her to meet him over on Highland Avenue to look at a house. He knew how badly she wanted to buy a place of her own. He'd sworn the house was just what she was looking for and the price was right, only he hadn't shown. He'd set her up. Gwen was certain of it. She wondered what he'd gotten paid for delivering her to the damned serial killer who'd almost killed Bobbie Gentry.

Please, God, don't let him kill me.

Tears flooded her eyes as fear and defeat welled in her chest. She didn't want to die.

Soft whimpers interrupted her desperation. *The children.* She wasn't hallucinating. There were children here. At least two. How could she lay here feeling sorry for herself when those children needed her? She swallowed against the awful taste in her mouth.

She had to get loose so she could help the children. First she swiped the edge of the duct tape covering her mouth against her arm over and over. She pushed at it with her tongue. Finally it came loose, and she was able to rub it aside. Then she tugged at the cloth that tethered her wrists above her head to something she couldn't see. Her legs were extended and spread wide apart, her ankles bound to the floor. Pulling on her right hand as hard as she could, she stretched toward the cloth and chewed at it. Over and over she ripped and yanked with her teeth. Finally the cloth ripped, and her heart leaped. Her right hand was free!

Turning to her left, she went through the same steps, tugging and tearing at the cloth. Victory seared through her veins as she freed her left hand. She sat upright and reached for her ankles, first one and then the other. Her heart pounding, she scrambled up from the awful mattress that smelled like the ones she'd helped remove from the beds of patients who'd died in a nursing home where she'd once worked.

She swayed, then steadied herself. Whatever he'd given her, her muscles were weak. *Hold it together, Gwen.* She could do this. The room was dark. She held still for a bit until her head stopped spinning. Her first instinct was to run; instead she listened for any sound beyond the whimpering of those kids. *Quiet.* Thank God. He was gone for now. He'd drugged her and then left her alone several times. He might be gone for hours.

Her fingers numb, she struggled with the rope around her neck. Hard as she tried she couldn't loosen it. The damned thing just bit more deeply into her skin. *Screw it!* She moved toward the window and looked out. In the distance she could see the lights of downtown. Her pulse raced faster and faster. All she had to do was get the children and get out of here. Her legs started to shake. *No. No. No.* She couldn't allow the shock to set in now.

Clothes, she needed clothes.

Gwen shook her head. Check on the children first.

Hands out in front of her in the darkness, she felt her way across the room. The first door she encountered was locked. She twisted and pulled hard on the knob, shook the door, but it was no use. The urge to run was nearly overwhelming. She wanted to kick and pull until the damned thing fell off its hinges.

"Find those babies—then you can run," she muttered, letting go of the knob.

She moved cautiously around the room until she felt another door. This one opened easily. The sobbing and whimpering was louder now. Her heart stumbled. She instinctively made shushing noises as she eased into the room. Their cries grew shriller. Even with her eyes adjusted to the darkness, she couldn't really see anything. If there was a window in this room, it was boarded up. She felt for the nearest wall and then moved slowly around the space. Stumbling into or over one of the children might injure one of them or her. They wouldn't be able to escape this hellhole if she was injured.

"Shh…it's okay now. I'll get you out of here."

The sobs grew more frantic, breaking her heart.

"It's okay. It's okay," she murmured as she moved closer to the sounds. Her fingers touched silky hair. Her heart pounded harder. "There you are." She squatted and felt the first child's face and then the other's. There was tape over their mouths. She started to peel it free but stopped. If she pulled off the tape the children would likely scream and that might alert him if he was somewhere outside.

Something moved against her leg. She roved her hands over the second child. Her body started shaking again. She had to get these children out of here while the adrenaline was still pumping through her veins.

More movement drew her attention beyond the second child. *Jesus.* How many kids did he have in here? She felt for the second child's hands. Wrists and ankles were bound together but not tethered to anything. She'd have to get them loose first.

"Don't worry," she whispered, "I'll get you out of here and take you home to your mommas."

The child's body trembled. "It's okay—it's okay," she promised.

More rustling of fabric against the wood floor drew her attention to the third child. She reached over to pat the poor baby. "Don't be afraid. It's okay now."

His hateful chuckle filled her ears before her brain registered the danger. He grabbed the rope around her neck and yanked her downward. A scream filled the room—*her* scream. The children's sobs grew louder. Gwen tried to fight. She twisted her body and clawed at the bastard with her both hands as he climbed atop her.

He grabbed a handful of her hair and slammed her head against the floor again and again. Her arms grew limp and so very heavy. Her body went lax against the floor.

He pressed his weight down on hers. "Did you really think it would be so easy?"

She couldn't see his face in the darkness, but now that it was so close to her own she could hear his heavy breathing, could feel his hot breath. "Please," she whimpered. "Do whatever you want to me, but let the children go." What in the world was he going to do with the children?

He laughed, the sound booming all around her like thunder.

Her head hurt, and the room wouldn't stop spinning. She tried to make her body move, but she couldn't...

He held her limp arms above her head with one hand and fumbled between their bodies with the other. She tried to rally the strength to fight, but she couldn't.

"When you chose rescuing the children over trying to escape," he murmured against her cheek, "I got so hard I thought I'd burst."

"Please," she murmured. "Don't hurt the children."

He rammed into her. She grunted...couldn't scream. *The children...*

Bile rushed into her throat. He rammed into her again. The body that no longer belonged to her jerked with the deep intrusion. A sort of numbness spread through her, as if her body was already dead. She heard the sounds of his assault but felt nothing.

As her mind faded to black, she thanked God for the darkness that prevented the children from seeing what the animal was doing to her.

Then the blackness consumed her.

Ten

Nick wasn't sure if he'd gotten Bobbie's full attention yet, but he was getting there. She was the first victim he'd interacted with—the victims of those he hunted were always deceased. That she was a cop created yet another challenge. The goal wasn't to impress her; it was merely to help her better comprehend the situation. She stood squarely between him and his objective. Her compromised emotional state made her far too unreliable to provide any value to the hunt.

If he was going to maintain his focus, he couldn't afford to be distracted by her. She needn't worry that sitting on the sidelines would hinder the outcome. Gaylon Perry would not escape. Nick doubted saying as much would yield the hoped for reaction. The detective wasn't going to thank him and go hide in protective custody. He had to tread carefully. This was, as she'd said, her jurisdiction.

"So if we add the three victims from France, and

the two students who disappeared from the university he attended, along with his friend Kevin Woodson, we still have one victim unaccounted for."

He nodded. "That's correct."

She moved along the wall, studying the photos. "So Perry—" she inhaled slow and deep as if saying the name was a tremendous burden "—goes off to France and has a wild summer with his equally weird friend and then he returns to settle into college life. But he's had a taste now. He has to kill again." She paused on a photo of Perry's father. "He's from a conservative family and community. From all accounts, his father was a strict disciplinarian, a religious fanatic some claimed." She met Nick's gaze again. "The father denies it, but I believe the scars on Perry's body were from being abused by one or both parents. It fits the FBI's profile."

Her eyes told Nick they shared the same feelings on the matter: too bad the old man hadn't killed him long ago. "I spoke to a few former members of the congregation and a couple of neighbors who weren't fans of his father," Nick said. "All said the same— he preaches fire and brimstone sermons and would stone sinners if he had his way."

"Who's this?" Bobbie reached up and traced the close-up of the hideously scarred body in the first of four photographs. Each showed a portion of a female body from the neck down.

"Perry's mother."

"His mother died of a stroke." Bobbie's confusion showed in her frown. "I've seen plenty of photographs of his mother and none—"

"Her husband abused her," Nick interrupted what he knew would be a repeat of one or more FBI reports. "Their entire marriage, I suspect. He was careful to ensure the damage was never visible. All the scars are below the neck and above the knees and elbows."

"Jesus Christ." Bobbie leaned in to more closely examine the photos. "How did we not know this? Some of the patterns…"

Her gaze met Nick's. She didn't have to say the rest. Bobbie's body was marked with similar patterns of torture, as was Perry's.

"His mother was quiet and kind and completely dedicated to her husband, the church and her son— in that order." Nick gestured to the other photos of Perry's mother that showed an overly modest woman who hid her attractiveness most likely to avoid additional beatings in the event another man dared look her way. "Her whole life revolved around obedience and sacrifice."

"How did you get these photos? There was no autopsy." Bobbie put a hand to her throat. "At the time of her death, no one knew Perry was the Storyteller."

Although Nick never revealed his sources, he felt her comprehension of the scope of his preparation was essential. "When I begin, everyone and everything related to the killer is relevant. Nothing is too insignificant. I don't wait for an opportunity to come to me. I search for and make the opportunity. These photographs were obtained from someone who had access to the body after her death."

"You mean you bribed a morgue assistant or funeral home attendant." She made a scoffing sound. "How could you be sure he would have photos, much less photos of this?"

"I couldn't, but I made it a point to find out."

She made a face. "Was your source some sort of necrophiliac?"

"Does it matter?"

For a moment her pale blue eyes held his, searching for answers he would never allow her to see. "No," she confessed, "I suppose it doesn't."

She turned back to his research. "The FBI profile concluded that when his mother died, he lost control and sought comfort by taking another victim." Her voice was distant now; the memories took her all the way back to the time and place that marked the beginning of the devastation to her world.

"He took a leave of absence from his position at the high school," Nick picked up from there, "to help his father with the funeral, and he never returned. He abducted and murdered Alyssa Powell, and then he became obsessed with you." He agreed with those conclusions in the FBI's lengthy report.

She hugged her arms around her chest and looked away. "No girlfriends, no wife, no history of any relationships outside the family."

"Other than Woodson," Nick pointed out, "that's correct."

"Family friends and neighbors, even the father, claimed Perry was too dedicated to his work and to the church for a social life." She shuddered and hugged herself tighter. "Do you agree with the FBI profile that the abuse his father staunchly denies triggered his need to kill? That it's the only way he can find sexual release?" Her gaze swung to his.

"I do." Nick had to look away. The dark shadows haunting her eyes now tugged at him in a way that was detrimental to his ability to stay centered on the task that lay ahead. "For the record, I don't agree with the part that suggests Perry's volunteer work with community youth groups was a way to make up for his bad deeds. In my opinion, it was simply another way of hiding in plain sight and proving his superiority. He was so clever, he could fool the whole town. To trust someone with your child is the deepest trust."

"And no one could see who he really was." She paused at the photos of his dead mother's scar-ravaged body. "Not even his own mother."

"Her son was the one thing that made her smile." Nick had heard that same statement from everyone he interviewed. He moved closer to the photos he had obtained from the albums in Perry's childhood home. "Even at twelve years old, he's standing closer to his mother than his father in family photos. See his right hand resting on her shoulder—that's a sign of protectiveness. No matter that he couldn't protect her—he wanted to. Every moment they shared away from his father was likely intense and filled with a kind of urgency and secrecy that one day things would be different. The two of them against the world."

Bobbie took a big breath. "Good thing he was an only child."

"There was another child born when he was ten," Nick corrected her, "but the infant died when he was only three months old. From pneumonia according to the death certificate."

"Something else the FBI didn't share." Bobbie stood back and surveyed the photos again as if seeing them for the first time. "How did you get all these photos? I don't think LeDoux has any of these."

"Family albums." Nick avoided eye contact. More of those details she didn't need to know.

"His father let you copy the family photos?" She laughed, the sound almost real. "No way. He gave one interview to LeDoux when Perry's identity was first discovered and then he lawyered up. The man did not willingly hand over these photos. In all the searches of his home, the FBI didn't bother with copies of these older family photos. Why did you?"

"Like I said, everything in Perry's world is relevant." Nick might as well get the other part over with. "As for how I got the photographs, I don't operate under the same rules that bind law enforcement."

Another of those almost laughs burst from her lips. The sound warmed him. He cursed himself. Another warning that she was a dangerous distraction. He had to find a way to distance himself. He was the one who wanted to laugh at that one. How was he supposed to distance himself from her when she was inextricably involved in what he needed to do?

"You broke into the man's house and took photos of all these," she guessed.

"I do whatever it takes." Nick did meet her gaze then. He was surprised to find no contempt or accusation. He would have preferred her distrust over the glimmer of respect he saw in her eyes. "Breaking and entering, however, is your theory about how I obtained the photos. You have no evidence to substantiate the allegation."

"I don't know who you are—" she searched his face for a long moment "—but if you can help me save those children and Gwen Adams, I don't care if you break every law known to man."

Anticipation expanded in his chest. Now they were getting somewhere. "Are you saying you'll stay out of the way and let me do what I need to do to stop him?"

She schooled her expression, exiling that glimpse of her true feelings she'd only just shown him. "No way. I'll take any and all help to save the hostages, but he's mine."

His frustration cranked up a few more notches. He had no one to blame for this situation but himself. He should have stayed in the shadows where he belonged. Her determination to end up a victim again had drawn him closer and closer. He'd stepped into her world to warn her and now he couldn't turn back.

"You want him dead. I get that, but you need to stop thinking of yourself and think about all his other victims for a minute."

Outrage darkened her blue eyes. "I am thinking of his other victims. I intend to make sure there aren't any more."

"And the ones we aren't certain about? Like the two college students? Are you willing to take peace away from those families?"

"So." She shifted her attention back to his collection of data. "His father's abuse murdered, in a manner of speaking, the little boy Perry was and created the monster he is today," she said, changing the subject. "The way he tortures and murders his victims tells the story he lived over and over as a child."

At least she was still talking. As long as they were communicating there was a chance she would listen to reason.

"Very good, Detective. You only missed one very important detail." He tapped a photo of Perry's mother when she was in her early thirties. "Look closely at her. Beyond the Puritan clothing and hairstyle."

When Bobbie's breath caught, he went on, "Do you recognize her? Long dark hair, light blue eyes and pale skin. Tall and slender. Every time he takes a victim, tortures and rapes her, he's torturing and raping his mother for not saving him." He looked straight into Bobbie's eyes and said the rest. "You look more like her than any of his other victims. That's why he couldn't resist you."

Bobbie drew back. "The FBI profile—"

"I know what the FBI profile says."

She stared directly at him then. "You want me to believe you know more than a trained profiler?"

"Believe what you will. After you left Perry for dead in the cabin, was the FBI able to trace his movements beyond the ride he hitched out of Mississippi?"

She glared at him without saying a word. There was nothing she could say, because the truth was they hadn't. She, like the authorities, knew Perry had made it out of the woods that day and caught a ride with a man just passing through the state. The unlucky guy's body had been found two weeks later. Since he was on vacation, the missing person's report hadn't been filed for days after his murder, and the connection to Perry hadn't been discovered for another month. That was where the FBI's search went cold.

"Like you," Nick explained, "Perry had some recovering to do. When you stabbed him, you missed anything vital, but you still managed significant damage." Lucky for Perry, the vintage Asian tattoo needle glanced off a rib. Too bad for the rest of the world.

When she made no attempt to interrupt, he continued, "It took me three months to trace his movements. I located the woman—a doctor—who provided medical care to him. The serial killer groupie stitched him up and provided shelter for six days."

Disbelief briefly overrode the anger and frustration. "Did you turn her over to the authorities?"

"I did, and that's where the trail went cold for me. I've been here waiting for him since. You have my word, Detective Gentry. I will stop him. I've never failed. I don't intend to this time."

For a long moment she only stared at him. "How do you expect me to believe you and all your research—" she gestured to the wall where he'd created the history of the case "—can somehow do what no one else has been able to?"

"I guess you'll just have to take my word for it."

She held up her hands stop-sign fashion. "How about you do your thing and I'll do mine?" She headed for the door.

Nick silently cursed himself. He'd long ago lost any people skills he'd ever possessed. "Wait."

One hand on the doorknob, she hesitated. "You know, my partner believes in you." She exhaled a big breath, shook her head. "He thinks you're psychic or something. A legend the FBI only whispers about."

Nick dared to move closer without the shield of anger. "What do *you* think?"

She turned from the door. Her blue eyes flared when she recognized how close he was. "I'm not sure. You operate outside the law to hunt down and stop serial killers, and I'm a cop. What should I think?"

"Maybe that I'm doing the right thing—the thing that no one else can do."

"You're a vigilante."

"And you're not?" The words were out before he could stop them.

Determination hardened in her eyes. "Don't pretend to know how I feel."

"I couldn't possibly."

"That's right. You couldn't. I don't want the son of a bitch to end up with life because some DA offers him a deal for sharing where he hid the bodies. I want him to die. I want him to die screaming."

A knock on the door shattered the silence that followed.

Nick kept his feelings on her admission to himself and waited while she moved aside. He checked the security viewfinder in the door. One of the officers from her surveillance detail was on the other side. Nick opened the door.

"Sir, I need to speak with Detective Gentry."

She stepped between him and the door and Nick backed away. He shouldn't have brought her here. Another misstep.

"What do you need, Officer Atkins?"

"Dispatch got a message for you from an anonymous caller."

She checked the cell fastened to her arm in an athletic band. "Why the hell didn't dispatch call me?"

"I don't know, ma'am, but the message was a little strange. It was nothing but a location."

"What location?"

"I-85 North, Exit 9. I believe that's the Taylor Road exit."

"Thank you, Atkins. I'll need a ride to the location."

Nick grabbed his keys before the uniform could respond. No way was he letting her out of his sight. "Let's go."

The MPD cruiser followed closely as Nick drove the mile required to access Interstate 65. Bobbie didn't say a word, but she didn't need to for him to understand she was worried the call meant Perry had made a move. It could be anything or nothing at all. Perry's MO was all over the map at this point. If he did manage to accomplish his goal of abducting and murdering Bobbie without being caught, he fully understood that his life as Gaylon Perry was over. Like a prisoner on death row, the Storyteller had little to lose, which made him far more dangerous than before.

"How about giving it some gas?" Bobbie tugged at the shoulder strap of her seat belt.

Nick pressed a little harder on the accelerator, the seconds ticking off like bombs in his head. Perry never took children. Sadly, Nick understood the goal of this unexpected move. He wanted to hurt Bobbie. He wanted to engage her emotions, making her more vulnerable. The more vulnerable she was, the more likely she was to make a mistake. She wasn't the only one headed down the wrong path.

Nick never allowed himself to obsess over any person involved in a hunt. Bobbie Gentry was a first.

The exit ramp for I-85 came into view, and he slowed for the turn. Gentry tugged her cell from its holder. "Detective Gentry."

Nick kept his attention on the road, but the escalating tension in her voice as she gave one-word responses to her caller warned the news was not good.

"We're almost there." She ended the call and shoved her phone back into its holder. "Step on it, Shade. Dispatch received three nine-one-one calls about a child on the interstate. Blue shorts, white tee. Blond hair."

Perry was taunting her with the memories of her own little boy's death. The bastard. He'd read Bobbie like an open book. He knew she was baiting him, and he was turning the methodology around on her.

"Those may be the nine-one-one callers." She pointed up ahead where three vehicles had parked in the southbound lane.

Nick braked to a stop. Blue lights appeared in the distance in front of them as well as in the rearview mirror. Bobbie was out of the car before he'd shifted into Park.

"MPD! Where's the child?" she shouted to the people standing outside their cars.

"There!" A woman pointed amid the stalled traffic on the northbound lane. "My husband is trying to catch him."

Bobbie burst into a run. Nick rushed after her.

The traffic that was still moving attempted to dodge them. *Idiots!* Why the hell didn't they stop? Couldn't they see the blue lights?

Bobbie darted between two vehicles. Horns blared. Nick skidded to a stop between them, allowing the second of the two to pass. He swore. She'd almost been hit by the second car.

"Joey!" she shouted.

The boy stopped running and turned. Hearing his name got his attention. Nick stayed back. The kid didn't need another strange man getting too close. He was far more likely to trust a woman. The child's eyes were wide with fear. His face was red and puffy from crying. One knee was bloody as if he'd fallen.

"Joey, don't be afraid, sweetie. I can take you to your mommy," Bobbie promised. "You stay right there. I'm coming to get you."

Two more cars approached, horns piercing the night air.

The boy held stone still. If he just stayed right where he was near the low wall separating the north and southbound lanes, he would be okay.

"You're doing good, Joey," Bobbie said gently.

Worry pounded in Nick's veins as two cars passed dangerously close. *Fools!*

Bobbie made it to the median. She reached for the boy, and he scooted away.

Nick rushed forward, a lane separating their positions, to cut him off. The child spotted Nick and froze. More headlights appeared in the distance.

Nick dared to move closer. "Your mommy's waiting for you, Joey. Let's go see her, okay?"

The boy ran into the line of traffic. Bobbie rushed forward and scooped him up, barely avoiding the third of the three cars.

Nick dragged in his first deep breath since the cop knocked on his door.

An ambulance raced into the fray, siren wailing.

Bobbie passed the boy to the closest cop and merged into the now-stalled traffic. Nick went after her. She moved from vehicle to vehicle, checking the passengers. Nick did the same. She was right to think Perry might be close by...*watching*.

Nick had almost caught up to her when a car cut from its lane and lunged forward, swiping past Bobbie, knocking her off her feet. Two MPD cruisers barreled after the vehicle.

Her face lined in pain, Bobbie was scrambling up when Nick reached her. "Are you all right?"

She pushed him away, limping in the direction the car had disappeared. "I didn't see his face. Was it him?" She rounded on Nick and demanded, "Did you see him? Was the driver Perry?"

"If they catch him, we'll know. You need to come with me." He took her arm to prevent her from taking off down the interstate.

"I can't leave." She glanced toward the ambulance that was departing with the child. "I should call his mother."

"Not until you've had medical attention."

Before she could argue, he scooped her up and started back toward the car.

"What the hell are you doing?"

"You're no good to anyone if you're broken, Detective."

She squeezed her eyes shut and shook her head. "Too late."

Eleven

Baptist Medical Center

Howard Newton swabbed his forehead with his handkerchief. A buddy in dispatch had called him and told him about Bobbie. He shook his head. What in the world was he going to do with her? She should have called him.

Shade had taken a position on the far side of the ER near the sliding doors used to enter the lobby from the parking lot. He had answered Newt's rapid-fire questions with short, curt answers when he first arrived, but he hadn't said a word since. He'd stayed clear of the cops who'd flocked to the hospital once word about the child's rescue and Bobbie's injury went wide. Reporters had swarmed into the lobby like flies to a rotting carcass. MPD's finest had herded them back outside and set up a barricade around the entrance.

Newt's gaze shifted to the set of white double doors next to the registration desk. The chief and the LT were back there with Bobbie now. Newt was going back as soon as Peterson and Owens finished chewing her out.

God almighty he didn't know how they were going to protect that girl. He closed his eyes and focused on calming his ticker. Damned thing needed to slow its galloping. The tightening band around his chest prevented a deep enough breath. To be on the safe side, he fumbled in his pocket for the pills he was forced to carry nowadays. His hands shook as he popped one from the packet and tucked it under his tongue. He breathed as deeply as he could and waited for relief. Next May, when it came time for his annual department physical, he'd have no choice but to disclose the newest red flag that he'd started to fall apart as soon as he'd hit fifty-nine. Why was his body so damned intent on reminding him he was barreling toward sixty?

When the pain first started, he'd figured all those years of smoking had caught up to him and the big C had invaded his lungs. The tests ruled out lung cancer and confirmed the coming need for a little tweaking of the arteries in his heart. He was putting it off because he knew what it meant—jockeying a desk. He was too damned stubborn to be taken out of the field. If he'd wanted to ride a desk and fiddle with paperwork he would have taken one of those promotions he'd been offered over the years.

When the discomfort in his chest had subsided, he stood and took a moment to regain his equilibrium. He spotted Shade watching him. *Good.* Newt had a few more questions for him and now was as good a time as any to ask them. He strolled over to the corner where the enigmatic man waited next to the rack of magazines no one wanted to thumb through since they were likely last year's editions.

Shade straightened from the wall where he'd been leaning. "If you walked over here to ask more questions, don't bother. You already know all I have to say."

"Maybe I do. Maybe I don't." Newt set his hands on his hips. "Neither of us can be certain until I ask the questions."

"Suit yourself." Shade waited, his posture relaxed, his expression clear of whatever he was thinking.

"You're here for Perry," Newt said.

"That wasn't a question."

Shade kept his attention on those white doors that separated the lobby from where the gurney had taken Bobbie. Maybe he was a little more worried than he wanted anyone to know. Newt had called Jessup again. He'd hated to bother the guy in the middle of the night, but there was no help for it. Jessup confirmed that Agent LeDoux was aware of Shade's presence in Montgomery. He'd also confirmed something Newt had suspected since the first time he met Nick Shade. The FBI had been attempting to monitor his activities since before he'd started hunting serial killers. Of course the reason was above Newt's security clearance, but it told him volumes.

There was something big in Nick Shade's past.

"Bobbie's important to me," Newt admitted. "I don't want anything you're here to do to get her hurt."

Shade met his gaze. It annoyed the hell out of Newt that his gave nothing away.

When Shade finally spoke, he said, "She doesn't need anyone to get her hurt. She's doing that all on her own."

Newt rubbed at his aching forehead. The damned pain in his chest had vanished, but now his head was throbbing. "Yeah, well, maybe you can help me out by keeping an eye on her."

"I'm not a bodyguard, and I'm not her keeper, Detective." He glanced at a couple exiting the lobby.

Newt held his temper when what he wanted to do was kick this guy's ass for being so damned arrogant. "I know what you are, Shade, and that's supposed to make you one of the good guys." Newt shrugged. "Maybe I misjudged you. I guess I'm just an old softie who still believes in heroes."

Shade leaned a little closer, or maybe it was Newt's imagination. His equilibrium still wasn't right.

"The one thing I'm not, Detective, is a hero."

Newt dragged his handkerchief from his pocket and blotted the sweat from his brow once more. He leveled a gaze on the other man that he hoped conveyed just how serious he was. "I hope you're being modest, Mr. Shade, because what Bobbie needs now is a hero."

Shade looked beyond him and Newt turned

around. The double doors were opening. Peterson entered the lobby. Newt hurried over to meet him. "How's our girl?"

Peterson tried his best to keep things official between him and Bobbie on the job, but tonight he didn't appear to be managing so well. The exhaustion and worry was heavy in his face and in the slump of his shoulders.

"She's okay. They're going to release her." He exhaled a weary breath. "She refuses to allow me to take her home. She doesn't want anyone in the department seeing me doing anything *extra* for her. It's bad for morale, she says. Maybe she's right." He passed a hand over his face. "I've been a cop for thirty-eight damned years and I don't know how I can keep her out of this, and I sure as hell don't know how to keep her safe."

Newt nodded. "It's impossible. She believes she's the only one who can stop him."

Peterson shook his head. "That's what the bastard wants her to believe."

The ER doors opened again, and Lieutenant Owens joined them. "She's asking for you, Newt. Room five."

He nodded. "I'll see that she gets home safe, Chief," he promised.

He left Peterson and the LT in deep discussion and headed for the double doors that separated the lobby from where the docs did their magic. As the doors opened he glanced back to see if Shade was still hanging around. He was gone.

Maybe he wasn't the hero Newt had hoped he was, but if he was the man his friend at Quantico believed, Nick Shade wouldn't let Perry get to Bobbie.

Worry weighted down his shoulders. A miracle would be required to keep Bobbie safe. Newt needed Shade to be that miracle.

He knocked on the door marked room five and Bobbie growled, "Come on in. Everybody else has."

Newt grinned and pushed into the room. Bobbie was already gathering her things to leave. "Hey, girlie. You about ready to ditch this joint?" She looked no worse for the wear, which made him feel loads better.

"You shouldn't be here," she fussed as she stretched her back. "You should be relaxing after such a monumental event."

Her grimace told him the soreness was already setting in. "You're like a third daughter to me. I couldn't *not* come."

When would she get it through her head that there were still people in this world who loved her? James and Jamie were gone, and James's folks had abandoned her, but she still had him and the chief, as well as the team. Hell, she had oodles of friends who cared about her, but she had pushed them all away during her recovery. He understood why; he only wished she did. She had needed to close out everything and everyone related to who she used to be in order to cope. At some point she had to come to terms with the idea that she couldn't keep who she really was away forever.

Sensing his frustration, she smiled—it almost made it to her eyes. "You're the best partner I've ever had." She threw her arms around him and hugged him.

He smiled and patted her on the back. "I'm the only partner you've ever had."

She drew back and gave him another halfway decent smile. "Damn it, Newt, you know I love you like a father."

For one fleeting instant she allowed a rare glimpse of the old Bobbie—the one who'd made him cry with tears of joy when she'd told him she was having a baby. The one who'd conspired with his wife and daughters to throw him a fifty-fifth birthday party he would never forget. The same one who'd organized a fund-raiser for a new playground in Washington Park after working a homicide in the neighborhood. God Almighty, he missed that sweet girl.

"Now go home and get some rest," she ordered. "My surveillance detail will take me home."

She went up on tiptoe and gave him a kiss on the cheek. Newt hugged her again before she could pull away. This time he said a little prayer. Whether she believed it or not, Bobbie needed all the help she could get.

She couldn't do this alone.

Twelve

Bobbie opened her eyes when the car stopped moving. As exhausted as she was, she was grateful to be away from the hospital. She'd already spent enough time in medical facilities for several lifetimes. This go around, she was basically unharmed. Tomorrow—wait, it was tomorrow—she would be sore as hell, but she would survive.

The driver who'd swiped her off her feet wasn't the Storyteller. Just a twenty-two-year-old jerk who'd had too much to drink and whose passenger and supposed friend possessed enough cocaine to continue the party once they got home. Now they were both in seriously deep shit, especially the driver. Bobbie couldn't remember ever being that stupid. All she'd ever wanted to do was be a cop like her father. She'd spent her entire childhood hanging on his every word and mimicking him. By the time she was eight, her mother had given up on making her wear frilly dresses and dainty shoes. Bobbie had been the quintessential tomboy.

That's one of the reasons I fell in love with you.

Her husband's voice swirled through her soul, making her heart ache.

She pushed the memory aside and turned her thoughts to the reporters who had shown up on Taylor Road and then at the ER. There would be no more keeping a lid on this. By the morning edition, she would be the top story on every news feed. LeDoux and his crew showing up only ratcheted up the media frenzy. She had escaped the horde at the ER because Newt had insisted on being the sacrificial lamb. He had provided a sound bite while she was hustled out a maintenance exit by her surveillance detail. Once outside, she'd found Shade waiting for her. The uniforms hadn't been happy about her going with him, but she'd outranked them both.

Her door opened. She snapped to attention. Shade stood in the vee made by the open car door. She hadn't noticed he'd gotten out of the car. Not a good sign considering she had refused pain medication.

She glowered up at the man, when her frustration had nothing to do with him. Or, at least, it shouldn't. "I don't need your help."

"Yeah. You said that already." He didn't move, just waited stubbornly.

Bobbie bit her lips together and climbed out of the car. Pain sheared upward from her right leg and through her hip. She swallowed the groan that burgeoned in her throat. Based on the X-rays taken at the hospital, the hardware was still right where it was supposed to be. No fractures. Nothing but soft-tissue injury. She would be bruised and sore for a few days.

She would get over it. What mattered was that Joey Rice was back with his mother.

But not Aaron Taggart. He was still out there. *And it's your fault. The Storyteller is doing this to hurt you.*

Ignoring the voice as well as the stomach churning pain, she made her way to the front door. She jabbed the key into the lock and gave it a twist. Before she could push the door open and step inside, Shade was ushering her aside. He crossed the threshold, and she followed, annoyed that he seemed to believe she needed him to take care of her. The man went through her usual routine of checking the rooms and windows. Digging deep for patience, she folded her arms and waited in the foyer.

When he returned, he walked right past her and locked the door. "A hot bath will help considerably."

What the hell did he think he was doing? "Thanks." She gestured to the door. "I appreciate your help out there. Enjoy the rest of your night."

Bobbie would analyze what the release of one child and not the other meant later, after she'd had some sleep. Her brain couldn't wrap around another thought until she shut down for a while.

"I'm not leaving you alone tonight."

She wanted to argue, but she was too damned

tired to put up much of a fuss. "Did my partner put you up to this?"

She wouldn't put it past Newt to prod this guy into playing bodyguard. It certainly wasn't the chief. Once he'd seen with his own eyes that she was unharmed, he'd been too busy raking her over the coals about the report the surveillance detail had given him. *Why on earth are you running at night alone? Why in God's name would you be associating with Javier Quintero? Who the hell is this Nick Shade that Newt told me about?* She'd like to hear how Newt explained that one.

"He has a tendency to overreact," she added when Shade didn't bother to answer.

"Your partner didn't put me up to anything." Shade jerked his head toward the hall. "Take a hot bath and hit the sack. I'll be on the couch."

He was serious. "No way." She moved toward the door. "You're leaving. Now."

Rather than debate the issue, he gave her his back and headed for the sofa. As she watched, he stretched out and laid his forearm over his eyes.

She opened her mouth to rail at him, but she heaved a breath and snapped it shut. What was the point? Obviously he was as stubborn as she was. Too exhausted and sore to physically remove him from her sofa, she gave up and trudged to her room. After she gathered a pair of lounge pants, a tank and underwear, she locked herself in the bathroom and filled the tub with steaming water.

Placing her weapons on the counter, she stripped

off her running clothes. She stared at her damaged body for a long moment before climbing into the tub. With a weary groan, she sank into the welcoming heat and closed her eyes.

Where the hell was the Storyteller? It was a good sign that Joey was uninjured, wasn't it? Did this mean he wouldn't harm a child? There were no incidents with children in his criminal history. Even LeDoux agreed that Perry had not taken the children for pleasure but to get to Bobbie. Leaving Joey on the interstate had been a reminder that her decision to send her child to the neighbors for help had gotten him hit by a car and killed. The memory gored into her soul like a dull spear plowing through her chest. If she hadn't pushed Jamie out the door that night, Perry would have killed him just to torture her. She knew this, and still the agony and guilt were unbearable.

Her lips trembled as more memories flooded her. She'd taught her little boy to run next door for help if anything ever happened to Mommy and Daddy. That night—Christmas Eve not even a year ago— she'd realized Perry was in the house. She'd pushed Jamie out the front door and screamed for him to run for help. Perry had grabbed her by the hair as she'd kicked the door shut. Then he'd dragged her to the kitchen, where he'd already killed her husband.

She had done the right thing. All she could have done under those impossible, heinous circumstances… and still her baby was dead.

No matter that she'd been reminded repeatedly

that she couldn't have known the neighbor's guests would be backing out of the driveway at that exact moment, she couldn't *not* blame herself. Tears escaped her best efforts to hold them back. Any way she analyzed and rationalized it, her actions had taken the lives of her husband and their son. She had agreed to work on the Storyteller case. Early in the investigation the concept had occurred to her that her looks—the same dark hair, pale skin, tall and thin body type of his other victims—might draw his attention. But the Storyteller never struck twice in the same town. If he took a victim or dropped a victim in a location, he was done there. He wouldn't be coming back to Montgomery and the opportunity to work on a case that had stumped the FBI for more than a decade was just too important an opportunity to pass up.

Bobbie had jumped at the chance.

Seemingly out of the blue the Storyteller suddenly changed his MO.

I couldn't resist you.

He'd said those words to her during the three weeks of torture she had endured. She'd lost count of the number of times he'd raped her. He'd carved her body to the point that between the scars from his work and those left by the surgeries she looked like some sort of female Frankenstein monster. At the time she hadn't known her little boy was dead, too. Believing he was waiting for her—that he needed her—was all that had kept her alive during those endless days.

Now she understood what no one—not even the FBI—had known at the time. The Storyteller's mother had died. Her death not only caused him to escalate—taking three victims in one year for the first time that the feds knew of—but also caused him to lose control. He'd gone into a frenzy in an attempt to assuage the loss he felt. That frenzy had prompted another first in the sick son of a bitch's murderous career: he'd made mistakes. She and her family had been part of those mistakes.

Bobbie would stop him.

And then what? Her life was over. If by some twist of fate she survived the coming battle, what was she supposed to do then? Was the fact that her broken heart kept beating her punishment for not being a better wife and mother? Maybe this miserable existence was her penance for putting her career before her family.

Do what you have to do, Bobbie. James always smiled whenever he said those words to her. *It's pretty cool being married to a superhero.*

Only she wasn't a superhero. She was a cop who'd taken a huge gamble and lost.

"I'm so sorry." Bobbie hugged herself and scooted down, drawing her head under the water to drown out the voices.

Thirteen

Nick sat in the darkness and analyzed the events of the past twenty-four hours. The hunt was his only true escape. Sleep brought the dreams and every waking hour reminded him where he'd come from. His only choice was to stay focused on what he had to do.

Immersing himself in the search for the most evil serial killers had always been easy. He'd studied them for years. He knew the way they thought, the reasons they killed and their need to leave signatures. When he started a hunt he absorbed all he could find about the serial killer he sought. One of the primary ways to understand who a serial killer was aside from the obvious was to study his victims. Since he tracked the ones no one else could find, the victims were typically deceased, which made maintaining the necessary mental distance a simple matter.

Bobbie Gentry was playing havoc with his ability to stay focused. He closed his eyes and tried again to immerse himself in the images and sounds, to cocoon himself in all that this day had brought. As hard as he tried, he could not block the scent of the shampoo she used or the whispers of her breath as she readied for bed. The door to her room was closed and still he sensed her every move. The hum of the hair dryer prompted images of her fingers working through long, damp strands. He'd studied her medical file. He knew every scar on her slim body. He imagined her cool fingers smoothing silky lotion over her skin and soothing balm over her lips.

Nick sat up. He should be back at his motel with its shabby carpet and lumpy bed where nothing belonged to him except the photos and reports related to what he'd come to Montgomery to do. What he always did. The sleeping arrangements, the city, the hunt, his survival…those were the variables that changed year after year. The rest stayed the same. *He* stayed the same.

Whoever or whatever he was. The woman down the hall had asked those questions. *Who the hell are you? Better yet, what are you?* He was no one. He was nothing. There were no photos in his wallet. No framed snapshots among his meager belongings. He possessed no mementos of his childhood or last year or yesterday, for that matter. Even his name was not the same as the one he'd been given at birth.

All that he was, was meaningless. He did what he did and time moved on, repeating itself day in and day out with nothing changing except the faces of victims and the MO of the killers he hunted.

He had no right to be in this place. He stood and

paced the room. He had no right to feel a kinship with her...the one victim who had survived to lead him to the killer he needed to catch. A very long time ago he had been in that awful place...the place where she was now. One of the most heinous and prolific serial killers to date had taken all that mattered to him. If only he could make her see that killing Perry would not bring her the peace she sought. She had to make her own way out of this nightmare that had taken over her life.

He inhaled deeply, drawing in the sweet scent of her that still lingered. He gritted his teeth and swore silently for allowing himself to come so close.

Twelve years he had stayed vigilant, never getting too close. Never failing in what he set out to do. Emotion was weakness. He knew better than to feel the need to protect or to desire something he could never have. The urge to protect was a distraction from the hunt, and desire was dangerous under any circumstances. As well versed as he was in these cold, hard facts, he could not deny feeling both. When that car had swiped her, his heart had stopped. Taking her into his arms and holding her had shifted something deep in his chest.

He could not have this... He could not be that man. Not for her. Not for anyone.

Tomorrow he would reset his boundaries.

For now he would search the perimeter of the property and ensure the house was secure. A shower and a couple of hours sleep would go a long way in clearing his head.

Careful not to make a sound, he slipped out the back door. An unhurried walk around the house and the adjoining yards slowly worked the tension from his muscles. He checked on the dog she pretended not to care about despite making sure the animal had food and water. It had only taken a few treats and a gentle stroke now and then to gain the creature's trust. Nick inhaled deeply of the night air, clearing her scent from his lungs, as he made his way back to the door. The surveillance detail remained in place.

He moved cautiously through the door and closed it without a sound. When the dead bolts were set, he stilled. He sensed her presence before he captured the subtle fragrance of her skin. He turned around slowly. She stood a few yards away, her Glock leveled on his torso.

He raised his hands in surrender. "Did I wake you?"

"What the hell are you doing?" she demanded, lowering the weapon.

"Perimeter check."

She shook her head. "I don't understand why you're still here."

With that she turned and disappeared down the narrow hall.

He doubted she would like his reason for staying any more than he did.

Fourteen

Gaylon was careful to stay within the posted speed limit, though it proved incredibly difficult. Fury and contempt churned inside him.

The dark-haired man was with his detective.

Whoever this man was, he would die. Bobbie belonged to Gaylon. He would not allow another man to have her—at least not until he was finished with her.

Clearly, his efforts to draw her attention were not sufficient. She was distracted.

Despite his anger and disdain, he was still aroused by what he'd witnessed on the interstate. He hadn't been able to stop for more than a few seconds as he would have liked to do. Staying with the flow of traffic had been imperative. Still, he'd watched as Bobbie rushed through the traffic to rescue the boy. She had looked so very heroic. So strong and capable in spite of all the things he had done to her. Her limp was scarcely noticeable. What a wondrous recovery.

When she'd handed the boy over to that other cop and rushed forward to look for Gaylon, he'd experienced a moment of panic. He felt immensely grateful to the fool who had suddenly shot out of the line of traffic and rushed away. Admittedly, he had been concerned at first. If Bobbie had been too seriously injured, his plans would have been foiled. But she hadn't been hurt badly at all.

Rage roiled inside him again as his mind replayed the dark-haired man picking her up and carrying her away. He'd watched as their images had grown smaller and smaller in his rearview mirror. The scene might have been considered romantic by some. Poor Detective Gentry. Had she finally found someone to replace the husband she'd lost?

A sneer pulled at his lips. He would know who this man was. He had taken Bobbie to the hospital. More than two hours later they had exited. She had climbed into his car of her own volition. Gaylon was most displeased with this turn of events. There was no time to revise his plan. He'd waited too long already.

The final scene was near. There could be no rewrites. There was no time!

It was glaringly apparent that Bobbie needed a reminder to stay focused.

First, he needed fuel. He turned into the parking lot of the convenience store to fill the gas tank. He'd been careful not to stop at the same place twice. But this morning he was going to make an exception. He parked at the pumps and noted that neither of the two clerks behind the counter was blond. Safe to go inside, he decided. People rarely remembered a face if they only saw it once. If they saw it twice, the odds of remembering went up considerably.

He reached for the glasses he'd taken from his father's bedside and tucked them into place. A glance at the rearview mirror and he smiled. The glasses gave him quite the eccentric air. With the track suit and running shoes he could be headed to the gym. He reached into the glove box and removed the envelope of cash he carried with him. His resources were running a bit low. Between his own savings and that of his parents, he had managed quite well. As long as he finished up on schedule, his funds would be adequate for slipping out of the country. He wished he could visit his mother once more but that would have to wait until things cooled off. In time the FBI and others would stop actively searching for him and he would become just another unsolved cold case stored in a cardboard box in some back room where no one bothered to go.

He tucked the envelope back in the glove box. His father hadn't been very happy about having to withdraw his life savings and turn it over to Gaylon, but he'd been fairly easy to convince. It was one thing for one of God's warriors to have the world discover his son is a closet serial killer, but entirely another to have his own secrets exposed. Oh yes, Wyman Perry had a few naughty secrets of his own.

Gaylon pushed the memories aside and emerged from the car he'd borrowed. Perhaps later, when he returned to visit his mother, he would castrate his father and send him to hell where he belonged. He'd considered doing so on his last visit, but once the money was in his hand there simply hadn't been time to do the deed right. He wanted to take his time and watch his father writhe in pain. He wanted to leave his body marked with hideous scars. Inspiration lit inside Gaylon. What a story he would leave on the old bastard's back.

The bell over the door jingled as Gaylon entered the convenience store. The two women behind the counter looked up and smiled at him. The shorter of the two said, "Good morning. You need gas, sir?"

Gaylon approached the counter and laid two bills there. "I do—" he glanced at her name tag "—Rory. You just keep whatever is left over."

She smiled. "Thanks."

She was moderately attractive in a rather ordinary way. Her mousy brown hair was neatly styled, and the dark eyes were clear. She might consider losing a little weight.

"Is your coffee fresh?" he asked, turning his attention to the other one, Gayle. She was far older than her coworker. A smart woman would have chosen to go lighter with her hair color as she grew older. As it was the dark brown gave her face an ashen look. Not attractive at all.

He had a friend down in Mobile who would have loved these two. When he was active, he'd preyed on the plain Janes of society. Age had never been relevant as long as they had all the right parts, he would say.

Gaylon's tastes had been far more refined. He preferred women like his mother. He wished she were still alive. He missed her so.

"Just made the pot," Gayle announced. "What size do you want and I'll get it for you."

He produced a smile. "That would be lovely, Gayle. A medium will be fine. One cream, no sugar. I need my caffeine before hitting the gym."

The two chatted about the heat and how they needed to work out. Rory brought up the news about the serial killer on the loose. They couldn't believe such an awful monster was right here in their town.

"I'm certain the police will catch him," Gaylon assured them as he accepted the coffee. "Be safe, ladies."

With a final smile, he left the store. When he pumped the gas he was careful to leave considerable change for the clerks. Before driving away, he tossed the coffee into the trash can. His mother always said Southern women were the sweetest.

"You're always right, Mother."

Fifteen minutes later Gaylon parked next to the house and got out. He'd been gone far longer than he'd intended. Hopefully his guests hadn't tired of waiting. He unlocked the chain on the front door. Inside was quiet. He turned on the battery-operated lantern he'd purchased when he'd selected his supplies for the big finale he had planned.

With the lantern on the table, its pale glow poured

over the woman stretched out on the mattress. This time he'd secured her wrists and ankles with the handcuffs he'd picked up at a spy shop he'd happened upon late yesterday. He hadn't bothered trying to locate the nylon rope he generally used. The hardware store where he'd stopped first had been out save a meager four feet. He had purchased what little the shop had on hand since it was absolutely essential for the noose and small lead. He'd actually intended to stop at another store, but then he'd gotten excited by the news of Carl Evans's suicide and forgotten. He'd had to rip apart Nurse Adams's clothes to restrain her.

A minor glitch. Later, when he'd considered how easy it would be for her to escape, he'd decided to make a game of it. So he'd sat in the darkness and listened to her efforts. Even without the aid of visual stimuli, it had been incredibly arousing, particularly when she touched him, thinking he was another child.

She hadn't opened her eyes since he returned, but she was awake. Her breathing pattern was far too uneven for sleep. He thought of Bobbie and how she would look stretched out here. He couldn't wait to marvel over all the scars from their last time together. He couldn't wait to take her apart.

He stood and moved to the other room to check on the boy. He lay curled into a ball. Duct tape bound his ankles and wrists. He'd had to install eyebolts in the floor for the nurse and the guests he'd be entertaining next. Since there was no bed frame with which to secure his guests, he'd had to devise his own system. It wasn't the first time the accommodations were somewhat less than suitable for his needs.

As much as he would like to entertain himself again for a while with the lovely nurse, sleep was essential to his ability to react sharply. He spread out the sleeping bag and slid his body inside. He would sleep for a few hours, and then he would check on Bobbie. He would show his nurse the photo he had snapped of the dark-haired man. If he was the same one who had visited Bobbie in the hospital, Gaylon would be concerned.

He couldn't wait for Bobbie to see what he had planned next. Each remaining step required careful orchestration to achieve the proper, escalating effect. By the time they were together again, sweet Bobbie would be more than ready for the end.

He closed his eyes and thought of her pale skin and dark hair. But it was her eyes that made his heart beat faster. They were the most unusual blue. So very light and pale…so very much like his mother's.

He burrowed deeper into his sleeping bag. She would be his again soon, and, like all those before her, her story would end with him.

Fifteen

Bobbie waited while Lieutenant Owens finished her call. LeDoux had called Bobbie at seven this morning and told her to meet him in the conference room. The chief had called her next and told her not to set foot outside her house or he would have her taken into custody. Then about fifty minutes ago he'd called back and told her to report to her commander's office.

Evidently there was a war happening between the chief and the feds. The chief wanted her tucked safely out of trouble's reach, while the feds wanted her in the middle of the fray. Bobbie wanted to tell them all to stay out of her way. Frustration stiffened her muscles, making her grimace. Her entire body felt like she'd been hit by a truck rather than side bumped by a car. She was sore as hell. The problem, as she saw it, was that until the Storyteller got what he wanted he would continue creating havoc.

Scott Taggart was dead. Gwen Adams and the

Taggart child remained missing. Bobbie closed her eyes. Who was going to stop Perry? No one had been able to stop him in thirteen years. They all— including Shade—needed to understand there was only one way to end this.

"Am I keeping you from your beauty rest?"

Bobbie snapped her eyes open and sat up a little straighter. "I'm sorry, ma'am. I was just thinking how I could be a great deal more useful to the investigation if I was out there—" she nodded to the door "—instead of in here."

Eudora Owens leaned back in her chair and scrutinized Bobbie. She had been the commander of the Major Crimes Bureau for five years. She was a beautiful, sophisticated woman. Not a single hair was ever out of place. She always wore skirts, never trousers. Not once had Bobbie seen her look anything other than elegant and polished. But those lovely features hid a woman who was best described as forged of steel and fire. Bobbie had a great deal of respect for her. A black woman from humble beginnings, Owens had worked hard to make her way through Alabama State University on her own. Her mother had been terminally ill during those years and her father had died when she was a child. Like Bobbie, Owens was an only child, so there had been no siblings to offer support. In her senior year, Owens had been raped and left for dead, but she'd survived. They had the latter in common, as well.

Bobbie wondered if the rape was the reason the lieutenant had never been married. God knew, Bob-

bie couldn't imagine ever allowing a man to touch
her again, much less sharing her life with one—
with anyone for that matter. The memory of Nick
Shade grabbing her up and carrying her to the ambulance last night intruded in an attempt to make
a liar out of her. She hadn't wanted him to touch
her but she hadn't exactly been in a position to resist. And then she'd melted into the warmth and
strength of his arms.

Not smart, Bobbie.

Thankfully he was gone when she woke up this
morning. She couldn't deny that his help might
prove useful, but she didn't like anyone bulldozing
his way into her personal space. The memory of that
wall in his motel room nagged her. He appeared to
want to stop the Storyteller almost as much as she
did. Had one of the victims been related to him or
a friend to him? She wasn't completely sold on the
idea of him not having a personal stake in this. He
was far too dedicated and wholly absorbed by the
case.

Bobbie dragged her attention back to Owens who
was reminding her that she was the only roadblock
standing between Bobbie and administrative leave.

When Owens paused, Bobbie interjected, "Yes,
ma'am, I'm aware that you're the sole reason I'm
even in the building today. I appreciate your support."

"Take my word for it, Detective," Owens warned.
"I'm not bucking the chief's edict for the fun of it

or even because I think you're the best detective we've got."

Owens paused to allow that news flash to sink in. Bobbie didn't take the admonition personally. She knew she was a good detective. One of the best for sure, but Owens never allowed anyone on her team to sport an oversize ego. Frankly, Bobbie felt confident that if her commander were anyone else in MPD, the chief would never have allowed his decision to be swayed. Bobbie suspected there was more to his relationship with Owens than anyone realized. Long ago when her father had still been on the force, the chief had held the position of Major Crimes commander. Maybe that connection was the special bond Bobbie sensed between them.

"I challenged his decision because," Owens continued, "the crazy bastard who almost killed one of my best detectives is back, and he's already murdered at least one person. He's abducted a nurse, and a child is still missing—all on my watch. I can't have that, Detective. I won't have it. No one knows him better than you do. I need you. Those victims need you."

Bobbie couldn't agree more. "LeDoux appears to want me on the case." Though she doubted his motives were as straightforward as the lieutenant's. Owens wanted the Storyteller stopped to protect the community. LeDoux wanted to be the hero—the fed who finally nailed the serial killer no one else had been able to find.

"I want you focused on Gwen Adams."

Bobbie couldn't see where Owens was headed with that statement. "What about the child?" The damaged organ in her chest squeezed painfully. *Don't let another child die.*

"Recovering the child will get the most coverage in the media. LeDoux and his team will be all over it. I want you to retrace Adams's steps. Lean on her boyfriend. With Evans dead, Neely is all we've got."

Made sense. "What do I tell LeDoux?" He'd already called Bobbie's cell twice.

"Don't tell him anything. You answer to me, not to him. Grab Newt and roll."

Bobbie stood. "Yes, ma'am."

When Bobbie opened the door to exit Owens's office, shouting had her bracing for trouble.

Newt stood between the short corridor created by the rows of cubicles and the LT's office, blocking the path of someone Bobbie couldn't see.

"Ma'am, as soon as Lieutenant Owens is available—"

"I've called twice this morning and she still hasn't called me back."

Marilyn Taggart. Bobbie walked quickly to where Newt was attempting to persuade the woman to return to the lobby and wait.

"Mrs. Taggart, how can we help you?"

Newt stepped aside, his face a study in worry. Bobbie gave his arm a squeeze.

Taggart shifted her attention to Bobbie. "You!" Her face twisted with anger. "This is your fault."

"Ma'am, why don't you come this way, and I'll

see if Lieutenant Owens is available," Bobbie offered.

Since LeDoux and one of his colleagues were in the conference room, she had no desire for them to hear what was obviously going to be a desperate mother and bereaved wife melting down.

"I am sick to death of hearing the same thing," Taggart shouted. She stabbed a finger at Bobbie. "You're the reason he's here. You're the reason he took my son and killed my husband. You should be out there trying to stop this monster."

Newt stepped between them. "Mrs. Taggart—"

"Mrs. Taggart." Lieutenant Owens's voice was direct and firm and somehow reassuring at the same time. "Step into my office, and let's allow the detectives to get on with their work. We want to find your son."

Taggart swayed on her feet. Before Bobbie could reach her, Newt took her by the arm and ushered her to the LT's office. As she closed the door, Owens gave Bobbie a knowing nod.

"We have to go." Bobbie took her partner by the arm and escorted him toward the exit. "I'll explain on the way."

"You sure look better today," Newt offered as they exited the building.

Bobbie stalled and looked at her partner. "She's right, you know. He's here for me. None of this would have happened if I hadn't survived."

"Bobbie." Newt took her by the shoulders. "At some point you have to stop blaming yourself. Perry is responsible for everything that's happened, not you. I wish I could make you believe that truth. It's time you took your life back."

Newt just didn't understand. Her life was over. Stopping the bastard who'd taken it and so many others was all that mattered now.

She hoped like hell she could make that happen before he hurt that child…or Gwen.

Highland Avenue, 11:10 a.m.

Bobbie waited for the convenience store clerk to complete the transaction and for the customer to be on his way with the pack of cigarettes he'd purchased. This place was only blocks from where Gwen's car had been found. It was as good a place as any to start retracing her steps. She flashed her badge and then showed the photo of Neely she'd taken with her cell.

"Have you seen this guy?"

The clerk studied the image, then he shrugged. "Maybe. I can't say for sure."

Newt pointed to the camera near the ceiling in the corner behind the clerk. "You have any other cameras besides this one?"

"There's two outside, but they don't work." The clerk nodded toward the one behind him. "That one doesn't, either. The owner keeps saying he's going to get them repaired, but he hasn't yet."

"Were you working on Thursday?" Bobbie asked as she tucked her cell at her waist.

He shook his head. "It was Leander Sykes. She

pulled a double. When I came in around seven on Friday morning, she was complaining." He rolled his eyes. "She's always complaining."

"How do we get in touch with her?" Newt pulled out his pocket-size notepad and pen.

"She's overseeing the unloading of the delivery truck." He pointed to the employees-only door at the rear of the store. "Just walk on through there."

Bobbie thanked him and followed Newt to the storeroom. The space was larger than she'd expected. An employees' restroom and a couple of lockers were surrounded by rows of shelves and stacks of boxes. A small overhead door was in the up position. As Bobbie watched, a man rolled a hand truck loaded with boxes through the open door. A woman, presumably Leander Sykes, held a clipboard and was busily checking off items. She looked to be in her midforties. Bottled blond hair was held up by a purple claw clip. Between her big eyeglasses, the high-waist straight-legged jeans and the polka-dot midriff-length crop top, she might have walked off the set of a 1980s television show.

"Leander?" Bobbie approached her. Newt stayed a few steps behind.

"You're not supposed to be back here," Leander warned.

Bobbie pulled her jacket aside and showed her badge. "Detectives Gentry and Newton, MPD. We have a few questions for you."

Newt gestured to the man with the hand truck. "Why don't you take a smoke break, buddy?"

The guy shrugged. "Fine by me." He reached for his shirt pocket as he headed for the open door.

"What's this about?" Leander held the clipboard against her chest like a shield. She blinked repeatedly, the generously applied blue eye shadow drawing attention to her brown eyes.

Bobbie showed her the photo of Neely. "Have you seen this man before?"

Leander stared at the screen for several seconds. "Can you zoom it in?" She tapped the frame of her glasses. "I need a new prescription."

"Sure." Bobbie zoomed in on the photo until Neely's face filled the screen.

Leander nodded. "Oh yeah. That's him." She pointed to Bobbie's phone. "He came in here Thursday afternoon. Well, after the lunch crowd, around three maybe. He was acting all weird."

"Weird in what way?"

"He said his car quit on him and wanted to know if he could wait inside for a friend. It was damned hot." She scratched her head with her pencil. "But we're not really supposed to allow anyone to hang around inside. Worked out okay since he suddenly changed his mind and hurried out the door. I think he spotted the camera above the cash register, and it freaked him out. Maybe he was planning on robbing the place. Thank God he couldn't tell the thing didn't work."

"Did he leave?"

Leander nodded. "As soon as he was out the

door he pulled out his cell phone and headed for the street."

Neely had gotten spooked by the camera. He'd called whoever he'd intended to meet and gone in search of a location without any security, Bobbie surmised.

"Did you see him again after that?" Newt asked.

"He didn't come back in the store, so I can't say whether or not he hung around outside. We get a crowd out there sometimes. The police come through every once in a while and the parking lot clears out. I can't say when he left or if he came back later."

Before moving on, Bobbie showed her a photo of Perry and asked if she'd seen him.

Leander asked her to zoom in again, and then she peered at the most recent photo taken of Perry before he disappeared last November.

Leander nodded slowly. "You know what, I have seen him. He was in here that same evening. A little later. But…" She made a face as if she was uncertain.

Pulse pounding, Bobbie said, "Look closely at his eyes and nose. Are you sure it was him you saw?"

More of the nodding. "Definitely. Except he was bald." She patted her head. "You know, slick as a baby's butt bald. And he wore glasses. They were too big for his face." She wrinkled her nose. "He kept pushing them up the bridge of his nose."

Bobbie exchanged a look with Newt.

"What time would you say he was here?" Newt asked.

"Around five thirty or six. I came on at two. Yeah." She hugged her clipboard again. "I remember because I was complaining about the assholes—" she pressed her hand to her mouth "—pardon my French. These two young guys had come in here showing their tails and being disrespectful." She shook her head. "I don't know why people don't teach their kids how to be respectful anymore."

"What did this man do or say?" Bobbie asked, hardly able to restrain the urge to shake the woman and tell her to focus.

"Oh, he was real charming." She blushed. "He called me by my name." One hand went to the name badge she wore. "He was just nice, you know." Her smile couldn't get any wider. "A real gentleman."

Bobbie opted against asking her if she ever watched the news. She steeled herself and went straight to the important questions. "Did you see what he was driving?"

Leander frowned and then made a face. "Sorry, I sure didn't. I got busy after that and I didn't even notice when he left."

"Was anyone else working with you that day?" Newt asked.

Bobbie's heart started to race as she waited for the woman's answer. No wonder Perry hadn't been spotted. He had shaved his head and wore big glasses. They'd expected he would disguise himself somehow. This was an important break.

"Yeah," Leander said. "Shelley was here, but she's pregnant and she has to run to the bathroom constantly. Between me and you—" Leander leaned a little closer to Bobbie "—I think she goes in there and gets on her phone. The woman is addicted to Facebook."

"Can you remember what he was wearing?" Bobbie pressed.

Leander hummed an uncertain note. "A shirt. Not a T-shirt. A shirt that buttoned up the front. I thought it was a little odd cause it was so hot and he had the damned thing buttoned to the neck. Sorry. I can't remember anything else."

"Do you recall what he purchased?" Bobbie moistened her lips and struggled to be patient.

Leander considered the question a moment. "A couple of bottles of water and some of those deli snack packs."

Food and water for Gwen and the boys. Bobbie looked to Newt once more, then back to Leander. "Do you remember anything else about him? Have you seen him since that day?"

The clerk shook her head. "No, ma'am. If either one of them has been back, I wasn't on shift." She looked from Bobbie to Newt. "What'd they do, rob a bank?"

"The bald man," Newt said so Bobbie wouldn't have to, "is Gaylon Perry, a serial killer. If you see him again, as soon as it's safe, you call this number." He handed her a card.

The woman went on and on about how she

couldn't believe she'd been that close to a serial killer. As soon as she paused to drag in a breath, Bobbie said, "You've been very helpful, Leander. Thank you."

On the way back through the store, Newt showed the Storyteller's photo to the man behind the counter and left a card.

Outside, the temperature was rising almost as fast as Bobbie's heart rate. She had to pass the update along to the LT now. LeDoux and his team needed to be alerted to the changes in his appearance.

Newt settled into the passenger seat of Bobbie's Challenger. "If Neely met with Perry in person..."

Bobbie was thinking the same thing. Since Neely didn't live in this neighborhood, it was the only explanation for the two appearing at this convenience store the same afternoon. "He could describe the car he's driving," Bobbie finished for her partner.

Owens had said to lean on Neely. The trouble was, what were they going to have to promise the jerk to get him to talk?

"We need to talk to him," Newt suggested.

"We do." Bobbie headed for the jail. Neely's bail arraignment wasn't until later today so they had a reasonable shot at strong-arming some information out of him while he was still desperate for his freedom.

After a few miles of silence, Newt announced, "I talked to my wife last night."

"You talk to her every night, don't you?" Bobbie

said as she made the next turn. She was pumped. The clerk had positively ID'd the Storyteller.

"Ha-ha. I talked to her about you," Newt clarified. "We're in agreement that you shouldn't be staying alone at your place right now. We'd like you to stay with us."

Bobbie cleared her head of the whirling thoughts and glanced at her partner. "I appreciate it. You tell Carlene I really, really do, but I can't do that."

"Bobbie—"

"I'll tell you the same thing I told the chief—I'm not making anyone else a target."

"Your face is all over the news this morning," Newt challenged. "There are those who think you should be run out of town so Perry will follow you. If we don't find the other two victims alive, this could turn nasty for all the wrong reasons."

Yeah, she'd gotten a glimpse here and there of the news. The people who were saying those things were afraid. Fear made people say and do things they wouldn't otherwise do. She worked hard to keep that in mind.

"I won't run from him, Newt. Not again."

"I just want to be able to sleep at night, girlie," he confessed.

Bobbie gifted him with a sad smile. "Sorry. But I have to do this my way."

He nodded. "I had to try."

She parked and they entered the jail. All they needed was one lead to get them on the right track. Just one. Neely could provide that lead. Anticipation hummed in her blood. She didn't care what she had to promise him to get him to talk. Legally, she couldn't promise him anything. Hopefully he didn't know that.

The sign-in sergeant stopped them as soon as Bobbie announced who they were there to see.

"Take a seat, Detectives." The sergeant gestured to the short row of chairs across from his desk. "Neely's meeting with his attorney right now."

Damn. Just their luck.

Newt chatted a while with the sergeant. Bobbie took a seat. As much as she appreciated and respected the Constitution, it annoyed the hell out of her that even scumbags like Neely were entitled to representation. She hoped he had the worst lawyer in the city. He sure as hell shouldn't have the best.

The low hum of Newt's conversation had her eyes drifting shut. She hadn't slept more than an hour or two at a time in months. Even if she never slept again she had to keep going. She had to finish this.

Last night had been particularly difficult. She hadn't wanted to sleep with Shade under the same roof. Besides Newt and the chief, she hadn't slept under the same roof with a man since...*before*.

She hadn't been able to get comfortable. Her mind kept going to the idea that he was in the house and that she really knew nothing about him. Yet she instinctively understood that he could help her somehow—even if she didn't want to acknowledge it. Maybe being under the same roof with her had made him uncomfortable as well since he'd been gone when she got up.

She closed her eyes and blocked thoughts of him.

Only one thing mattered…stopping the Story-teller.

Sixteen

12:28 p.m.

"You're sure there're no cameras or recording devices?"

Neely was nervous. Understandable. Nick hoped he endured far more discomfort before this was over.

"You have my word, Mr. Neely," Nick assured him. "Our conversations are completely private and fall under attorney-client privilege. You may speak freely and no one, other than myself, will ever hear what you have to say."

"It was Carl's idea," he said as he leaned forward and braced his elbows on the marred tabletop. "He wanted to save his kid, you know? I had to help him. It was the right thing to do."

"What occurred between you and Carl Evans is not the FBI's highest priority, Liam. May I call you Liam?"

"Sure." He frowned. "If that's true, then what am I doing here? That crazy bitch read me my rights like I was a criminal. I was just trying to help a sick kid. Anybody with a heart would have done the same thing."

"I completely understand." Nick restrained the contempt mounting inside him. "Any parent would understand."

"You have kids?" Neely asked hopefully.

"I do," Nick lied. "I would do exactly what you did for them."

Neely relaxed back in his chair. "Good to know. So, how do you get me out of here?"

"Before we take any steps," Nick began, "it's imperative I understand any and all issues that might present a problem in our case."

More of those frown lines deepened on Neely's face. "What do you mean, issues?"

"Anything you did that the authorities might discover in the course of their investigation. It's always better if I'm prepared to contest anything they throw our way. All you need to do is start at the beginning and tell me everything you did as it relates to Ms. Adams and those files."

Neely tapped his thumb against the table. "It's your job to be on my side, right? You won't like—" he shrugged "—get all judgmental or anything."

"I have a responsibility to the court to represent you to the best of my ability." Nick opened the briefcase he'd brought along and removed a pad and pen. "My sole purpose is to listen and determine the proper avenues for navigating any legal obstacles that arise."

"Okay." Neely nodded. "Okay. About a week and a half ago I heard Gwen and Carl arguing. She flat-out refused to give him the records. Since she's a nurse at the hospital and with home health, she has access to all their records."

"Did she tell you what Carl wanted?"

"Nah. I asked him myself." He picked at his fingers. "At first he wouldn't tell me. Eventually he opened up. The guy who wanted them was some big movie producer from out in LA. He wanted to do a movie about what happened with that Detective Gentry. He offered Carl a hundred grand for the records. I told Carl for ten I would get them for him." He looked from his fingers to Nick and back. "I've been out of work for a while. Ten grand went a long way toward getting me back on my feet."

Nick nodded. "I noticed you made an additional deposit." MPD and the bureau didn't have Neely's bank records just yet, but Nick did.

His eyes went wide. "How do you know that?"

"The police have your bank records." He picked up a manila folder from his briefcase. "They had to turn over any evidence discovered so I can properly prepare your defense."

Neely groaned. "Oh man. I knew I shouldn't have deposited any of that money. But the car dealer wouldn't sell me the car without a cashier's check." He laughed. "Since when did people stop taking cash? Anyway, the bank wouldn't issue the cashier's check unless the money was deposited in my account first."

"Where did the additional money come from?"

Neely shifted in his chair. "You gotta understand, Carl and I didn't know the person we were dealing with was this serial killer freak. We really thought he was a movie producer."

Nick pretended to make a few notes on his pad. "What did he want besides the records?"

Neely moistened his lips. "He wanted to interview Gwen personally."

Nick forced his pulse rate to slow. "Was she willing to talk to this *movie producer*?"

Neely made a dismissive sound. "She would never have agreed to it." He inhaled a big breath and let it go. "So I arranged the meeting."

"How did you do that?"

"I told her about this house I saw. She's been saving for a house. I knew that would get her attention."

What a piece of shit. "What name did he use?"

Neely frowned. "What do you mean?"

"You said Gaylon Perry represented himself as a movie producer. What name did he use?" It was a struggle to keep the fury out of his tone.

"Quentin somebody. I can't remember, but it sounded authentic."

"When you discovered Gwen was missing, what did you do?"

"I called her phone a bunch of times. When I found her abandoned car in the middle of the night, I called Carl. We both looked everywhere and couldn't find her. It was insane. We had this big argument. He said he'd been doing some research and that this movie guy wasn't who he said he was. He called the number the bastard had given us, and the guy said a bunch of crazy shit. Carl was real upset. I mean really freaked out. He went home, said he was calling the police. I kept driving around looking for her." Neely cleared his throat. "Then I got scared so I went home and got high."

"This was the morning Carl Evans shot himself?"

Neely nodded. "You have to believe me, I had no idea who this motherfucker was. We never met face-to-face, just talked on the phone. After I made sure Gwen was headed to the house, I called him and that was the last time I heard from him until Carl called him. I did drive by the house after Gwen got there. She was still sitting in her car." He shook his head. "The whole thing was fucked up."

Nick forced himself to make another fake note in order to get his temper under control; then he lifted his gaze to the fucking idiot seated across from him. "This is very important, Liam. Did you see any other vehicle near the house while Gwen was there?"

Neely shrugged. "I lived in that neighborhood as a kid, you know. I'm familiar with the streets, so I parked on the next street for a little while to watch. Just to make sure she was okay."

"Is this when you got high, Liam?" Nick asked. "Maybe you couldn't wait until you got home."

He nodded. "Yeah. I snorted a little coke."

Great. "And what did you see?"

"A black car pulled into the driveway behind Gwen." He cleared his throat. "A man wearing a baseball cap and sunglasses got out and went up to her car, and the two of them went inside the house. So I left. I figured if she went in with him, he must have been okay. Gwen is nobody's fool."

Except yours, Nick kept to himself. "Can you tell me anything about the car?"

"It was an Altima. Black four-door Altima."

"Were there any decals or a license plate?"

He shook his head. "I couldn't see any from where I was parked, but it had to be a rental, didn't it?"

Nick ignored his question. "Was the car old or new?"

He made a face as if he were thinking hard. Nick suspected this was something he rarely did.

"Not brand-new, but maybe last year's model."

"Is there anything else you remember? Did he suggest any other meeting place?"

Liam moved his head from side to side. "Nothing."

"He didn't mention any other locations?" Nick repeated.

Neely shook his head. "No. He never wanted to stay on the phone long, like he was always in a hurry."

Nick tossed his notepad and pen back into the briefcase and closed it. He stood.

"Wait! What happens now? When am I getting out of here?"

Nick shrugged. "I have no idea." He reached for the door.

"But aren't you supposed to figure this out and give me some kind of advice?"

Nick hesitated. He really should keep going. Before he could stop himself he turned around. He leaned across the table and put his face in the idiot's expectant one. "Here's some advice for you, Neely. Bearing in mind what you've done, before they haul your sorry ass off to prison—I'm thinking Atmore, a real shithole—do the world a favor and kill yourself."

The fool's irate bellowing followed Nick out the door.

As he reached the security checkpoint, he stopped.

Bobbie Gentry and her partner were walking in his direction.

Seventeen

Bobbie looked from Shade to the corridor. "Why are you here?" And why was he wearing a suit and carrying a briefcase? A bad, bad feeling temporarily stifled the exhilaration she'd felt only minutes ago. *Oh hell.*

"Let's talk outside." Shade gave her a look that urged her to listen.

Newt took hold of her arm and ushered her after Shade. "We'll be back," he said to the desk sergeant as they passed.

Once they were out of the building, Bobbie wheeled on Shade. Was he insane? This was not an episode of some television series where cases were solved by going around the law. *What about you, Bobbie?* She dismissed the voice. The steps she took were different. "What the hell are you doing here, Shade?"

He looked from Bobbie to her partner and back. "You're looking for a Nissan Altima. Black in color. Relatively new, maybe last year's model. Possibly a rental."

"You talked to Neely?" she demanded.

He dared to walk away. She stormed after him. "I could arrest you right now, Shade. What you did was—"

He halted. "Like I said, we play by different rules, Detective."

When he headed for his car once more, Bobbie would have followed but Newt stopped her. "He gave us a lead. Let's not waste time arguing the law with him."

Her partner was right. She watched Shade drive away. "Are we still talking to Neely?"

Newt harrumphed. "You think he's going to talk to us now?"

"Damn it!" Bobbie loaded into her Challenger. What the hell had Shade been thinking? "If he screwed up any chance we had of learning something from Neely—"

"I'm thinking he may have given us a hell of a break." Newt tapped a few keys on his cell. "We can start with Alamo and work our way through the alphabet."

Bobbie set a course for the address Newt spouted off. They'd barely gotten a mile when her cell rang. She pulled it from her waist and groaned. "It's Owens." Bobbie hit the accept-call button and braced for questions she couldn't answer. "Gentry."

"Detective, what the hell is going on over there? I just received a call informing me that Liam Neely is screaming something about being harassed and questioned under false pretenses. Have you and Detective Newton questioned him?"

"No, ma'am. We got a tip and decided to follow up on it first." Bobbie glanced at Newt. It was one thing for her to risk damaging her career and entirely another to jeopardize his. He gave her a confirming nod. "Newt and I never made it into the interview room. When we first arrived the desk sergeant said Neely's attorney was with him. Then we got this tip and we're following up now."

Owens sighed, the sound conveying her frustration. "I won't ask for the source of your tip, but I would like to know what this lead is."

"It's possible Perry may be using a rental car. A black Nissan Altima. We're hitting the rental agencies now."

"I want an update every two hours."

"Yes, ma'am." Bobbie ended the call and tucked her cell away. "We're off the hook for now. But—" she glanced at Newt "—the security video at the jail will show the make-believe attorney who visited Neely was the same guy who went to the hospital with me last night. I don't want Shade dragging you into trouble, Newt."

"Don't worry about me, girlie." He relaxed into the seat and flipped the sun visor down. "I was busting heads as a beat cop when Owens was still wearing cheerleader skirts."

Bobbie sent him a surprised look. "Owens was a cheerleader in high school?"

"She was. My mother was a member of the Christian Ladies League, and she heard about one of the cheerleaders needing a little help. So she bought the girl's uniform and paid the fees related to her participation."

"They don't make them like your mom anymore, Newt." Bobbie lost her mom when she was only twelve. Cancer sucked. Life sucked. She just wished she could have been a better mom.

Maybe she could be a good cop for a little while longer.

Long enough to get this son of a bitch.

Gardendale Drive, 7:58 p.m.

Bobbie backed into her driveway. Her surveillance detail parked at the curb. She locked the car and headed for the front door. She and Newt had hit every car rental agency in the city, including those at the dealerships and at the airport. No one had rented a car to anyone who matched the Storyteller's description—the old description or the new one.

A total of thirteen Altimas had been rented. Ten of those were definitely legitimate, the other three were unconfirmed. She shoved the key into her lock. There was always the chance Perry had stolen the car and it hadn't been reported yet. Cars went missing on the larger car lots and often weren't noted for days. Newt had requested the names and addresses of everyone in the county who owned a black Altima manufactured in the past two years.

She opened the door and cleared her mind. She listened and inhaled deeply, confirming the sounds and smells of her place hadn't changed. Once inside with the door locked, she went through the house and performed the usual checks. *Clear.*

She flipped on the living room light, stripped off her jacket and tossed it on the sofa. As she reached for the weapon at her waist, a knock echoed from the back door. Palming her weapon, she eased in that direction. She stood well clear of the door and cracked the blinds shielding the window nearest the rear exit.

"It's Nick Shade."

She drew back from the window. How was it he always knew when she was looking at him? An educated guess? Coincidence?

After releasing the dead bolt, she opened the door. "Is there something wrong with my front door?"

He came inside, closed the door and locked it. "After what I did today, you might not want to be seen with me."

"Neely is threatening to sue the department." Bobbie tucked her weapon back into its holster. "They printed a shot from the surveillance video, but it's difficult to see your face. I'm guessing you've done this before."

The dim glow creeping toward them from the one light she'd turned on as she came in allowed her to see what might have been the ghost of a smile. Then again, she might have imagined it.

"I may have taken a similar opportunity once or twice."

"Lieutenant Owens and Special Agent LeDoux have the person on the security video footage figured for an ambitious reporter. They're on the lookout for you, Shade."

"Should I be concerned about your loyalty?"

She hesitated, mostly to see his reaction. He kept whatever he felt to himself. "No, and I don't think they'll be able to identify you from the video." Getting to what she assumed was the point of his visit, she said, "We got nothing from the rental car angle."

"Neely sold an interview with Gwen to Perry for ten thousand dollars. He never met Perry in person, but he saw him in the driveway of that house where Adams's car was found."

"Yeah." Bobbie had already heard. "He copped a plea two hours ago. The DA dropped the potential accessory to murder charges in exchange for his full confession. They've got him on suicide watch now. Apparently, someone suggested he take his life before he got sentenced to Atmore."

Rather than comment on her obvious accusation, Shade said, "A neighbor near the Highland Avenue house saw a man in a black car, possibly an Altima, driving around the neighborhood Thursday afternoon. He parked on the street. She couldn't remember the full license plate number, but there was a JDHS sticker on the bumper."

"Then it's not a rental. JDHS is Jefferson Davis High School. The owner has kids in school." Bobbie quickly sent Newt a text with the information. She studied Shade for a long moment. "Why didn't we find this woman when we canvassed the neighborhood?"

"She left Friday morning to visit her daughter in Huntsville. She only returned home today."

Bobbie rubbed at her forehead. She was so tired. "Thanks. I hope you'll keep me informed of anything else you find." She reached for the door. The sooner he was out of here, the sooner she could do a little research of her own on *him*. If the FBI knew about him, others did, as well. She'd been a cop long enough to have a few friends in high places. Like the US marshal she'd once worked with. He was in New Orleans now, but she could call him. His son was about the same age Jamie would...

"I'll be on your couch," Shade announced.

He walked past her as if her permission wasn't required.

Bobbie closed a mental door on the memory of her baby and concentrated her attention on the moment. "Wait just a minute, Shade."

When he turned back to her, her cell rang, cutting off whatever he might have said. Bobbie snatched it from her waist and stared at the screen.

She froze.

The number was her home number... The house where she and James had lived with...their child.

She slid a finger across the screen, tapped the speaker button and held her breath. "Hello." The single word was so hollow she barely recognized the voice as her own.

"Mommy? Please come get me."

A volatile mixture of emotions exploded in her veins, at once red-hot and ice-cold. "Who is this?"

"Mommy, I'm scared."

Her heart kicked in her chest. The voice wasn't Jamie's, but it definitely belonged to a male child around the same age.

"Aaron?" Bobbie's heart rose into her throat. "Is that you, Aaron?"

"Come home, Mommy."

Sobs echoed across the line.

The call ended.

"I think that was the missing boy... Aaron." Her gaze locked with Shade's. "He was calling from my house."

Shade was ushering her toward the front door before she remembered taking a step. He grabbed her keys and they rushed out the door. When they reached her car, he guided her to the passenger side.

"I'm driving," he said.

There was no time to argue. While he drove, she alerted Newt, who would send word up the chain. Unless there was a unit in the area, she and Shade should arrive first. Whatever was waiting at her house, she wanted to find it first. The surveillance detail was right behind them, so they had some measure of backup.

Bobbie calmed her breathing and cleared her mind. If the voice was Aaron's, that meant he was still alive. She wanted him to be alive and safe. She glanced at the speedometer and then out the window. Five minutes. They would be there within five minutes.

Not soon enough.

She hoped the son of a bitch was waiting for her, but intellectually she comprehended that he wouldn't make such a foolhardy mistake.

Bobbie stared at her cell for a long moment before tucking it back at her waist. *Be there, you bastard.*

Ryan Ridge

Shade made the turn into the subdivision and shut off the headlights. The surveillance detail did the same. No other cruisers appeared to be in the area. Shade stopped a block from her house. Dusk had fallen, making it more difficult to surveil the area.

"I'm getting out here," he said. "I want you to pull into the driveway and wait in the car until I tell you it's safe to get out."

"Sure." He was clearly out of his mind. Bobbie wasn't waiting.

He hesitated before opening the door. "Listen to me, Bobbie. Don't go inside until I've checked out the situation."

"Right." She didn't look at him. Instead, she focused on the dark house that had been her home for five wonderful years.

Now it was nothing more than a headstone for her dead life.

Shade disappeared into the encroaching gloom.

Bobbie scooted across the console and shifted her car into Drive. She turned the headlights on once more and slowly rolled the final block to her house. The turn into her driveway made her stomach sink. She shoved the gearshift into Park and shut off the engine.

The cruiser stopped on the street and waited.

Any minute now a full onslaught of official vehicles would arrive. LeDoux would likely show up and they would all trample through the painful memories of her life.

Bobbie started to shake. She couldn't watch that scene play out. She needed to have a look now so she could stand back when the evidence techs and feds prowled through the place. She couldn't be part of that. She just couldn't do it.

"To hell with you, Shade." She didn't take orders from her partner; she sure as hell wasn't taking any from him.

Her weapon palmed, she made her way to the front door. On second thought she decided to go through the garage. She moved around to the side of the garage and unlocked the door. She flipped a switch, and fluorescent lights blinked to life, gleaming against the charcoal BMW that was her husband's birthday present from her four months before he died. It wasn't one of the really expensive models, but it was the best she could do on a cop's salary. The decade-old black Subaru was hers. She walked between the two, her heart aching at the sight of the matching car seats, one in each vehicle.

The garage smelled the same. A little like gas and oil from the lawn mower. The blank space on the top storage shelf where the Christmas ornaments usually sat was dusty now. The decorations and the tree were still right where they were the day her life ended. She inserted the key that still hung on her key ring into the lock and gave it a turn. Shoving the keys into her back pocket, she opened the door slowly and eased into the laundry room.

Unable to help herself, she closed her eyes and inhaled the scent of home. The fluttering in her chest made her tremble.

Without turning on a light, she slipped into the kitchen. After Jamie was born, she and James had installed night-lights in every room. *No more stumbling over furniture and toys*, he had insisted after taking a tumble while going for a middle-of-the-night bottle. Images from that last night he'd been in this kitchen flashed one after the other in her head. Her husband lying on cold white tile, deep crimson pooling around him. His beautiful gray eyes open and unseeing.

Don't look back, Bobbie.

Tonight the house was silent. Outside in the distance the wail of sirens reverberated. Her senses on alert, Bobbie moved through the kitchen and into the long center hall. The memory of pushing Jamie out the front door and her head snapping back as the Storyteller grabbed her by the hair arced through her brain.

Pounding on the door made her jump.

"Detective Gentry, are you in there?"

One of the uniforms from her detail. She flipped on the overhead light and squinted at the brightness. Surveying the hall she moved backward toward the door. Long dead pine swags scented the air. Red, green and silver ornaments filled a large glass bowl on the table next to the door.

Bobbie unlocked the door and allowed the uniforms inside. "No one moves past this point until I say so," she ordered.

"Yes, ma'am," echoed in unison.

She made her way to the living room—the last place where she sat cuddled with her precious son. They'd been watching *Rudolph the Red-Nosed Reindeer*. James had been in the kitchen baking cookies for Santa.

The artificial tree they'd decorated that very morning still stood before the towering palladium window at the front of the room. Giggles and happy chatter echoed through her mind. Those hours were the last that felt real to her. Everything since was like functioning on autopilot and just cruising through time.

The gifts sat unopened under the tree. Her breath caught beneath her breastbone. All these months later and she still couldn't bear the idea of opening the ones from her husband and baby. She simply couldn't. If she left everything exactly as it was maybe she would wake up from this pretend life—this nightmare—and find her family here, smiling and happy and waiting for her.

"They're here, ma'am."

The officer's voice dragged Bobbie from the painful memories. She was out of time.

With a last look at the Christmas tree, she returned to the entry hall. "I'll take a look upstairs. Tell them to stay down here until I give the go-ahead."

Bobbie climbed the staircase, memories of the first time she and James had opened the front door flooding her senses. He had carried her across the threshold and later that night he'd carried her up the stairs after hours of lovemaking on the bare living room floor.

The doors along the upstairs hall were closed, the way she'd left them, except one. There were four. Three bedrooms and a hall bath. The first on her left was the bathroom. She approached the one on the right. Jamie's room. The one door that remained open. Jamie never liked his door closed.

Downstairs raised voices sounded. The deep insistent chords of Shade's voice clashed against the more uncertain tone of one of the uniforms. Ignoring the ruckus, Bobbie reached for the switch and bright light flooded her baby's room. The blue race-car bed and the dresser James had painted to match, even adding racing stripes, made her heart ache. Jamie's Legos and cars were scattered around the floor where he'd left them. His favorite stuffed animals—a fox, a bear and an elephant—waited on the bed. The bear was almost worn-out, one eye missing...

Bobbie trembled as she leaned down to visually

examine the one thing that didn't belong. The note left on the pillow. Broad red strokes of what looked far too much like blood spelled out the words.

You can't save them.

She squeezed her eyes shut and fought the burn of tears.

Footfalls echoed on the staircase. Bobbie dragged in a breath and scrubbed back the damned tears. She cursed herself and faced whoever was about to appear at the door of her son's room. *Shade.*

"We need to close down the area and look for the boy."

She had no idea what he was talking about but the urgency in his voice, on his face had her moving toward him. "You think the child is still here?" Bobbie surveyed the room once more. It was possible the little boy could be hidden somewhere in the house. Her pulse shifted into a faster rhythm. Would they be lucky enough to have the second child delivered unharmed?

"We rescued a child in traffic last night," Shade reminded her. "You got a call from a child—from this house. He may be hoping to reenact what happened that night. He wants to cause you pain, Bobbie."

Understanding hurtled into her. She rushed out the door and down the stairs.

"Shut down the neighborhood. No one comes in or leaves until we check all the driveways, garages, beneath cars—anywhere a child might be in danger of being run over."

The way Jamie had been…the night she pushed him out the door to what she hoped would be safety.

Shade caught up with her on the sidewalk. "If his goal is to make you live through that horror again, that means he's close by. Watching."

Bobbie surveyed the street she had loved so very much before… Fury roared through her. *Come on, you bastard, show yourself.*

They searched every house, garage and parked car in the neighborhood. No one had seen Perry or the Black Altima he drove. And the boy was not here.

Bobbie wanted to scream in frustrated agony. She wanted to turn this whole county upside down, but they didn't have the manpower or the time for that kind of manhunt.

Reporters waited outside the entrance to the subdivision. She could feel their zoom lens following her every step.

Where the hell was Shade?

He'd disappeared again. She'd noticed that he kept his back to others, particularly reporters, as often as possible. Was he worried about his face ending up in the news? Could he possibly have a criminal record under another name? Hell, he could be a fugitive for all she knew. *Doubtful*, she amended. The authorities were aware of him. Newt's friend at the bureau had confessed as much.

She walked back to the house she had once called home and went around to the side the reporters couldn't invade from their position. Leaning against the brick wall she closed her eyes and reached for some semblance of professional focus. Where would he take the child? Was he keeping him in the same place he was keeping Gwen? God, Bobbie hoped not. No child should see what she knew firsthand Gwen was going through.

Bobbie had never been much for church, not as an adult anyway. Her mother had insisted they go every single Sunday without fail. After her mother died, Bobbie and her dad hadn't felt compelled to attend Sunday services any more. They had found special ways to spend their Sundays together. After all, if God had abandoned them, why wouldn't they abandon him?

Made perfect sense to a twelve-year-old.

Bobbie squeezed her eyes shut a little tighter and did that thing she hadn't done in about twenty years.

She prayed little Aaron Taggart would be returned safe and sound to his mother. She prayed Gwen would come through this alive, as well. And she prayed for the strength and courage to do what needed to be done. She opened her eyes and pushed away from the house.

She would find the Storyteller and she would kill him.

10:50 p.m.

A full half hour later Bobbie climbed into the back of a cruiser and closed her eyes as the two uniforms who'd followed her to the Ryan Ridge house drove her home. Shade had taken her car, damn him. Not that she actually cared, but she'd intended to drive around for a while.

Don't kid yourself, Bobbie. The Storyteller is long gone by now.

And so was Aaron. Agony swelled in her chest and she fought the urge to cry. *Not here. Not now.* The bastard would never spare Gwen and the boy's lives. He'd likely meant for Joey to be killed on the interstate.

Bobbie hugged her arms around herself and stared out at the passing lights. This would end soon. The Storyteller wouldn't keep pressing his luck. The FBI's current profile indicated he expected to survive and move on after he finished here.

Not if I can help it.

The cruiser slowed and made the turn onto Gardendale Drive.

"Looks like your friend is here," one of the officers said, interrupting the long span of silence.

Bobbie sat up just as the cruiser's headlights flashed over her Challenger. Shade leaned against the hood. Her heart reacted. Why in the world it suddenly mattered to her that he was here waiting for her made no sense at all. Just another indication of how total exhaustion messed with a person's head.

She climbed out of the cruiser.

"We'll be out here if you need us, Detective."

She thanked them as she closed the door, or she thought she did. Hoped she did. Her attention had landed on Shade and stayed there. Some part of her needed to hear him say he'd left before her because he'd spotted the Storyteller. She wanted desperately to hear him say he'd found him and it was all over.

Bobbie stopped three or so feet away from him. Not once in all these months had she wanted to hear that someone else had captured or killed the Storyteller. She wanted it to be her. She wanted to take his life the way he had taken hers. Except she was so tired, so very, very tired. For the first time she wanted it to be over.

As if he read line and verse on her face, Shade said, "I didn't find him."

Those four little words crushed her. Tears brimmed in her eyes, and she swayed on her feet.

He reached for her, and she held up her hands. "Don't." She shook her head. "Don't touch me."

He glanced at the street. "Let's go inside."

His soft words made her angry. Anger gave her strength. She stormed to her door and went inside. It was unlocked; he'd obviously already checked to see that the house was clear. She went straight to the bathroom and tore off her jacket. It hit the floor. One by one she tossed her weapons on the counter, her gaze glued to the tormented face in the mirror.

She was no closer to stopping the son of a bitch than she had been more than eighty-some-odd hours ago when Carl Evans blew his brains out. The Storyteller was playing with her, and she was helpless to stop him. The entire department and the illustrious team from the FBI were helpless...just like before. The damned blouse hit the floor next. She flattened her palms against the cool counter and closed her eyes.

You failed then and you're going to fail this time, Bobbie.

A sob rose in her throat. How had she ever expected to do this? She should have known that Perry would use her desperate need to get him against her. He'd taken Gwen and those babies. He'd killed the Taggart boy's father. All on her watch…all with her waiting, wishing he would come for her. But no! He wanted to punish her some more first.

The tears she struggled to hold back spilled past her lashes. *Goddamn it!* She sucked in a breath and scrubbed them away. In the mirror she saw Shade watching her from the doorway. She hadn't even shut the fucking door. She closed her eyes and swore again. "Enjoying the show?"

He moved behind her, and she grimaced. With her blouse on the floor he would see the scars and the words the bastard had inscribed on her back.

When she would have told him to go away, he stepped over her clothes and knelt next to the tub. He turned on the tap and adjusted the water temperature. Before she could summon a rant, he was standing behind her again. Somehow she mustered enough dignity to say, "This is one thing I can handle myself."

His dark eyes searched hers for a moment. Despite her best efforts, her lips trembled. Before she could launch another protest, he reached beyond her and turned off the light. His hands landed on her waist, and she gasped. Bobbie opened her mouth to argue, but his fingers slipping beneath the back of her bra stole the words. He released the clasps and slid the plain cotton garment down and off.

Trembling, she moistened her lips. "What're you—"

"Shh…"

The sound hummed against her cheek. She wanted to make him stop but she couldn't summon the wherewithal to manage the feat. He slipped her belt free and let it fall to the floor. He knelt and removed her shoes and socks. When he reached up to draw her trousers down her hips, she clutched at the counter and dragged in a deep breath of the steam-filled air. His fingers traced back up her legs, lingering on the scars before slipping into her waistband and tugging her panties down next. A distant ache began deep inside her.

He pushed to his feet, and she held her breath, uncertain what would happen next. Part of her wanted to demand he stop, the other desperate part wanted him to do anything to make her forget for just a little while. In the darkness he wouldn't be able to see the real her and she could pretend for just a little bit that she wasn't the broken Bobbie anymore.

He scooped her up into his arms and held her against his chest. She savored the smell of his skin. Before she lost all sense and dove her fingers into his hair, he settled her into the tub. Warm water splashed around her, over the side. He shut off the faucet and the silence closed in. For a moment she couldn't breathe. What was she doing naked and alone in the dark with this man? A man she didn't even really know? Maybe she had lost her mind. All this time she'd been so certain she knew exactly what she was doing—what she had to do.

Now she wasn't sure of anything.

His hands plunged into the water and sought her body. He guided her deeper into the water and washed her hair, the feel of his fingers on her scalp chased away all other thought. Then those long-fingered hands moved to her body, slowly, gently gliding the soap over her skin. Her shoulders, arms and torso and then her legs. He placed the soap in her fingers and used her hand to wash the most intimate part of her.

The water was cooling by the time he helped her from the tub and dried her body. He rubbed and squeezed her hair with the towel until it was nearly completely dry. Then he took her in his arms and carried her through the darkness to her bedroom. He drew back the covers and tucked her in.

"Sleep," he murmured against her forehead.

Then he was gone.

The woman she had been certain had died in that shack all those months ago roused, and for the first time in 248 days Bobbie felt something besides pain.

Eighteen

"No, that's not acceptable." Tony LeDoux stared at the pale circle on his finger where his wedding band had once been. Five years. The woman he had loved—still loved—was willing to throw it all away over a few snags.

He heaved a heavy breath. "If you keep the house in DC, I get the cabin in Virginia. That's my final offer, Giselle. If that's not acceptable to you, then we'll let a judge figure it out." He ended the call and tossed his phone on the bed. He tunneled his fingers through his hair and wished for a drink.

His drinking was another of the issues she claimed had ruined their marriage. He rolled his eyes and plopped down on the foot of the bed. When a guy worked the kind of cases he did, he needed a stiff drink when he got home. What kind of wife didn't understand that?

His soon-to-be ex-wife, apparently.

He thought of Bobbie Gentry and the bullshit

game the Storyteller had put her through tonight. The bastard had murdered her husband, caused her kid to be killed and almost killed her. Now, seven months later he tortures her with other kids he abducted. Amazingly Giselle couldn't understand why he didn't want to have kids?

Any man in his right mind would feel the same way after seeing the things he had seen. God, he'd seen children cut into pieces and mailed to a parent. He'd uncovered remains of children brutally beaten to death—as often as not by their own parents. Every day children were burned, stuffed into garbage containers and thrown into rivers like an unwanted litter of kittens. How in the hell could he work up the courage to participate in the act of bringing a child into this world? He'd seen too many taken out by the worst kind of killers.

He loosened his tie. The search in Bobbie's neighborhood had given them nothing. The Taggart boy hadn't been found. Chances were he had never been in Gentry's house. Perry may have recorded the kid's cries and played them from the house phone. Whether or not the kid was there, Perry had been there. He was torturing Gentry and relishing every move made by her and every law enforcement officer involved.

Watching the devastation sucked. Tony had been on the Storyteller case for six long years. Until November last year they'd had nothing but thirteen bodies—a female victim taken from one state and her body dropped in another for each year the Storyteller had been active with that MO. Then on the third day of December a second body in the same year had been deposited at a drop site. Twenty-one days later Bobbie Gentry had gone missing.

They hadn't known until she escaped in late January of this year who the Storyteller was. Based on Gentry's observations of the bastard's methodology and his own scars, much of their original profile had been confirmed. A lot more had been revised. Bottom line, he was still out there. It had taken Tony and his team months to piece together his killing history and to understand that his mother's death had apparently sent him over the edge.

Perry was a psychopathic serial killer of the highest order.

He was also a major contributor to the breakdown of Tony's marriage. Unsolved cases were the ones that kept an agent from sleeping at night. As horrific as many of the cases he investigated were, if the killer was found and brought to justice he could at least sleep at night.

Perry had stolen that ability from him for more than six years now.

A soft rap on the door drew Tony in that direction. He checked the security viewfinder. Male. The man wore a hotel uniform and held an envelope.

"You have something for me?" Tony asked without opening the door. He'd learned the hard way that serial killers could be incredibly clever. He'd had one get all the way in his room once pretending to be maintenance.

"A message left for you at the desk, sir."

"Just slip it under the door."

Tony removed a five-dollar bill from his wallet and slid it under the door for the guy.

"Thank you, sir."

Tony watched as far as the viewfinder would allow as the guy walked away. Then he gingerly picked up the envelope. The flap wasn't glued so removing the folded paper inside was easy enough. With the tips of his fingers he opened the single page.

I can tell you how to find Perry. Meet me at Union Station.

Anticipation lit inside him. In all probability it was a trap or maybe a nutcase wanting attention. Either way, Tony couldn't ignore the potential lead. The old Union Station was only a block or so from the hotel. He grabbed his coat and shouldered into it. He could be there in under five minutes, but he wasn't a fool.

He reached for his cell phone and rushed into the corridor. By the time he was on the elevator, he was calling Jacobs. Jacobs was the newest agent assigned to Tony's team. He'd rather have brought a more experienced member but they were stretched too thin as it was. There hadn't been anyone else he'd felt comfortable pulling from their current assignments. So he'd brought the new kid.

Special Agent Smith Jacobs didn't answer until the third ring. The out-of-breath quality in his voice warned it wasn't because he'd been asleep. "Meet me in the lobby now," Tony ordered.

"Ah… I'm not in my room, sir."

Son of a bitch! "Where the hell are you?" As Jacobs asked his friend how to get from where they were back to the Renaissance, Tony burst out of the elevator into the lobby. He headed for the front desk. He dragged the note from his pocket and held it up for the clerk to see. "Do you remember who left this note for me? Was it a man or a woman?"

The clerk looked confused. "I'm sorry, sir. I only came on duty an hour ago. No one's come to the desk until you did just now." She pointed to the envelope. "It was lying here when I came on duty so I sent it to your room."

Jacobs was saying something in his ear. He was at the Embassy Suites, which was a matter of only a few blocks. "I'll pick you up at the front entrance," Tony said. "Be ready or this will be your last assignment on my team." He ended the call and turned his attention back to the clerk. "Call whoever was on duty before you and get her or him here ASAP." He showed her his credentials. "Call the manager. I'll need to see the security video for the lobby and the parking lot." When the clerk simply stood there staring at him, he pounded his fist against the counter. "Now!"

She jerked. "Yes, sir." She grabbed the phone, her hands shaking.

Tony hurried out to the parking lot. The valet turned to him, but he shook his head. Tony never used a valet when he was on assignment. He wanted to know where his vehicle was at all times. He hustled across the parking lot. The damned place had been packed when he arrived just after ten. Parking slots had been few and far between.

He spotted his SUV, hit the remote unlock and hustled over to the driver's-side door. His cell rang. He dragged it from his pocket. *Jacobs. Damn it. What now?*

"What?"

When the agent announced that he didn't have his weapon with him, Tony barely restrained the urge to throw the phone across the parking lot. "Be at the goddamned front entrance in one minute." He ended the call and shoved the phone into his pocket; then he reached for the door handle.

Pain pierced his neck. He reached for his weapon and tried to turn around, stumbling in the process.

He felt himself falling, but he couldn't catch himself.

His back hit the asphalt. His SUV and the car next to it seemed so far away.

His eyes were closing and he couldn't seem to stop them.

The last image he glimpsed was Gaylon Perry's smiling face staring down at him.

"Hello, Agent, it's been a while."

Fuck.

Nineteen

The piece of shit made the final turn in the fourth eyebolt. He looped the steel handcuff through the hole and snapped it shut. He sat back on his heels. "Now."

Gwen shuddered. She'd pretended to be asleep when he'd come inside dragging a body. Fear had thundered in her chest. Once the man was laid out on the floor she'd been able to see his chest rise and fall. He was alive. Thank God.

Maybe he would be able to help her escape before it was too late. Perry had been gone for hours today. Early this morning he'd shown her a photo on his phone. The man carrying Bobbie Gentry was the same one who'd visited her in the hospital back in February. Perry seemed disturbed by her answer. He'd paced the small room for what felt like hours. She'd spent every minute worried that he would touch her again. Her entire body shuddered at the idea. She felt like a hollow shell. Even the many cuts and bruises he'd made on her body no longer hurt, not really. She'd gone numb.

Thankfully, when his pacing stopped, he'd left again. She'd tried so hard to get free but the handcuffs he'd used to secure her were impossible to escape.

Each time he had raped her she closed her eyes and tried to disappear from this awful place. The most sickening part had been the feel of his semen seeping between her thighs. If she survived this nightmare, there was no telling what diseases he may have passed on to her. She thought of the endless days Bobbie had suffered his torture. Gwen recognized now just what a true miracle it was that she had survived. All those months Bobbie had struggled to regain her strength and balance. Gwen remembered the first time Bobbie had tried to run a lap around the gym. She'd fallen three times before she made it. Gwen had run with her. By the end of the fourth week, Bobbie could outrun her. In all her life Gwen had never seen such determination.

Please find us, Bobbie.

While Perry stripped the man, Gwen dared to stretch her neck to look toward the other room. He'd brought the little boy back earlier tonight. She hadn't seen any sign of blood, but he had been whimpering. Hopefully he was okay. She squeezed her eyes shut. *Please, God, let the little boy be okay.* Perry had already taken one away, and she feared the worst. She had tried to recall the things he'd done in the past, but she could only remember that he raped and murdered women. Bobbie had told her the story about how her little boy died. The Storyteller hadn't killed him—not directly. Why would he start killing children now? Did serial killers change their MOs?

As if she'd asked the question out loud, he whipped his attention toward her. She closed her eyes. *Too late!* He'd seen her!

The rustle of fabric brushed her ears, and she braced for his disgusting touch.

"Well, well, look who's peeking." His fingers dragged down her rib cage. "It's almost time, Nurse Adams. You and I should prepare so that we're ready to begin when our new friend awakens."

Her heart pounded harder. "Please. No more."

He smiled. How could a man with such a normal face and seemingly caring smile be such a monster?

"I'm not going to hurt you anymore, Gwen. I'm going to hurt Bobbie by killing you right in front of her."

The sobs rose so fast Gwen couldn't hold them back.

He moved away for a moment, but quickly returned with a hypodermic needle. "Time to go to sleep."

She tried to draw away but he jabbed the needle into her neck. The burn rushed through her veins and her body immediately went still. Her vision dimmed until the faint lantern light was gone.

As her mind drifted away she felt him loosening her restraints.

She knew what would happen next...he would tattoo her story on her back.

She remembered what that meant: *the end.*

Twenty

"We've interviewed the clerk who spoke with Agent LeDoux last night before he left the hotel." Special Agent Kent Mason pointed to the whiteboard, where a timeline had been created. "The time was just after midnight."

Bobbie tried her best to focus on what the new agent who'd showed up before daylight this morning had to say. Mason was new to her, but apparently he had worked the Storyteller case with LeDoux at some point over the years. Newt had called Bobbie around one this morning and told her LeDoux was missing.

What the hell was Perry doing? How was he handling all these hostages?

She and Shade had gone to the scene at the Renaissance Hotel. Shade continued to surprise her. He read a crime scene like a trained investigator. Too bad the scene had yielded the same as the Storyteller's scenes always yielded: nothing. The new agent on the scene as well as the ones she'd worked with before were all baffled.

As if she'd said the words aloud, an agent—another one she hadn't met before—stood. "My name is Angela Price. I'm a profiler, and I'd like to address the abrupt changes we've seen in Gaylon Perry's behavior."

Peterson shifted in the chair next to Bobbie's. He was not happy about her being here. They'd gotten off on the wrong foot first thing when he demanded she explain Nick Shade. She'd shrugged and said he was a serial killer expert recommended by one of Newt's old friends at the FBI. Peterson had looked at her with the same expression he did each time she told him the session with the shrink went great. He recognized she was lying, but it made life easier to pretend he didn't notice.

The memory of the gentle way Shade had bathed her last night and then tucked her into bed made her feel restless even now. Why had he done that? Why the hell had she let him? She was glad he'd headed in a different direction from her this morning. He'd told her he had a source he wanted to check in with and that he might be gone most of the day.

Be careful, Bobbie. Don't get yourself dead.

Bobbie pushed the memories aside and surveyed the room. Owens was seated on the other side of the chief, next to the sheriff. The rest of her team, including Newt, was in the field helping with the search. Bobbie wanted to be out there. Owens could brief her on what the damned profiler had to say. Why was she wasting time sitting here?

Despite her impatience and frustration, Bobbie listened while the profiler reviewed the Storyteller's MO—as if anyone in the room was unfamiliar with who and what this son of a bitch was and how he did things. Frankly, she could be up there doing a better job. Giving the agent grace, Perry had changed things up considerably.

Apparently she sighed too loudly since everyone in the room turned her way. The chief nudged her foot with his own. Owens, on the other hand, wasn't nearly so subtle. "Did you have something you wanted to share with the task force, Detective Gentry?"

Hell. For a split second Bobbie considered letting everyone in the room know she thought they were wasting valuable time. But then something Shade said to her bobbed to the surface of her frustration. "Each time he takes a victim it's about his mother."

"Did Perry share this insight with you?" The profiler flipped through the folder in front of her. "I don't recall reading that in any of your statements."

"He didn't mention his mother." Gaylon Perry's face flashed in front of Bobbie's eyes. "I've spent a lot of time thinking about the way he reacted to her death. Everything he's done has been about her." She fell silent, but when the room waited for her to continue, she said, "If you look at photos of her when she was young, you'll see his typical victim." She had everyone's attention now. "I believe he's punishing his mother for not protecting him from his abusive father."

The profiler nodded. "Interesting theory, Detective. I'll certainly look into it." She directed her attention back to the room at large. "Moving on, it's clear that Perry has regained control and is now on a mission." Her gaze slid to Bobbie again. "His intent is to reclaim the one victim who escaped. To do that, he's collected what he feels are marketable assets. At some point very soon he'll either use them to help accomplish his goal or he'll want to trade."

The next several minutes were spent with Agent Mason and Chief Peterson going over how the manhunt had been expanded and how a media blitz had been launched to further warn the community about Perry and to potentially garner useful tips. All blond-haired, gray- or blue-eyed children between the ages of two and five were at risk, as were females who met the criteria of Perry's previous victims. The goal was to make it impossible for him to show his face anywhere without being recognized. Photos of Perry with and without hair were being circulated.

The security camera footage from the hotel had shown him, sporting a baseball cap and glasses, dropping the letter on the desk in the lobby. The black Altima had been picked up as well, but not the license plate. All additional camera footage in the city was being reviewed for any glimpse of the vehicle. The work was time consuming, but it could pay off. For now, all black Altimas spotted were to be stopped and checked.

Bobbie closed her eyes. She could only imagine the condition Gwen was in at this stage. Bobbie wished she could have saved her from this. *And LeDoux, damn.* There was no way to guess what Perry might do to him, beyond killing him. As concerned as Bobbie was about Gwen and LeDoux, it was the child who worried her the most. He was the most fragile of the victims. Why hadn't Perry left him at her house? What purpose could the child possibly serve now? Had he intended to leave him and something went wrong?

Notebooks closed and fabric rustled, alerting Bobbie that the briefing was over. She stood and surveyed the group. Sheriff Young was the first out the door. A representative from the State Police as well as the Alabama Bureau of Investigation had been among those present. No one could be left out of the loop with a serial killer running loose in their jurisdiction.

Before Bobbie could escape, the chief and Lieutenant Owens cornered her. "I want you sticking close to Detective Newton," Peterson said.

"I'm headed to his location now." For good measure, she added, "My surveillance detail will be right behind me."

"You haven't mentioned your thoughts about Perry's pre-killing history before," Owens noted. "I'd like a full report on any other interesting discoveries you've made from whatever sources you've *stumbled* upon."

Owens danced all around it, but what she really wanted to know was who Nick Shade was and if Bobbie had gleaned any part of her theory from him. Before Bobbie could deliver a reasonable explanation, the profiler joined their huddle. "I was about to request the same," Price announced with a smile meant to show her team spirit. "I don't think I've seen photos of his mother any younger than fifty."

"I'll be sure to give you a copy of my report," Bobbie said. Since she didn't have one, she supposed she'd have to write one up.

"I'll walk you out, Detective," the chief said before Price could fire away with whatever other questions she had.

As if she understood the chief wanted privacy, Owens stayed in the conference room and initiated a conversation with Price.

The chief waited until they were in the parking lot before he launched his interrogation. "You're up to something, Bobbie." He stopped near her car. "I'm not satisfied with your answer about this man—Nick Shade."

"I told you he's an expert." She shrugged. "Didn't you ask Newt? He'll tell you the same thing. The FBI knows he's here and following the case."

"I spoke to Newt, yes." The chief searched her face for a moment. "I may not have jurisdiction over your off-duty life," he said, repeating words she had thrown at him many times, "but I have a right to be aware of anything or anyone who might affect your ability to do the job."

"Newt knows him," she hedged. "He's helping me deal with *this*." Bobbie realized for the first time since Shade bulldozed his way into her life that it was true. She hitched a thumb toward the driver's-side door of her Challenger. "Speaking of my partner, I should get out there."

When she would have slipped away, the chief touched her arm. "I'm worried, Bobbie. Really worried."

"I know and I appreciate your concern." He and Newt loved her, and she loved them. She swallowed at the lump rising in her throat. It didn't mean she felt the loss of James and Jamie any less to admit she loved the two other people closest to her.

Or that you felt something when Shade touched you? The realization startled her. She pushed it away.

The chief held her gaze a moment longer. "I expect to hear from you once you've reached Newt's location."

"Yes, sir."

Newt and the others were working the area downtown hoping to find a witness to LeDoux's abduction. Bobbie climbed into her Challenger and rolled. The MPD cruiser followed. She checked her cell to see if she'd gotten a call or a text from Shade. Whoever he had to see, she hoped he learned something useful. Just now, she would take any help she could get.

She shook her head, surprised by the admission. Maybe it was time to admit she couldn't do this alone.

Court Square, 11:20 a.m.

Bobbie parked on Commerce and walked over to the fountain where Newt and Michael Hadden, the agent from the local FBI field office, were pointing to a camera high atop the Winter building. A frown tugging at her brow, she double-timed it over to see what they'd found.

Bauer and Holt had rolled to follow up on a call from the hotline. None of the tips had panned out so far, but there was always the chance one would be the real thing.

Newt saw Bobbie coming and put his phone away. "I was about to call you."

Hadden held up a plastic evidence bag. "We just fished this out of the fountain."

Bobbie took the bag and inspected the silver chain and the cross it held. Even if the initials hadn't been engraved on the back, she would have recognized it. A fist drove into her stomach. "This is Gwen's." She handed the bag back to Hadden. "It was in the water?"

"Along with all the coins." He glanced at the scattering of coins under the water. "It's a miracle I noticed it."

"We were checking the cameras in the area."

Newt pointed to the two cameras positioned high overhead. "We figured while we were here we'd take a walk around the fountain. Just in case."

Alyssa Powell's body had been left here. At the time, there had been no cameras downtown. Not that it would have mattered. If the Storyteller hadn't wanted to be seen, he would have taken precautions. He hadn't gotten away with murder all these years without a highly developed sense of self-preservation.

Bobbie surveyed the fountain, remembering the day Powell had been found. Her murder had been the beginning of the end of Bobbie's life. She came here often. Always in the middle of the night. She glanced up at the cameras. She supposed the FBI was about to learn that sad fact about her.

Bobbie followed Newt and Hadden to city hall. One of the city's media technicians, Lane Knott, had set up three monitors for watching the playback.

Lane adjusted his eyeglasses. "The playback will move forward quickly, otherwise we'd be here forever. When you see something you want to look at more closely we can change to slow play. We can zoom in. We can do all sorts of things."

He tapped a few keys on the keyboard and the feed from the first of the two cameras monitoring the fountain appeared on the screen. "We've begun our search on Thursday, August 25."

By the time the video reached Friday night, they'd all taken seats. The playback might be on fast-forward, but it took some time. When her car appeared on the screen, followed by her surveillance detail, Newt glanced at her. Hadden kept his gaze locked on the screen. She shifted in her seat, no longer comfortable, as she watched herself climb out of the car and cross the courtyard. For what she knew to be several minutes, she stood alternately staring at the fountain and surveying the square. The silence in the room was deafening. Finally, the video showed her walking back to her car, and then driving away.

Daylight came with morning, and then afternoon traffic whizzed around the fountain. Pedestrians strolled along with no idea or no care their every move was being captured on video. Dusk fell, the street lamps came on and night claimed the city once more. The time stamp on the screen passed midnight, and a black Altima stopped near the fountain.

"There he is!" Bobbie scooted closer to the screen. "Back it up."

Lane went back to where the Altima first appeared on the screen and changed the setting to slow play. The Altima parked and the driver emerged. He wore the same baseball cap and tee as in the hotel video. He walked over to the fountain and tossed something into the water. Bobbie reminded herself to take a breath. Then he turned and looked up at the camera. He removed the cap and smiled, his bald head gleaming in the moonlight.

"Can you zoom in a little closer?" Newt asked.

Bobbie loosened her grip on her chair arms.

"Sure thing." Lane tapped a key or two, and the face on the screen rushed forward as big as life.

Bobbie drew away, her chair almost tipping backward.

Newt reached out and squeezed her hand. "You okay?"

She nodded, dragged in a breath. "I'm good." She cleared her throat. "Can you run that last few seconds back for me, please?"

Lane reduced the zoom a little and backed up a full minute. He gave a nod to Bobbie. "This should be better."

This time Perry's face didn't fill the screen, but his image was as clear as if he were standing across the room.

"Sweet Jesus," Hadden muttered.

"Wait." Newt tapped the screen. "Zoom in on the car. What's that in the backseat?"

They all leaned forward, hoping to make out the glimpse of something in the backseat of the Altima. Black or dark blue...then a flash of a man's face.

"It's LeDoux." Ice hardened in Bobbie's veins. "He's got LeDoux in the backseat."

"Back it up once more," Hadden said, "to the point where the Altima appears in the shot."

Lane reduced the zoom and went back to the requested starting point. They watched Perry arrive and emerge from the vehicle. He threw Gwen's necklace into the water, and then he stared up at the camera. After removing his cap, he smiled and then he reached up and blew a kiss.

Bobbie's stomach hit the floor. She clamped her jaw shut to prevent the bile that rushed into her throat from spewing forth. Perry climbed into the Altima and drove away. Unfortunately his path and the camera's angle didn't intersect on the license plate.

"Let's pull the feed from all the cameras downtown," Newt suggested, "one by one and see if we can track him."

"I believe Agent Price already has someone on that," Hadden offered.

Newt nodded to Lane. "A second look never hurt."

Bobbie pushed out of her chair. "I need a minute."

Newt glanced up at her.

"I'm only going to the restroom. I'll be right back."

Bobbie struggled to keep her stride steady and unhurried. The bitter bile burned like fire in her throat. She pushed through the door, locked herself in the stall and bent forward in the nick of time. The violent heaves emptied her stomach of the coffee she'd had this morning. She hadn't eaten—not that a failure to fuel herself was uncommon. She couldn't care less if she ate.

She grabbed a length of toilet paper and wiped her mouth and nose. Closing her eyes she leaned against the cool metal wall of the enclosure. He'd been watching her closely. Why hadn't he made a move toward her? Why the big production with all these victims? *Jesus.* Why hadn't he taken her instead of LeDoux?

Shade.

Nick Shade was the problem. The surveillance detail wouldn't be a problem to work around. She knew it, and so did Perry. Shade, though, presented an unknown variable who had planted himself inside her home the past two nights.

Maybe she'd been wrong. Maybe Shade's insights weren't worth the obstacle he presented between her and Perry. The idea that he'd made her feel things she didn't want to feel was like…cheating. Her jaw hardened as she made up her mind. As soon as he showed up again, she intended to tell him to stay away. Whatever insights he had, he could share with Newt and her partner would pass them along to her.

The sooner Perry had a clear path to her, the sooner this would be over.

She couldn't allow anyone else to die.

Twenty-One

Nick signed his name on the visitor's log and tossed his driver's license on the counter.

The guard looked at his license, then eyed Nick for a moment. "Empty your pockets."

He'd expected the inconvenience, so he'd left his cell and change in the car. He placed his wallet on the counter.

The guard studied Nick a moment longer before jerking his head toward the gate. A warning buzzed and the gate slid open.

"This way, sir." Another guard walked with Nick.

The corridor was long and gray. Fluorescent lighting overhead added another layer of starkness to the facility. Nick had only been here once, and he hadn't made it this far. Even now his palms were sweating and his heart pounded. Fourteen years ago he'd gotten as far as signing his name to the log, and then he'd walked out. Part of him wanted to turn around and make that same mad dash now.

Not today. He had to do this for Bobbie. He thought of the way it felt to touch her. He'd wanted to show her she could feel again. He'd wanted to prove to her that it was possible to live again.

Except he hadn't lived in more than a decade and a half—who the hell was he to show her anything?

The one thing he could do was help her stop Perry, and this might very well be the only way. He needed leverage to get a step ahead of Perry. Nick hadn't felt this kind of desperation since the beginning.

He clenched his jaw as he considered what he'd come here to do. There were men in this world who didn't deserve to share the same airspace as the rest of the human population. One of those men was in this facility. As much as he hated that man, he knew things—things only a vicious killer would know.

Nick needed a no-holds-barred tap into that cesspool of disgusting, yet valuable information.

Just this once.

"Your attorney called the warden and made all the necessary arrangements," the guard, Malcolm Clinton, explained.

The attorney wasn't actually *his* attorney, but Nick saw no reason to correct him.

"The prisoner is only allowed outside his cell one hour a day. Today, this will be his hour."

"I won't need an hour."

Malcolm glanced at him. "You just let the two guards waiting outside the door know when you're finished. The prisoner will remain fully shackled during your visit. You are not to touch him or pass anything to him. He'll undergo a full-body and cavity search after your visit."

The thought almost made Nick smile. He hoped the guard who performed the cavity search had big, careless hands. No one on the planet deserved abuse more than the vile serial killer he'd come here to call on.

As Malcolm had said, a guard waited on either side of the interview room. At the door, Malcolm paused to give Nick final instructions. "Bear in mind, Mr. Shade, that this prisoner has mutilated and murdered forty-two victims, including his own wife. Before he was sentenced to life in prison, he was a renowned psychiatrist. Do not trust him in any capacity."

"I'm well aware of his crimes." Nick reached for the door. "I wouldn't trust him in a pond full of alligators."

Nick took a breath and entered the interview room. He stood just inside the door for a moment before taking a seat. Randolph Weller's arms were manacled to the belly shackle at his waist. Beneath the table where he sat, his ankles were shackled together, and then to the floor. The table was a long narrow conference table. A chair sat on either side. Against the wall on the south end of the reasonably large room were four more chairs. There were no windows. More of those harsh fluorescent lights lit the space.

Lastly, Nick allowed his attention to settle on

the man in the baggy prison jumpsuit. His sandy-blond hair had long ago grayed and receded, leaving him with an inordinately high forehead. His face was pale and lined with age. His hazel eyes sparkled with something like pride. The concept made Nick queasy.

Hundreds, maybe thousands of times over the past decade and a half he had wished this pathetic excuse for a human dead. He'd actually tried to kill him but he'd failed miserably. No matter that fourteen years had passed since Nick had laid eyes on him, he still longed to reach across that table, wrap his fingers around his repulsive throat and choke the life completely out of him.

"Imagine my surprise when Lawrence called this morning to say you were coming." Weller smiled. "I'm certain the world must be coming to an end and the guards failed to inform me."

Nick reached deep for his faltering determination. This meeting was necessary. It was a first, but life was full of unpleasant firsts. *Just get it over with.* He pulled out the chair on his side of the table and sat, his spine rigid.

"You're looking well," Weller said. "Lawrence told me you'd changed your name."

Lawrence Zacharias was the bastard's attorney.

"I came here to ask—" Nick swallowed his pride "—you a question related to a case I'm investigating."

The slight smile Weller had brandished from the moment Nick entered the room disappeared. "Your career choice is a rather dangerous one. Lawrence worries that you've become quite self-destructive."

"I don't care what Lawrence worries about." Nick stared unflinchingly at the man across the table. "I know you have ways of getting information in here. I'm certain you keep up with all your old *friends*. Who among your network is acquainted with the Storyteller?"

The older man's eyebrows reared upward. "The Storyteller. Ah. Quite a vile fellow, that one. His work is self-centered and completely lacking in originality. He's next, is he?"

Nick said nothing. He had no desire to share unnecessary exchanges.

Silence stretched between them with the bastard staring unblinkingly at Nick.

"Winston Fletcher," Weller announced finally.

Nick was surprised to hear that name. "My sources list him as deceased."

"Not quite," Weller refuted. "You'll find him using the name Willie Finley. He operates a rather rudimentary fishing business in Mobile Bay, Alabama. While Perry was attending the University of Minnesota in Duluth, he and Fletcher became chums. They shared a penchant for rather brutal sexual intercourse with their victims. I'm confident they've kept in touch over the years. It is, after all, human nature to catch up with old friends."

At least now Nick had a good idea where Perry had disappeared to after leaving his friend the doctor who patched him up. Nick wasn't surprised he'd hung around in Alabama. Perry had wanted to stay close to Bobbie. What better way to avoid capture than to remain close to the scene of the crime? The world had expected him to run far and fast.

The name was all he'd come for. Nick stood and pushed in his chair.

"Perry is a simple man. Why don't you ask me anything else you'd like to know? I've studied most of the high-profile ones." Weller chuckled. "Even a few who aren't so famous. One of the perks of agreeing to assist our friends at the prestigious FBI."

Nick grudgingly met his gaze. *Why not?* The bastard's infinite knowledge of murder and murderers was another of the reasons he'd bypassed the death penalty. Nick pulled out his chair and settled in it once more. "What's the one thing Perry would do anything to protect?"

His expression one of amusement, the serial killer named Randolph Weller cocked his head and studied Nick. "How you disappoint me, Nicholas. You should know the answer to that question. It's so very elementary."

Fury roared through him but he held it back. He refused to rise to the bait. "My life's goal is to disappoint you."

Weller considered him for a moment. "Be that as it may, I wouldn't want you to have come all this way for nothing."

Nick reached for patience. "I'm listening."

Weller smiled. "His mother, of course. She is

the one thing he would go to any and all lengths to protect."

Nick gritted his teeth for a moment before responding. "His mother is dead."

"But he still loves her, worships her actually. You see, dear Gaylon is a regular Norman Bates. He loves his mother more than anything. He wanted to protect her from his father, but he never could, not until he was a man himself anyway. All those years he was forced to listen to his mother being brutalized as well as to endure the way his father brutalized him. Love, hate and the purest form of obsession. An incubator for evil, as they say."

"He chooses victims who look like her," Nick pointed out. "When he rapes and murders them, he's punishing her for not saving him." He refused to acknowledge that some part of him wanted to impress the bastard.

Weller gave a conceding nod. "You are so very close."

Nick restrained the anger that continued to build with his every word. "Why don't you enlighten me then?"

Weller gave a nod. "Deep down Gaylon resents that his mother didn't protect him—that's true. But he resents even more that all those times he listened to his father torturing his poor mother he grew aroused. His first experience masturbating was likely to the sound of his father raping his mother. As he matured he yearned for that sort of power, for the raw, animal sex. The need was overwhelming and eventually he gave in. The only way to hide what he'd done was, of course, to murder the victim. So, you see, Nicholas, when Gaylon takes a victim, he punishes himself by becoming the thing he hates more than anything else—his father."

Silence thickened, pushing the air out of the room.

Just when Nick would have again stood to go, Weller added, "What better medium than the silky skin of his victims on which to convey his tortured story. Learning the art of tattooing was his one truly creative act. I suspect his old friend Fletcher had something to do with that."

As interesting as his additional theories might be, Nick had what he'd come for. His body rigid with mounting tension, he stood.

"Before you go," Weller ventured, delaying Nick's exit, "please tell me. Have you felt it yet?"

Rage ignited in Nick's gut. The urge to reach across the table and rip off the bastard's head blazed through him before he could quiet it. "I'm nothing like you."

"I remember the first time." Weller closed his eyes as if recalling. "The urge was overwhelming. It swelled like the tide and I was helpless to its power. That's the way of it. When it comes, you're completely helpless. You'll see."

Nick turned his back and started for the door. He would not listen to another word the monster had to say.

"Elizabeth would be proud of you, Nicholas."

He whipped around, rage battering against him anew. "Never say her name. Never."

Weller sighed. "Very well. Please accept my deepest apology."

His movements stiff, Nick reached for the door once more.

"It was good to see you, son."

Twenty-Two

Criminal Investigation Division, 5:50 p.m.

Clutching her desk phone to her ear, Bobbie rolled her chair deeper into her cubicle. The receptionist answered on the second ring and recited her practiced spiel. "This is Detective Bobbie Gentry." She spoke barely above a whisper. "I need to cancel tomorrow's appointment."

She waited through the expected calendar check for next week's appointment. "Sure," Bobbie agreed. "That works. Thanks." She placed the receiver back in its cradle and glanced around just to be sure no one had walked up while her back was turned.

The chief would surely understand her skipping this week's appointment with the shrink. She stood, went up on tiptoe and peeked over the cubicle wall to see if Newt had finished his report. His chair was empty. She frowned. Where did he go? She hadn't realized he'd left his desk.

"I finished the report."

She jumped and turned around to face her partner. "Great."

He offered her one of the two cups of coffee he held. "It's been a long day."

She accepted the cup and tried to appear at ease. "There's still more than two hours of daylight. Should we check in with the search team commander?"

Agent Mason was in charge of the grid search. Bobbie and Newt had spent the entire afternoon reviewing footage from the city's cameras. Too bad they'd gotten nothing for their trouble. The Storyteller had prepared well. He knew the areas to avoid. But he was out there somewhere. Every wasted minute was one stolen from his hostages. Jesus, she still couldn't believe he'd gotten the drop on LeDoux.

He got the drop on you, didn't he?

She blinked away that reality and sipped the too-strong, too-hot coffee. Maybe the bitter burn would clear her head.

"Listen." Newt tipped his cup to his lips and grimaced. "We're overdue having dinner together. How about you follow me home for a good home-cooked meal?" She readied herself to decline, and he tacked on, "Carlene will really be disappointed if you don't come. I gave her my solemn promise I'd talk you into it."

Bobbie caved. *Why the hell not?* If it made her partner happy, she could give up a couple of hours. "How can I say no?"

Newt shrugged. "Feel free to invite Shade."

She hadn't seen him since early that morning when he announced he had a source he needed to check in with. "He's following up with a source."

"Just the three of us then." Newt confirmed with a wink. "Nothing like having two lovely ladies at the dinner table."

Bauer bullied into their huddle. "Holt wants to see all of us in her office."

Since Holt had a cubicle like the rest of them, her office was code for the men's room. The ladies' room wasn't an option since Owens might walk in.

"What's up?" Bobbie asked as they headed in the direction of the men's restroom.

Bauer shrugged. "Got no idea."

"Liar." Bobbie jabbed him in the ribs with her elbow. He never had been a good liar.

"You'll see." Bauer shot her a grin.

"Have a little patience, partner," Newt added.

Uh-oh. Whatever this meeting was about, it was feeling more and more like a setup.

Once all four were in the men's room, Bauer placed an out of order sign on the door. A smile tugged at Bobbie's lips. She hadn't met with the team like this since...*before*. She had missed these people so much. Bobbie hesitated, waiting for the guilt to surface. It didn't come this time. She'd spent every waking moment since leaving the hospital feeling guilty that she had survived. She didn't know how to feel about suddenly *not* feeling that way.

Holt rested her hands on her hips and looked straight at Bobbie. "Things are getting messy."

That was a hell of an understatement. Bobbie glanced at Newt. Just what did these three have up their sleeves?

"Since Perry took LeDoux, Bauer and I have been talking," Holt explained. "We're a team, Bobbie. You know each of us is doing all within our power to make sure that piece of shit doesn't get away this time. We just wanted to make sure you understood you can come to us for anything you need—on or *off* the record."

Bauer draped his arm around Bobbie's shoulders. "You're not in this alone. We've got your back." He hitched his head toward Holt. "We're following up on every damned tip coming into the hotline. We will find him. Don't hesitate to come to us if you need us *beyond* the job, if you get my drift."

Newt gave a nod of agreement. "We're here for you, Bobbie. Anything you need, day or night."

Bobbie tried her damnedest to keep it together. Tears crowded her vision. "I really appreciate it more than you can know."

"You're doing great, Bobbie," Holt assured her. "Not many people could have come back from what you went through. We let you down last time. We'll make sure he pays this time—one way or another."

Bobbie hadn't stopped to think that her team might feel in part responsible for what happened with the Storyteller. The hurt in their eyes told the tale. She'd been so busy pushing them away that she hadn't noticed. "You've always had my back. There's no one else I'd rather be with on a team."

Newt clapped her on the back, breaking the tension. "Good. Let's get out of here and have a nice, relaxing evening."

"What's the deal with the guy I've seen hanging around with you?" Holt asked as they exited her "office."

Images and soft sounds from her bath last night whispered through Bobbie. "He's a friend."

"He's an expert on serial killers," Newt said.

"Whatever he is, he's damned hot," Holt said with an approving glance at Bobbie.

"What?" Bauer griped. "You don't even like guys."

"That doesn't mean I'm blind."

Bobbie laughed; the sound startled her.

Newt squeezed her hand and smiled. "There's my girl."

As they exited CID, Bobbie wished she could get back to this—to the way things used to be. But going back wasn't possible. It meant a great deal to her that these people would risk everything to help and to protect her.

The problem was, they couldn't. They'd just end up dead. She couldn't let that happen.

She had to do this…alone.

Crestview Avenue, 8:30 p.m.

Bobbie couldn't eat another bite. "Carlene." She set her napkin aside. "That was incredible."

She couldn't remember the last time she'd had a home-cooked meal. The roast had been divine.

The peas and potatoes utterly delicious. She'd eaten two rolls. Tonight she'd have to run at least two extra miles just to burn off the homemade lemon icebox pie.

Carlene smiled. "I'm so glad you enjoyed it, Bobbie. We need to do this more often."

With one daughter in Nashville and the other newly married and settling in Louisville, Bobbie suspected the two got a little lonely. "Are you still planning that cruise?"

Newt groaned. He did not want to spend fourteen days on a ship.

Carlene's attractive features spread into a smile. "I can't wait! We're leaving the first of November." She stood and started to clear the table. "I'm dragging Howard to the post office to get his passport on Saturday."

"Really?" Bobbie shot him a look as she stood and gathered her plate.

Newt rolled his eyes.

"You two go chat while I take care of this," Carlene insisted. "Police work is your domain—this is mine."

"You heard her." Newt ushered Bobbie from the dining room. "Wonderful dinner, sweetheart."

Bobbie followed him out onto the back patio. The air was still too warm, but there was a gentle breeze. As hard as she tried she couldn't help wondering where Shade was and who he'd gone to see.

"When this is done—" Newt gestured to one of the big rockers he and his wife used "—we need to do one of those interventions on Bauer. I smelled alcohol on him at work today."

Bobbie dropped into the big comfortable rocker. She had noticed the bloodshot eyes. "He blames himself for Leyla's death."

Newt shrugged. "Whatever's driving him, Holt told me she's planning to give him a verbal warning when things settle down."

"He's a good guy—a good cop, but Holt's right," Bobbie agreed. Her cell vibrated, and she dragged it from her pocket. *Unknown caller* flashed on the screen. "Gentry."

"It's me."

Shade.

That her heart beat a little harder annoyed her. "You have news?" She had no intention of allowing him to believe she wanted to hear anything else.

When Newt gave her a questioning look she mouthed *Nick Shade.*

"Nothing concrete," Shade said.

A few seconds of silence lapsed. If he didn't have anything, why did he call?

"I wanted to check on you," he said as if she'd asked the question out loud.

Be careful, Bobbie. Don't get yourself dead. Even as her pulse reacted to his words she reminded herself that Shade had an agenda. He didn't really care about her beyond her connection to the Storyteller. The weight on her chest seemed to get heavier.

Why did that realization bother her so much?

More important, why didn't she just tell him to stay gone?

"Any new leads on your end? Anything on Le-Doux?"

She shook her head. "Nothing."

The idea that another day had come and gone and they were no closer to finding Perry made her sick. *Where are you, you son of a bitch?*

"It'll be morning before I'm back in Montgomery," Shade said, drawing her from the troubling thoughts. "I'm in Mobile checking up on an old friend."

He's in the way, Bobbie. Standing between you and Perry. "Let me know if you find anything." She ended the call without saying goodbye or waiting for anything else he might have to say.

No one could get in the way of what she had to do.

She turned to Newt. "This was a great idea, partner."

Why not enjoy the evening with Newt? No one had the promise of tomorrow.

Twenty-Three

Killer Fishing, Mobile, Alabama, 9:00 p.m.

Nick parked two blocks from his destination and walked the rest of the way. He'd spent the past three hours worried about Bobbie. Hearing her voice had done little to assuage his concerns.

As much as he tried to deny it, a bond had developed between them. He had to stop Perry before he got to her. The memory of touching her, of needing desperately to comfort her, tore at his soul. As damaged as he was himself, she made him want to heal her.

Maybe he could do nothing about that unexpected need, but he could end Perry's reign of terror. He could give her that much.

Starting here. He scanned the dark yard once more. Winston Fletcher, aka the Lady's Man, forty-one years old, had raped and murdered at least half a dozen women according to some sources. He'd been a person of interest in three cases, but no evidence had ever been found connecting him to the crimes. According to Nick's off-the-record sources, Fletcher had died four years ago. No new victims with his killing signature had been found, which seemed to confirm that conclusion.

Apparently Nick's sources had been wrong. It happened. Most of the people he reached out to were either cops or criminals. The percentage of reliable information was about as good from one as the other. As much as he needed a break, he hated like hell that the information had come from Weller.

He dismissed that particular frustration. He had more pressing concerns. Coming here straight away had been essential. For whatever reason Weller hadn't shared this information with the feds already, but they would certainly know it by now. His cell and the interview room were no doubt monitored.

Nick had to hurry. Stopping Perry was not the issue. He would make that happen. It was Bobbie whose unpredictability made his work particularly time sensitive. She was the only reason he had gone to Weller.

Like Weller said, Fletcher had purchased a home with river access and set up his fishing guide operation under the name Willie Finley. Nick imagined Fletcher got a good laugh every morning at the idea that no one would ever understand the inside joke as to why he'd named his operation "Killer Fishing."

Nick shook his head at the irony and surveyed the area once more. There were other homes nearby, and all appeared to be occupied. Nick had been watching the house for an hour. No one had come in or out. The blinds on the windows prevented him from seeing inside. He'd considered going in through an upstairs window, but he'd decided that knocking on the front door would be the stealthier access since Fletcher wouldn't be expecting a straightforward approach.

Before he reached the front door, Nick checked the only weapon he had selected for the encounter, a stun gun. He stretched his neck and then knocked on the door.

"Who the hell is it?" the male voice shouted from inside.

"I hate to bother you," Nick called back, moving to the right side of the door. "My car won't start and your neighbor Mr. Henagar said you might have some jumper cables."

"I need a name and some ID," echoed through the door.

"Nick Shade." He removed his driver's license and slid it through the mail slot since there was no other way to show the man on the other side.

Silence.

Fifteen seconds later, he decided Fletcher had no intention of responding. Nick braced to kick in the door, but the knob turned and the door opened a crack. The same voice as before said, "Come in."

Tension throbbing in his pulse, Nick pushed the door inward. Winston Fletcher sat in a wheelchair. He weighed at least 350 pounds and his long hair was pulled back into a ponytail. He wore a sleeveless T-shirt that showed off his many elaborate tattoos and cutoff sweat pants that revealed frail legs.

Fletcher pointed to the license still lying on the floor. "You can never be too careful." He looked Nick over again.

Without taking his eyes off Fletcher, Nick picked up and pocketed his license. "Like I said, I hate to bother you, but your neighbor Mr. Henagar said you had jumper cables. He never mentioned…"

"Don't worry about it." Fletcher jerked his head. "They're in the toolshed. You'll have to get them yourself. Both my helpers have gone for the day."

"Henagar said he'd give me a jump if you provide the cables," Nick added. His instincts warned this guy was not as harmless as he pretended. "He was pretty sure you keep them for the boats."

"Can't do without 'em." Fletcher rolled through the living room and the kitchen and into what had once been a back porch that now served as a mudroom of sorts. "Out there." He pointed to the back door. "Walk straight to the first shed, they're hanging on the wall right inside the door."

Nick didn't move. He hadn't spotted a weapon, but he sensed that if he turned his back—

Before he finished the thought Fletcher reached between his right leg and the chair. Nick grabbed his beefy arm and wrenched it behind his back. Fletcher howled in agony and dropped the .38 he'd snatched from its hiding place.

Nick seized the weapon. "I guess you figured out I'm not here for jumper cables, Mr. Fletcher."

Face red, Fletcher shook his head. "The man you're looking for is already dead."

"Is that right?" Nick opened the screen door and pitched the .38 outside. "I'm glad to hear it. Maybe you can help me with something else."

"My neighbors know I'm crippled," he warned. "If they get suspicious, they'll call the police. You said you spoke to one of 'em. He'll remember your face."

"I'm not here to kill you, Fletcher. I have questions. Answer my questions and I'll leave, and then call the police. You'll have time to do whatever you chose, make a run for it or end this yourself."

Recognition flared in Fletcher's eyes, and he gave a chuckle that sounded more like a cough. "Well, I'll be damned. I guess you're real after all. My money was on myth. I didn't think there was anyone left out there who cared enough to be a monster slayer."

"Answer my questions," Nick repeated, "and then you can make your decision."

"As you can see, I can't make a run for it." Fletcher gestured to the wheelchair. "Four years ago I bought this operation looking for warmer temps and fresher meat, if you know what I mean. I was sick of the cold-ass weather up north. Anyway, I was on the roof making some repairs and I fell, fractured my spine. Came home from the hospital paralyzed from the waist down. Now when I get those old urges I have to watch somebody else doing it on the internet."

Nick ignored his sob story. "Gaylon Perry is in hiding somewhere in Montgomery. I hear the two of you are old friends. What do you know about where he is?"

Fletcher shrugged. "The two of us go way back, yeah. I ran into him at a college hangout back in Duluth about twenty years ago. He was a student, and I was keeping a low profile after a close call with cops in Detroit." He laughed. "We were both looking for a little fun. We shared a couple of sweet little cunts from the college."

"Where is he now?" Nick demanded. Time was his enemy. Fletcher could save the walk down memory lane for his next stop.

"I told him to let it go," Fletcher went on, evidently choosing the scenic route to get to the answer Nick wanted. "But he just couldn't do it, man. He said he had to fuck that bitch cop one more time before he finished her off."

Nick restrained the need to beat the worthless scumbag to a pulp. "I need a location."

"He stayed here for a few months." Fletcher frowned as if he were considering what to say next. "He cut out about two weeks ago. Said it was time to finish the bitch's story. I haven't heard from him since."

Frustration expanded inside Nick. "Did he leave any maps or notes? Maybe he used your computer."

"Nah. He's too smart to do something that stupid."

"Maybe I should make that call while you try to think of something useful," Nick suggested.

"Wait! Do you know what he's driving?" Fletcher asked, looking far too cocky for a guy about to pay the price for his crimes, whether to the justice system or to his maker.

"Do you?" Nick countered.

"His mother's gray Prius. It's a couple years old. About a month ago he took a bus back to Nebraska. Perry's old man gave him the car and some more cash. Final payment for his silence." Fletcher shrugged. "He changed the license plate before he left, so I can't tell you what it is."

Nick had to ask, "Why would his father need Perry's silence?"

"Let's face it," Fletcher said with a laugh. "Most of us don't get this way without a little help from the family. Perry's old man horsewhipped him about every day of his life. He carved symbols and shit on his flesh—told him he was the devil's spawn. Fucked him up big-time. His momma didn't do shit about it. She was too afraid." He made another of those raspy chuckling sounds that warned he'd smoked too much for too long before deciding to quit. "Eventually Perry got the bastard back, though. Right before he went off to college his old man started beating on his momma again and Perry half killed him. He told him if he ever laid a hand on her again, he would finish the job. Perry was real protective of his mother."

"Is that right?" As much as he hated to admit it,

Weller had been right so far. Then again, what had he expected? Dr. Randolph Weller was the foremost authority on serial killers alive today…maybe because he was at the top of the evil scale himself.

"Oh yeah." Fletcher nodded. "Jealous, too. His mother had another baby when Perry was about nine or ten. Another boy. He couldn't stand that the baby took all the time she used to give him. He said the baby was always sick so when he suffocated it no one seemed surprised to hear it had died. His baby brother was his first kill. Like Cain and Abel, man. Really fucked up."

"The infant brother died of pneumonia," Nick argued, but even as he did he knew Fletcher was right. There was the missing male victim. That his first reaction was an urgent need to share the information with Bobbie took Nick aback.

"If the reverend said it died of pneumonia," Fletcher countered, "who was going to challenge him? According to Perry, back then no one would dare defy the reverend. He was a big deal, still is to the old-timers."

"Why would Perry tell you all of this?" Nick didn't actually doubt the specifics. Fletcher had basically confirmed Weller's conclusions.

Fletcher shrugged. "Since I'm stuck in this chair I spend a lot of time in psychology chat rooms. I wanted to know what made me the way I am." He shrugged. "I learned how to get people to talk. How to read 'em. For example, I knew you were here for me the second I looked into your eyes."

Nick wasn't convinced on that last part. If Fletcher possessed such well-honed insight he would have shot first and offered the jumper cables later. The idea that this scumbag could have stopped Perry made Nick want to use the stun gun until his black heart ceased to beat. *Have you felt it yet?* Nick pushed the intrusion away.

As if Fletcher sensed a shift in Nick's tension, he offered, "If you really want him, make him come to you. He'd do anything to get to that cop."

Nick balled his fingers into fists and restrained the fury building inside him. "Goodbye, Mr. Fletcher."

"If the cop's not an option, his mother then."

Nick hesitated and Fletcher grinned. "Yeah, that would do it. Dig the bitch up and tell him if he wants her to rest in peace he'd better come get her. Trust me—he'll go bat-shit crazy."

Nick had to give the man credit, he was creative. "Before I go, do you have what you need?"

Fletcher gave a nod. "Shotgun propped by the bed."

"You have fifteen minutes before I make the call to the authorities."

Fletcher was already wheeling out of the room as Nick left through the back door. Before he reached his car, he heard the blast of the shotgun.

One less case to clog the justice system.

Nick started the car. He needed to get back to Montgomery…to Bobbie.

Twenty-Four

Ted Peterson raised up on one elbow. He stared down at the beautiful woman in the bed next to him. Her rich dark skin against the cool white sheets made him want her again. She was the most amazing woman he had ever known. Intelligent, beautiful, like-minded. She completed him in ways he hadn't known were possible.

Guilt nudged him, but he couldn't help how he felt.

"What're you thinking?" she asked as she trailed a rich red nail down his chest.

"How very much I want to repeat the last hour again and again. Right now. In the morning. The day after that..."

She smiled and reached up to stroke his jaw. "I must say, you outdid yourself, Ted."

He leaned down and kissed that lush mouth of hers. Every day he struggled not to touch her at work. On the job they had to be Chief of Police Theodore Peterson and Commander of Major Crimes Lieutenant Eudora Owens. But after hours, every chance they got, they were lovers and best friends. She was the one person he could talk to about the things he didn't dare say to anyone else.

"One day we won't have to sneak around like this," he whispered against her throat. He drew back and searched her dark eyes. "I want to introduce you to the world as mine."

She sighed and looked away. "You know we can't do that. Not now. Maybe not ever."

"I'll be retiring in a few years," he reminded her. He was sixty-two, more than a decade older than her. Once he was retired, the job would no longer interfere. Lately he'd wondered why he waited to retire, and then he remembered the other reason they couldn't be together.

"Work isn't the only issue we have to think about." She hugged his chest to her breasts, making his body stir with desire once more. "Be that as it may, I am very happy with things just as they are," she promised.

He wasn't so sure that was true, but he also knew Dorey would never pressure him to ignore his other obligations. She was too good and kind. Too selfless.

"I can't keep asking you to put your wishes aside for my obligations." He didn't deserve her. He traced her cheek with the pad of his thumb.

Dorey scooted out of his arms and reached for her robe. "Did you visit her on Sunday?"

His dear, dear, sweet wife. He sat up, reality collapsing onto his shoulders. "Not this time. With the Storyteller case, I couldn't get away."

"Of course." She smiled sadly. "Her condition continues to decline?"

Ted nodded. He and Sarah had married right out of college. They had never been blessed with children and then, a decade ago, she had developed early-onset Alzheimer's. She rarely even recognized him anymore. Still, he visited her every Sunday unless there was serious trouble at work that required his attention. Whatever she needed for the rest of her life, he would go to the ends of the earth to ensure she received. As hard as he had tried to remain faithful, a part of him had started to emotionally disengage the day her illness took her from their home. It was the only way he could let Sarah go.

He had needs, too. He'd gone many years with those needs unfulfilled until one particularly late night at work he and Dorey had lost control. It had taken another six months before either of them felt comfortable making regular arrangements. Still, here they were a year later sneaking every possible moment together where no one could see. What started as a need had turned into something far more…far deeper. He loved Dorey. He loved her with all his heart. He was so tired of hiding those feelings.

To prevent saying more and sounding as if he were feeling sorry for himself, he turned his attention to more immediate concerns. "I'm worried about Bobbie," he confessed, dragging on his discarded boxers. "She's pushed me away completely the past few months. The only relationship we have at this point is that I'm her superior, and even that one is strained."

They both preferred not to talk about work when they were together, but that distinct break was not always possible to maintain.

"Newt's watching her closely." She reached for his hand. "Let's have a glass of wine."

He placed his hand in hers and followed her down to the kitchen. This grand old historic home had been Sarah's dream home. He should sell it and find something more manageable. All these years it felt wrong to sell it as long as she was alive. Funny how he couldn't bear the idea of that perceived betrayal and yet he in no way saw his relationship with Dorey as being unfaithful. Two years ago on one of her rare lucid days, Sarah had urged him to move on with his life. She had pleaded with him not to die along with her. He'd ignored her words for as long as he could and still he second-guessed his decisions.

Time to stop overanalyzing the subject.

"What do you know about this so-called serial killer expert who keeps showing up with her?" he asked as Dorey gathered stemmed glasses. "He was there when the Rice child was rescued, and then I saw him again at the hospital."

"I thought he was a friend of Newt's." Dorey

frowned. He reached out and traced the lines on her brow with his finger. Her frown relaxed into a smile. "He and Bobbie certainly seemed close at the hospital."

"As far as I can determine he's a private citizen who hasn't broken the law. Agent Mason sidestepped the subject when I asked about him, but I got the impression they were familiar with Shade. Newt insists that's the case." Ted had found nothing on the man—no criminal history, no credentials. "I can't exactly drag Shade in for questioning. At least not until I have cause." Ted heaved a sigh. "I want to trust Bobbie's judgment, but she's been through so much. If her involvement with this man proves a mistake..." He shook his head. "I keep hoping the day will come when she can smile again. When she's happy again."

"Oh, sweetheart." Dorey drew him into the circle of her arms. "You're looking for the old Bobbie to come back. The one thing I can personally guarantee is that the woman you knew before won't be back. She's gone forever. Trust me on that one."

Ted held her tight and closed his eyes against the truth in her words. "I just can't bear to see her keep hurting."

Dorey drew back and gave him a sad smile. "I'm afraid you can't protect her from the pain...not as long as Perry is out there. She's not going to allow herself to begin the process of healing until he's no longer a threat to her or anyone else, and then, for her, the real work will begin—rebuilding her life *alone.*"

That was the part that worried him the most.

Twenty-Five

Gaylon lifted the drowsy nurse from the waste bucket and dragged her back to the mattress. He carefully lowered her facedown and secured her wrists and ankles. She moaned and whimpered with every move. He despised allowing a piss break once he'd begun the story.

He might as well end his work for the evening. His shoulders were tired from stooping over. He should have found a way to elevate the mattress from the floor. The working conditions were less than optimal. He wasn't nearly as organized as usual. Certainly his choices in tools and other assets had been limited.

A sigh escaped his lips. "See how much trouble you've been, Bobbie."

"She's going to kill you."

Gaylon spun around to stare at the agent secured facedown against the filthy wood floor.

"That's right," LeDoux said. "She won't let you get away this time."

"The way you have so many times?" Rage burgeoned before Gaylon could tamp down the nuisance. "Do you think she'll swoop in just in time to save you and my other lovely guests?" He laughed. "We'll see, Agent. We'll see."

"Fuck you."

"Oh my." Gaylon turned his hands up. "I've lost all track of time. You're been here an entire twenty-four hours, and we've hardly shared any quality time."

Gaylon walked over to the table and surveyed his tools. He picked up the hammer. "This will do nicely."

LeDoux's respiration sped up as Gaylon approached him. The reaction sent a thrill through him. He'd considered many times that someone needed to pound some insight into the agent's thick skull. Since Gaylon had other plans for him, a less vital part of his well-toned body would have to do.

He knelt next to the agent's long, muscular legs. "I've watched you run on a number of occasions. You're quite the athlete."

LeDoux's body stiffened.

Gaylon smiled. "I've often considered popping in to visit your lovely wife, but I fear Giselle is not my type. Far too self-centered and quite lazy."

"Stay away from my family, you son of a bitch!"

"Now, now, Agent, there's no need to get nasty. I wouldn't fuck your bitch wife with your dick." Gaylon braced one hand on LeDoux's left calf and swung the hammer with his other.

The small toe flattened like the proverbial pancake. Gaylon grinned at the spurt of blood. LeDoux howled between clenched teeth.

"Come now, *Special Agent* LeDoux—is that the best you can do?" Gaylon swung the hammer again. The fourth toe flattened. Blood spurted. Another wounded howl issued from LeDoux's throat. Gaylon flattened the middle toe. This time LeDoux screamed long and loud. "Now that is a healthy scream."

After a few minutes of enjoying his whimpering, Gaylon left him be. There was plenty of time for more fun and games. He gathered his tools and put them away. The agent's warning regarding Bobbie played over and over in Gaylon's head. He looked forward to the fight. His body stirred with excitement.

Very soon she would be his.

The time was near.

Perhaps his detective needed another reminder that he was waiting and that three lives depended on her cooperation. LeDoux's abduction hadn't resonated with her as Gaylon had hoped.

Fury fired in his belly once more. It was the dark-haired man. He was shielding her somehow.

Very well. Gaylon picked up LeDoux's credentials case.

It was time to remind her that she could not avoid what was coming.

Her story was his to finish.

Twenty-Six

A sound whispered across her senses.

I will find him.

Bobbie's eyes opened, and she bolted upright. Her fingers went instinctively to the Glock under her pillow. She tried to filter the sensations and images before they faded. She'd been dreaming. She was back in the hospital after she'd tried to take her life. Newt and her uncle Teddy took turns holding vigil at her bedside. The sounds of their pain— tears, whispered words begging her to come back— whirled in her head and then vanished. *Come back, Detective Gentry. I will find him.*

Who had said those words?

The sound—the one that awakened her just now—came again. The knock at her back door echoed through the house.

Relief loosened her muscles. Someone was at her back door. It had to be Shade. She threw the covers off and walked through the darkness, the Glock in her hand. She hadn't seen him since yesterday morning. He'd called, which had felt strange, but she had to admit she'd been relieved to hear his voice. She'd known him all of three and a half days. Didn't matter that he'd made her feel something for the first time since her life was taken from her. She understood that he was standing between her and the Storyteller.

In the kitchen she went to the window and checked. As he always did, Shade looked directly at her as if he knew she was watching him. With a deep breath, she released the dead bolts and opened the door. All she had to do was tell him to go and to stay gone this time.

His gaze roved slowly over her face as if he sensed trouble. "Have there been new developments?"

"We found Gwen's necklace in the fountain." Bobbie pushed the hair back from her face. It was the middle of the night. She supposed she could wait until daylight to tell him he had to go. "Which didn't really give us anything useful."

"Nothing new on LeDoux?"

"We backed up the video footage from one of the cameras that overlooks the fountain." She still couldn't believe the audacity of the bastard. "Perry drove right up to the fountain in that black Altima and tossed the necklace. Then he looked up at the camera and blew a kiss." The image made her sick. "LeDoux was in the backseat. We couldn't see enough to determine if he was dead or alive, but he was in the car."

Shade seemed to consider the news for a moment. Then he said, "We should get some sleep."

Wait just a damned minute. "What about your source or sources? You came back empty-handed?"

"We'll both be able to analyze what I learned better after some sleep."

She started to argue but decided letting it go would make what she had to do in the morning a little easier. "Fine."

Come daylight he would tell her what he'd learned and then he had to go.

6:30 a.m.

Bobbie pulled on her jacket and checked her reflection in the mirror. She'd fastened her hair into a ponytail. A dab of concealer had done basically nothing for the dark circles under her eyes. Her appearance didn't matter. No one really noticed how she looked anymore. She was poor, broken Bobbie. She would never get over losing her family. There were some things in this world that weren't meant to be survived.

But she had survived... James would want her to go on. Jamie...

Bobbie shook her head, exiling the thoughts as she shoved her Glock into its holster. She clipped her badge and phone to her belt. A strong cup of coffee, a quick chat with Shade, and she would head to the office.

Leaving the bathroom, she considered going back to her room and making the bed. She didn't know why the idea crossed her mind. She hadn't made a bed in 250 days. Why start now? Funny that she even thought about it.

Maybe it was the man who'd slept on her couch for the third time. He somehow interrupted her ability to stay disconnected from her emotions—from the world. All the more reason he couldn't stay.

The cup she used for coffee sat on the counter. She shoved a pod into her single-serve coffeemaker and pressed the necessary button. The machine chugged and sputtered, and the scent of coffee filled the air. There had been a time when that smell had made her smile. It meant the start of a new day. She'd loved her life, her work…her home.

"Morning."

She looked up as Shade appeared at the passageway between the living room and kitchen. "Morning."

"I could use your help."

This from the man who had warned her to stay out of his way? "How so?" Didn't really matter what had changed his attitude. She could hear him out before she told him to be on his way. He'd said he would fill her in on what he'd learned yesterday. Maybe his abrupt statement had something to do with what he'd learned.

"Perry was in Mobile for a while before coming here. He probably completed a number of scouting expeditions before he came to Montgomery to stay about two weeks ago—according to my source. Once he arrived he needed supplies. Urge the task force to start canvassing convenience markets again as well as hardware stores. We know he prefers to stay away from the big chain stores. They typically have security cameras that actually work." Shade opened a cabinet and retrieved a mug. "Whether he stocked up before he took Adams or after, someone has seen him since last Thursday."

While he brewed a cup of coffee, Bobbie weighed the scenario. If this was the intelligence he'd spent twenty or so hours collecting, then he needed to reevaluate his sources. "The feds are running a media blitz." She sipped her coffee. "Call-ins about sightings are off the charts, but none of them have panned out so far. What you're suggesting could be a waste of valuable time."

"If they're still looking for the Altima, that may be why they're not getting the responses they need."

The cup she held suddenly felt too heavy. "You believe he has some other means of transportation."

The smile he so rarely showed made an appearance. "He's driving his mother's gray Toyota Prius."

"Why didn't you mention this already?" Why would he hold on to that kind of information three—no four—hours? Her temper flared and she sat her cup on the counter. "Did you know this all along or just since yesterday?"

He gave her a look that answered the question. "I learned this information late last night."

"I thought you went to Perry's family home

months ago." Uneasiness stirred. Had he made a trip to Nebraska in the past twenty-four hours?

"I did. Both vehicles registered to his parents, the Prius and the Suburban, were in the garage. The feds found the same when they searched the home a month after I did. According to my source, his father gave him the Prius as a token of his appreciation for Perry's continued silence."

Bobbie withdrew her phone and sent a text to Owens who would pass it on to Agent Hadden. The sooner someone followed up on this lead, the better. She glanced up at Shade as she hit Send. "His father doesn't want the world to know he isn't the godly man they think he is."

Shade leaned against the counter, the warm mug cradled in his hands. "You got it."

She shook her head. "That's just great. The father is as guilty as the son."

"There's more." Shade waited until she met his gaze before he continued. "The little brother who died when Perry was ten, the infant, was his first kill. He suffocated him."

"Holy shit." Bobbie's hands shook. She tucked them under her arms. "Was he afraid his mother would love the new baby more than him?"

"He didn't want to share her attention."

"Now we know why he strangles his victims in the end." Bobbie touched her throat. "In a roundabout way he's repeating that first murder over and over, watching the bodies stop struggling." Whatever else was in his DNA, his parents had helped create the heinous killer Perry had become.

"It gives him a feeling of complete control," Shade added.

"How did you find this new information?" Even if he went to Nebraska, Perry's father would never have willingly shared these details. "Who's your source?"

His dark eyes settled on hers. "I don't reveal my sources. Let your friends at the FBI know they need to make a follow-up visit to the Perry home. Maybe his father will be a bit more cooperative if his freedom is in jeopardy."

She reached for her cell. "His father may have a way of contacting him." At some point she would have to tell Owens where all this information was coming from. Just not today. On second thought, rather than try to put all this in a message she decided to call Newt and give him the update. Despite having gotten the information from Shade, she walked away from him as she filled her partner in. Newt would see that Owens and Holt were briefed. Since both Bobbie and her partner were supposed to be working with Hadden on the grid search, Newt urged her to follow this new lead with Shade. He would cover for her.

Newt was right. She could do more good focused on this new intelligence. She might as well take advantage of Shade's help today. He could be on his way tonight. She thanked her partner and turned to Shade. "We'll start canvassing hardware stores.

Newt will see that the task force is briefed. He'll cover for me."

"I hoped you would say that." Nick pulled a map of the city from his back pocket. "Let's start with the outlying neighborhoods. Wherever he's hiding, he needs privacy and some amount of distance from any other occupied buildings or houses. I've searched a good number of areas already—we'll start with the areas I haven't checked."

She surveyed the areas he'd marked. "He usually goes more remote than what I see here."

"I think he's close this time. Close enough to see you regularly. He likes watching you and knowing you're not far away."

She grabbed her shoulder bag. "I'm driving."

Shade didn't argue.

As usual, he exited before her, did a quick check and then waited for her to follow. Part of her wanted to trust him completely and share her fears. He had gotten her through some tough situations. Like on the interstate when the Rice child was released and at her house after that call from the Taggart child. Maybe when this was over, if she ran into him again.

Wait, when had she started thinking in terms of what she would do when this was over?

Didn't mean anything. She checked her mirrors. The surveillance detail fell in behind her. When the chief reviewed her detail's report he would know she hadn't spent the day with Newt and Hadden. Nothing she could do about that. She'd just have to deal with the fallout when the time came. For now, this was the right move.

After about five minutes of nothing to focus on other than the smell of Shade's skin, she announced, "I should know more about you."

The silence continued for another mile or so.

"You know who I am and why I'm here. What else do you need to know?"

Bobbie considered what she wanted to ask first. She doubted his cooperation on the subject would last long. "Where's your family?"

"I don't have any family." He leaned against the headrest.

"Where are you from?"

"All over."

She rolled her eyes. "Where were you born?"

"Atlanta."

"Where did you go to college?"

"You didn't do a background check on me?"

She took the ramp to 85. "I think you know what your background check reveals. Besides, I haven't had time." The truth was, since her initial thoughts on the matter she hadn't taken the time. As long as he was a mystery she could...what? Hope? Believe? What was wrong with her head? She hadn't hoped or believed in anything in the past 250 days but her desire to get Perry. *Something is wrong with you, Bobbie.*

"Florida State, but I dropped out."

"Why?" She couldn't shake the idea that he was well educated. If he'd dropped out he had done so near graduation or he'd spent a great deal of time since educating himself.

"Personal reasons."

"You married?"

"No."

"Children?"

"No."

"What was your last job before undertaking your current venture?"

"A three-year tour in the military."

"Why didn't you make it a career?"

"Personal reasons."

"If you can't be hired," she ventured, "how do you afford the rental car you're driving? Or the motel? Food?"

Another stretch of silence.

"I inherited a great deal of money," he finally said. "I have an investment manager who keeps it earning for me, and this is how I spend it."

She braked for a light and glanced at him. "Your family was well-off?"

"In every way except the one that counted." He stared out the window.

"What happened to your parents?"

"Dead."

There was something they had in common. "My mom died when I was a little girl." Bobbie thought of her mother. She used to watch the old family videos every Christmas just so she could remember the sound of her mother's voice. Whenever she smelled Miss Dior tears burned her eyes. Her mother wasn't much for wearing perfume, but every Sunday before church she'd dabbed the scent behind her ears.

"You were twelve," Shade said. "Your father died ten years later while you were a senior in college."

She nodded. "He kept the blood pressure issue a secret from me. For years I was angry with Uncle Teddy—the chief of police—for not telling me."

"Peterson is your godfather."

She shouldn't be surprised he knew so much about her. Whatever or whoever his sources, they seemed to be thorough. "And my boss. Mostly he's a pain in my ass."

"When you became a detective, he purposely ensured you were partnered with Howard Newton."

She glanced at him as she took the first exit circled on the map. "How do you know that?"

He shrugged. "I don't. I just know what I would do if I had a goddaughter I wanted to keep safe on the streets. I would partner her with a senior detective—a father figure."

Shade was right. She'd accused the chief of exactly that when she'd gotten the assignment. At the time, Lieutenant Owens had been in another division and Major Crimes was a good old boys club. Romey Larson, the former commander, would have done anything the chief asked. Owens challenged him frequently. The woman had moxie.

It wasn't that Bobbie had anything against Newt back when she first started in Major Crimes. She'd liked him but she'd wanted to be partnered with someone more her own age. Someone who wouldn't be so old-fashioned and set in his ways. Now she couldn't imagine being partnered with anyone else.

Maybe she wouldn't ask Shade any more questions. He might get the idea that he could do the same. She didn't like that he could read her so well or that he'd done so much research on her.

Mainly, he made her think about things she didn't want to think about anymore.

Noon

Not one damned person they interviewed had seen the gray Prius or the black Altima. Bobbie's stomach warned she should eat soon. Maybe after they stopped at the next hardware store on the list Shade had compiled.

Newt had called. The search of video footage had picked up the black Altima on 85 the night the Rice boy had been dropped. He'd put the kid out and driven away. Mud was smeared on the license plate to ensure it was unreadable. The Altima continued south on 85 until there were no more cameras. The ground search was proving less productive. They had nothing so far. Bauer and Holt hadn't interviewed a single caller whose story had panned out.

When this stop was finished she and Shade would have the north side of Montgomery covered. There was still east and west and even south. Someone somewhere had seen him. He'd obviously moved about in the city far too frequently to go completely unnoticed.

Shade had taken over the driving four stops ago.

Considering how many calls and texts she received from her team as well as the chief, the change was probably a good thing. When Shade climbed out, she did the same. There wasn't much happening. Not the first car in the parking lot. The temperature was climbing rapidly toward the high of ninety-eight the meteorologist had forecast. Just walking from the car to the storefront had sweat beading on her forehead.

Shade opened the door the way he had every time, and then waited to follow her inside. The bell over the door jingled and the clerk looked up from his work stocking the shelves. He set the box he held aside and offered a big smile.

"Welcome to Myers. How can I help you folks?"

Bobbie shifted her jacket aside and showed the badge clipped at her waist. "Detective Gentry, MPD. This is my associate, Mr. Shade. We have a few questions for you, sir."

He looked surprised. "Is this about the robbery last month?"

Bobbie shook her head. She showed him the photos of Perry she had saved on her phone, the one with hair and the one without. "Have you seen this man? He may have been wearing a baseball cap and glasses. We believe he would have been looking for items like duct tape, chains. Nylon rope. The kinds of items you'd use to secure something." *Or someone.*

"He looks… Wait." The clerk looked at Bobbie. "He was here. Last week. Thursday, I believe. I was off on Friday. Had to be Thursday." He scratched his head. "He bought a couple of lengths of chain and eyebolts. A lock." His brow furrowed in concentration. "Follow me." He hurried down an aisle to the rolls of chain. "This is the chain he bought." He hustled over one aisle. "These are the eyebolts and bolts." He gestured to two of the metal bins. "He also bought a hammer, a battery-operated drill driver and a large flat-tip screwdriver. He wanted some nylon rope but I was just about out. He bought what I had anyway."

"Can you recall the vehicle he drove?" Shade asked.

"As a matter of fact, I do. It was a newer Toyota Prius. My wife has been nagging me to buy one for her. I think it was silver or gray."

Anticipation sliding through her veins, she looked around again for cameras. "Do you have security cameras?"

The clerk shook his head. "We were supposed to get them after the robbery last month, but it hasn't happened yet."

"Did he say anything beyond what he needed?"

The clerk shook his head. "Not that I can think of. It was one of our busier days. I didn't have a lot of time to chat like today." He shrugged. "He was friendly, as I recall."

"Did you notice which way he went as he left?" It was a long shot, but Bobbie had to ask.

"I didn't. Once he was out the door and in his car, I was on to the next customer."

"Can you tell us how he paid?"

"Cash. Our credit card machine was broken, and I had to do everything by hand. It was a real pain. I was really grateful to anyone who brought in cash."

Bobbie withdrew a business card from her jacket pocket and passed it to him. "If he comes back, call me, text me, whatever you can do."

He nodded. "I'll do it." Recognition flared on his face. "He's that serial killer. That Storyteller guy."

"Thank you." Bobbie hurried away before he recognized her, as well.

When they reached the car, Shade climbed behind the wheel again and handed her the map he'd made notes on. "Wherever he is, he's closer to this side of town than any other."

She fastened her seat belt, then squeezed her hands together to prevent him from seeing how they shook. "How can you be certain? He may have driven around and chosen this store at random."

Shade backed out of the parking slot and rolled onto the street. "He was here before he took Adams. He was in preparation mode. When a serial killer is in prep mode, everything is about efficiency. He's focused on getting ready for taking down his prey. He won't waste time driving around."

Made sense. "How do you know so much about serial killers?"

"I spent a lot of years studying cases. Not just the famous ones—every one I could get my hands on."

"Why only serial killers?" She glanced at him as she unfolded the map.

"I'm only one man, Detective." He looked at her and she looked away. "I had to draw the line somewhere."

"So, how do you know so much about people in general?" As a cop with several years under her belt, she had better than average insight, but Shade was like a shrink—maybe too much like one.

"After I left the military, I immersed myself in psychology and human nature. Like now, I can see you're anxious."

She studied the map and made a dismissive sound. "I'm a cop. We have three victims out there somewhere with a serial killer. Anxious is an understatement."

"You're worried about the victims, but you're anxious because you're afraid I'm in the way of the goal you've set."

He was guessing. "Even if you'd hit the nail on the head, how would you know something like that? I thought you said you aren't psychic?"

"You glance at me repeatedly, then look around. You keep checking the time, hoping the day will be over so you can go to your house and shut out the world until you're ready to emerge again—in the dark, alone. You want to do this alone because you believe that's the only way Perry will approach you."

"Where are we going next?" She kept her attention fixed on the map. No way was she letting him see the truth of his words in her eyes.

"We're going for food," he said in answer to her

question. "The way you keep grimacing and show-ing signs of fatigue, you need to eat."

He knew too much already.

Her cell vibrated with an incoming text from Owens. Briefing at 1. Be there.

"I guess we'll have to hit a drive-through."

The briefing couldn't be about a new develop-ment, Newt would have let her know.

She stared at the passing landscape. They were getting close.

We're going to get you, motherfucker.

Bobbie stilled. She glanced at Shade. There was no "we." What was wrong with her brain today?

Twenty-Seven

West Montgomery, 3:30 p.m.

"I have to go." Lynette bit back the other words she wanted to shout, but that would only make bad matters worse. She glanced at Bauer, who pretended to be messing with his phone. No matter that they'd been partners since before she got her promotion to sergeant, she still felt the weight of his judgment about her alternative lifestyle. He swore he didn't care, and maybe he didn't. Maybe it was her paranoia. "Really, Tricia, I have to go. Yes. I'll see you when I see you."

Lynette ended the call and tucked her phone back at her waist. "Is this our turn?"

"Yeah. Right there on Erskine. Make a left."

Slowing, she made the turn. She blew out a breath and shoved back a strand of hair that had come loose from her bun. She would be so damned glad when this case was over. Any time the feds were crawling all over the city, the chief was on everybody's ass. The damned heat didn't help.

"I'm still pissed that Owens sent Newt and Bobbie with Agent Hadden," Bauer grumbled. "I was hoping to work with the feds this time. Instead, we're stuck following up on every lunatic who decides to call in about Perry."

"I noticed. You've been pouting all morning." There were many things about the job that got on her nerves, but a whiny male was by far the most annoying.

"I am not pouting. I'm frustrated." He heaved a big sigh. "You sound pretty damned frustrated yourself. Trouble in paradise?"

Lynette wanted to slap his smug face. Life was so easy for good-looking heterosexual males. He had no idea what she had gone through in her life. At sixteen when she'd realized she was gay, she'd lost her best friend. When she was twenty-two and came out of the closet, she'd lost her parents. They still pretended that life was normal between them, but she knew they merely tolerated her choices. College, the job, every fucking thing was harder when you were gay. Even her love life had come with more ups and downs than the average. By the time she reached her midthirties, she no longer gave a shit what anyone else thought. Then she'd met Patricia Underwood. She had fallen madly, deeply in love with her. They'd gotten married two years ago and were expecting their first child. Lynette had provided the egg and Tricia carried the baby. It was perfect.

Except Tricia seemed to be having trouble staying at home alone. The baby was due in two weeks, so Tricia had started her leave from the bakery. From the day she began staying at home, she had started calling Lynette every other hour.

"She's pregnant," Lynette snapped. "Pregnant women have extra needs."

"Remind me never to get a woman pregnant." He smirked. "Are you ever going to tell who the sperm donor was?"

"Go fuck yourself, Bauer." She flashed him a smile. She wanted to add that at least her lover hadn't committed suicide, but she bit the mean words back. No matter that Bauer tried to pretend that he was over that tragedy—it had been two years he would remind her—it was obvious to Lynette he wasn't. He was an ass a lot of the time, but Leyla's death had hurt him badly. He did such a good job of pretending he didn't care about a damned thing that she often forgot that beneath that I-don't-give-a-shit exterior was a decent guy...for the most part. One who she suspected was drinking way too much. When this was over, she had to address that issue.

"I will never have to worry about that, Sergeant." He leaned back in the seat and tried to stretch his legs. "You see, I'm so charming and so damned good-looking that if I live to be a hundred I won't be able to bed all the babes who want me."

"I'm sure." She had to laugh. The guy was so full of himself. Truth was he was damned good-looking, and he could be charming. He was also smart and a good detective. Since his girlfriend died, she wouldn't trust him in the room with her seventy-year-old mother. The guy would screw anything.

Rumor was he was cheating on his fiancée, she found out and OD'd on sleeping pills. Lynette knew better. He had loved that woman with everything he had. Still, she didn't ask. If he wanted to talk about his personal life, he would.

"You think Bobbie'll ever be the same?"

Lynette parked in front of the house belonging to the tipster who'd called in on the hotline claiming he had seen Perry. "She's still a good detective. She takes some serious ass risks. Like walking into that house with Carl Evans. That was way out of line."

"Oh yeah," Bauer agreed. "Miller is still bitching about it."

Lynette harrumphed. "Miller complains about everything. I don't know how he ended up SWAT Commander. The man is a whiny bitch."

"That might be true, but he kicks major ass in the field. Have you ever gone out on a call with him?"

Lynette opened her door. "You just like that he throws grenades and kicks in doors."

"I should sign up for SWAT." He looked over the top of the Crown Vic at her. "I'd be badass, Sarge."

"Yeah, but you might ruin that pretty face."

"Seriously, though," he said. "I miss the old Bobbie. She was the one who brought cake every time it was somebody's birthday. She made us laugh no matter what else was going on."

Lynette remembered. She would never forget the way Bobbie held Bauer's hand at Leyla's funeral.

She never left his side. For weeks after the funeral, she made sure he got out of bed and came to work. Lynette was the one who put him to bed every night for the first month or so. He'd drink himself unconscious wherever he happened to be. Ten on the dot every night she hustled over to wherever he'd crashed and dragged him to bed. She wondered if he would do the same for her.

Shaking off the bad memories, she surveyed the house for the first time. "Are you sure this is the right address? The place looks abandoned."

A long barrel suddenly poked through a broken pane of glass.

"Gun!" Lynette hit the ground and rolled as the blast of the shotgun ruptured the silence. She drew her Glock and took aim.

Bauer went down and rolled in the other direction. Another shot thundered and hit the ground between them.

"Mr. Hennessey, you okay in there, sir?" Lynette shouted. The caller had given that name.

A few yards away Bauer was calling for backup.

"Mr. Hennessey, it's Sergeant Holt and Detective Bauer. Remember you called us about a tip on Gaylon Perry?"

According to the operator who'd taken the call the tipster sounded like an older African American gentleman. Lynette hadn't gotten a look at the shooter. At this point she couldn't be sure who or what they were dealing with.

The barrel withdrew from the window. Bauer

took off, staying low as he scrambled around the end of the house. Lynette moved closer to the front door, using the concrete porch for cover. The snap of the weapon indicated he'd reloaded. The barrel extended once more through the broken window.

Damn it. She still couldn't see the shooter.

The best she could do was to keep him talking while Bauer sized up the situation.

"Mr. Hennessey, did we do something wrong? You did ask us to come?"

"I'll tell you what you did wrong," he shouted. "You've killed one too many of my people. It's time we evened the score."

Fuck! If they couldn't disable this guy before backup arrived, this would not end well for the man inside.

Her cell vibrated. She checked the screen. A text from Bauer.

House is empty. Only the shooter. Old man. Going in.

She quickly entered a response. No deadly force unless no choice.

"Mr. Hennessey," she called as she put her phone away. "Why don't we put down our weapons and talk about this?"

"The only talking I'm gonna do is with this twelve gauge."

Shit! "What about your family, Mr. Hennessey? If you shoot one of us, you're going to jail for a very long time. You'll hurt your family, sir."

"You killed my grandson, Tyrell. You shot him dead and he didn't do nothing wrong. Now I'm going to shoot you dead."

"I didn't shoot him, Mr. Hennessey. Maybe you need to talk to the person who shot him and find out what really happened." Lynette remembered the case. Six months ago, Tyrell Pride entered a convenience store and robbed the clerk at gunpoint. When he'd exited the store, a cruiser just happened to pull into the parking lot. Tyrell started shooting, and the officer had no choice but to return fire. Tyrell died three days later.

"I know all I need to know." The old man fired in her direction. A piece of concrete chipped off the edge of the porch.

Fuck!

"Drop the weapon, Mr. Hennessey!" Bauer shouted.

He was inside. Tension rushed through Lynette's limbs.

Hennessey still had one round in the chamber. If he wheeled on Bauer, he'd have no choice but to defend himself and then an old black man would die, making two white cops look like the bad guys.

Lynette scrambled up and ran. She zigzagged back and forth, making for a hard target. She didn't have to look to know the barrel tracked her movements.

The shotgun discharged.

She hit the ground.

When pain failed to streak through her body, she looked toward the house.

"Stay down, sir!" Bauer's voice echoed from inside.

Her partner had him. *Thank God.*

Lynette got up and double-timed it to the door. The wail of sirens signaled backup was almost here.

In the vacant living room, Bauer had cuffed the old man and put his weapon out of reach. Hennessey screamed profanities, mostly about cops.

Lynette leaned against the wall and took her first deep breath since they arrived.

She suddenly wanted to talk to Tricia…just to hear her voice.

She shook her head. Sometimes she hated this job.

Twenty-Eight

Bobbie was ready to tear out her hair. First there was the pointless briefing that had consumed an hour with nothing but rehashing what they already knew. Then, they'd spent every minute of the past five and a half hours combing the back roads on the north side of Montgomery and found nothing.

"A needle in a haystack," she muttered. Her cell vibrated and she checked the screen. *Newt.* "Hey, partner." Bobbie wondered how he was enjoying his time as Hadden's partner. Later, when it was just the two of them, she would ask. She was grateful he was covering for her. Owens and the chief thought she was with him and that made things far less complicated.

"Agent Mason passed down word that we should call it a day," Newt told her. "Briefing's at eight in the morning."

"Got it. Thanks, Newt."

"Hey," Newt said, "Hadden asked some questions about Shade. I did a lot of hedging and tossed out the same story we've been giving."

Bobbie digested the news. "Okay. Good to know. See you in the morning."

"Night, girlie."

Bobbie put her cell away and opted not to mention the agent's interest. Shade wasn't a fool. He expected questions. "Agent Mason is sending the troops home for the day."

"It'll be dark soon," Shade commented. "We should do the same."

She surveyed the landscape. *Where are you, you son of a bitch?*

The drive back to Gardendale didn't take long since they were on her side of town already. The idea that Perry could be only minutes from her house made her want to turn around and continue searching until she found him or she was too exhausted to continue. It didn't seem right to stop just because the sun had gone down.

"Since we're doing this together," Shade began, "like partners, I want you to know that I'm working on a potential angle for luring Perry out of hiding."

"What kind of angle?" Why was she just hearing this? "Is it legal?" Did she really care?

"It involves his mother—that's all I can say." He pulled into her driveway. "I'll tell you more as soon as the details are in place."

She started to protest but a package on her porch where the beam of the headlights rested derailed whatever argument she'd intended to make.

"Did you order something?"

She opened her door to get out. "No."

Shade was out of the car and hustling up the sidewalk right behind her. She withdrew a pair of latex gloves from her jacket pocket and tugged them on while he used his cell as a flashlight and shined the beam into the open box.

Pale blue shirt...*blood*.

A black leather credentials case lay on top of the wadded shirt. Her heart hammering, Bobbie reached for the case and opened it.

Special Agent Anthony LeDoux.

Damn.

She placed the case back on the shirt and moved away from the box. "I'll call it in."

Forty minutes later her yard was lit up like a stadium. Newt and three evidence techs, along with Agents Mason and Hadden were inspecting every blade of grass. Bobbie and four other members of the task force were going from door to door canvassing the neighbors. Shade stuck with her, though she was confident he'd rather not have been under such close scrutiny from all the law enforcement personnel on the scene. He usually faded into the background or disappeared whenever anyone else was around.

She wondered what he had to hide.

"You take this one," she said as they approached the next house. "I've got a call."

While Shade knocked on the door and asked the same questions—Have you seen this man? Did you see a gray Prius or black Altima in the neighborhood today?—Bobbie stayed at the street and called her friend Andy Keller, who was currently combing her yard for evidence.

"Hey, can you do me a favor?"

"I can and will."

It was easy to imagine the big goofy smile on his face. He was a good guy who asked her out at least twice a month. Bobbie didn't have the heart to tell him not to waste his time. She was damaged goods.

"Don't tell anyone, okay? I'd like you to lift a few prints from the steering wheel of my Challenger and see what you come up with?"

"You trying to find yourself, Detective Gentry?" he teased.

"Just checking up on something. I'll owe you big-time."

"Dinner would be payment enough," he said, the humor gone from his voice now.

She moistened her lips and did what she had to do. "Dinner it is then." Before ending the call she tacked on, "Let me know what you find. The sooner the better, okay?"

"You got it."

Bobbie put the phone away just as Shade headed back down the sidewalk. He shook his head. "Same answers as all the others."

No surprise there. People in this neighborhood went out of their way not to see things. Sometimes what you saw could get you killed.

"Let's grab that one before anyone else gets to it."
She pointed to the house at the far end of the street.

"I take it that one belongs to your pal Quintero?"

"That's the one."

They walked to the end of the block. The few
street lamps that worked provided little light. Good
thing the sky was clear. She could see four—no
five—of Javier's boys lounging on the porch. Six
or seven vehicles were parked in the yard. How did
this bastard continue to operate so efficiently under
the MPD's radar?

As she walked through the chain-link gate, one
of the men asked, "What you want, bitch?"

Bobbie set her hands on her hips, pushing her
jacket open and showing off her badge and weapon.
Not that any of them didn't already know who she
was. "Not you, that's for sure." When the laughter
died down, she asked, "Where's Javier?"

"He's busy right now."

She took the first step up to the porch. "Tell him
I'm here."

Shade moved up beside her.

The silence lasted a beat longer than she would
have preferred.

The one who'd been doing all the talking told
one of his boys to get Javier. He did this in Spanish.
Bobbie spoke enough of the language to understand.
No one said a word while they waited. Down the
street the sounds of cops banging on doors echoed
through the darkness.

Finally the door opened, the light from inside

slicing across the porch, and the guy who'd gone inside came back out. "He said come on in, *mami*."

Her stomach always got queasy when the bastard called her that. She wasn't his baby or his lover. "Thanks."

Bobbie was grateful no one attempted to stop Shade from going with her. Of course they were all heavily armed. She had her Glock and her backup piece but she was relatively certain Shade was not armed. She was yet to see him carrying.

Another mystery to solve. Why would a man who hunted serial killers walk around unarmed?

Inside the dump of a house was surprisingly well furnished. Javier was kicked back on a sectional that seemed to go on forever watching an even bigger television. Not at all the picture she had expected to find.

Javier held up his long neck bottle. "You want a beer, *mami*?"

"No thanks."

"How 'bout your friend?" Javier shifted his attention to Shade. "Maybe your *sombra* would like a beer."

Shade held the other man's gaze for a moment. "I'll pass."

"Someone left a package at my door, Javier. Did any of your people see anyone messing around my place?"

Javier stared at her for a moment. "Maybe. Was you expecting a package?"

"Don't give me any grief, Javier. Just tell me what your people saw."

Javier pushed to his feet. "We need to speak privately."

Bobbie looked to Shade. He turned and walked out the door. She was surprised he didn't argue.

"If you waste my time," she warned the jerk eyeing her as if he could eat her up, "I will make you regret it."

Javier grinned. "I love it when you talk tough to me, Detective." He grabbed himself. "Makes me hard."

Bobbie rested her hand on the butt of her weapon. It was the same every time. "Let's hear it."

"The guy—the one on TV—has been coming around. I first noticed him about two weeks ago, but I didn't know who he was until they started plastering his face all over the news."

"You mean the Storyteller." Her heart rate climbed rapidly as she waited for a confirmation.

"Yeah. Him. Anyway, he cruised through again today and dropped off a box. This time he was driving one of those shitty little hybrid cars. The kind the queers and tree huggers like."

"What was he driving before?"

"First time I noticed him it was a black Nissan. One of those knockoff Maximas. But today was the Prius."

"What time did he make the delivery?"

"Around eleven this morning."

"Do you remember what he was wearing?"

"Jeans, baggy ones, and a hoodie. My boys were laughing 'cause it's hot as hell and the dumb fuck was wearing a hoodie."

"Did he do anything else while he was here?"

"Drove right on out of the hood after that." Javier took a long swig of his beer.

A thread of tension worked its way through her muscles. *He* had been to her house. "I need you to do something for me, Javier."

Javier moved closer to her. Since they were about the same height, he looked directly into her eyes. "I would do anything to fuck you just one time, Detective. What can I do to make that happen?"

"I'm serious, Javier." One of these days she was going to take this asshole all the way down. "Will you help me or not?"

He sucked another swallow from the bottle and licked his lips. "Maybe."

"If you see him again, call me."

He shrugged. "Look, *mami*, if you want that fucker dead, just say so. He comes back into my territory I will kill him dead."

"No. Just call me. Okay?"

He smirked. "I see how it is. You want him all to yourself." He looked her up and down. "I guess I can't blame you for that. I would really like to watch, though."

"You help me catch him and I'll definitely let you watch."

"Deal." He turned up the bottle and finished off his beer.

Before she reached the door he said, "You should watch the *sombra*."

Bobbie glanced back at him. "The guy with me? What about him?"

"His eyes," Javier said with a forked gesture toward his own. "He has the eyes of a killer."

Bobbie opened the door and walked out. Shade waited for her on the porch. None of Javier's men said a word as they walked away. Bobbie was glad. The mood she was in she might have shot anyone who did.

The evidence techs had already packed up and headed to the lab. Bobbie would give Andy a call in the morning to see what he found. Running the prints through the usual databases wouldn't take long.

She thought about Javier's comment. He might be more right than he knew when he called Shade a shadow. But was he a killer?

"Are you going to tell me what he said?"

Ah, Nick Shade didn't like being left in the dark. D-Boy stretched to the end of his chain and wiggled his tail as they walked past his yard. Bobbie made another mental note to call the landlord. "He saw the Prius. Perry delivered the box around eleven and drove away."

Shade said nothing.

She was just about to demand his thoughts when Newt and Hadden met them at her driveway.

"No one appears to have seen anything," Hadden complained. "This is some neighborhood you live in, Detective Gentry. If I were your superior, I'd be concerned that you're suicidal."

Shade touched her elbow, preventing her from sticking her foot in her mouth. "I'll be back in a few hours."

Where the hell was he going?

"I have a few questions for you, Mr. Shade," Hadden called to his back.

Shade didn't turn around. He climbed into his car and drove away.

"Agent Mason doesn't like having any unofficial parties involved in this investigation," Hadden warned Bobbie. "Your friend has shown up once too often. It's beginning to look as if he's attempting to insinuate himself into our investigation."

"Hold up, Hadden," Newt countered.

"Javier Quintero saw Perry deliver the package," Bobbie announced, cutting off the explanation that would likely drag Newt deeper into the mess she'd made. Giving up Javier was the best way to divert attention from Shade and to keep Newt out of the equation.

Thankfully a call drew her partner away from the huddle before he could say more on the subject of Shade.

"Who is Quintero?" Hadden demanded.

Bobbie gave him a quick rundown on the local gang leader.

"This Quintero is a friend of yours?" Hadden eyed her speculatively.

She smiled. "Not really. He's just my neighbor. He lives at the end of the block."

Newt returned to her side as Hadden walked away.

"I'll talk to him," the agent called back as he headed for his car.

When he'd driven away, Newt said, "Suddenly I do not like that man. Ever since that Agent Price arrived he's acting all pushy and arrogant. I think he's trying to impress her."

"Maybe he's trying to fill LeDoux's shoes." Bobbie hoped the prick was still alive. As much as she despised him, she didn't want him to die like this.

Newt grunted in agreement.

"Javier thinks Shade is a killer," she said without qualifying the statement. Not that she put any real stock in what Javier thought, usually anyway.

Newt walked quietly beside her for a moment. "Has he shown you any reason to believe that's true? I definitely didn't get that impression from Jessup."

"As far as I can tell he doesn't even carry a weapon." Bobbie glanced around to ensure Shade hadn't reappeared. "I had Andy pull his prints from my steering wheel. I need to know more about him."

"Good idea." Newt heaved a big breath. "The chief called. Your detail informed him that you were with Shade instead of me today. He wants to see us both first thing in the morning."

Bobbie had expected as much. "I'm surprised we've avoided the issue of Shade this long."

In the past seventy-two-plus hours Shade had been coincidentally involved at the scene on the interstate and at her Ryan Ridge house, both of those incidents could be explained away since Bobbie had been with him and off duty when she received the calls. Today, however, was different. Today and tonight he'd gone door to door with her in the course of an official investigation. They'd both understood the move would not go unnoticed even with Newt covering for her. Or maybe the chief or Mason had finally figured out it was Shade who'd represented himself as an attorney and interviewed Neely. Probably not, she decided, or Shade would be the one with a face-to-face with the chief.

Maybe this was the answer to her concerns. If the department and the FBI started asking questions Shade might feel compelled to stay away from her.

That was what she wanted, wasn't it?

"I wish you'd reconsider protective custody or staying with Carlene and me."

Bobbie dragged her attention back to the here and now. How many times would they have this conversation? "Carlene said the wedding was amazing. Are the newlyweds enjoying Barbados?"

"Okay, okay, I get the hint." He threw his hands up. "The wedding was amazing. Since you couldn't come I'm going to make you watch the video with me when this is over."

"I'll bring the beer and popcorn."

"It's a date." Newt poked his hands into his pockets as they walked. "We haven't actually talked to the kids, but the pictures they're sending make my heart glad."

Bobbie hugged her arms around his. "Hearing that makes my heart glad."

Few things had the power to make her feel anything anymore. Her partner's happiness was one of those few.

The way Shade had made her feel nudged her. A glitch, she decided. A shattered piece of who she used to be trying to resurface. That woman was dead and gone.

When they reached her house, Newt insisted on coming inside and ensuring that all was clear. As soon as he was gone, Shade knocked on her back door. Funny how quickly the strange became normal.

When she let him in, she backed toward the hall. "I'm gonna hit the shower." Memories of the way he'd held her and bathed her had her heart thumping.

"I'll call in a pizza order," he offered.

"Sure."

"Wait."

She hesitated when every instinct warned she should keep walking.

"I should tell you about that angle I was working. It may actually work out after all."

Now he had her attention. "Oh yeah?"

He moved toward her. His coming closer in the narrow hall made it difficult to breathe.

When he stopped right in front of her, he looked

away a moment. "You might find my methods un-conventional."

Was he worried what she would think of him? "Trust me, Shade—at this point convention, ethics, the law—" she shook her head "—I don't care any-more. All that matters is that I stop him."

He nodded. "The new source I discovered was an old friend of Perry's. He suggested I make Perry come to me by using his mother."

"She's dead." Bobbie felt certain there was more coming. She hoped there was more.

Nick held up his cell and showed her a photo. Bobbie recognized the woman in the red dress. The bastard's mother. Her closed eyes, made-up face and the padded satin upholstery around her warned that she wasn't asleep on a sofa. "She's…in her coffin?"

Shade nodded. "Well, she was. At the moment she's in a freezer at an undisclosed location only I know about."

Disbelief or something on that order stopped Bobbie for a moment, then she said, "You have a resource in Nebraska who was willing to dig her up and snap a photo." Just when she thought noth-ing would surprise her.

"Digging wasn't necessary." Shade tucked his phone away. "Her body was borrowed from the family mausoleum."

"And you believe this will get a reaction from him?" She had to admit the scheme could work.

"I believe so."

"How do we let him know? It's not like we can

run an ad in the paper or on television. None of the burner numbers he's used are still in service."

"The time will come," he assured her, "and we'll have the leverage we need."

Bobbie wasn't sure which scared her the most... what Shade had done or the idea that she found the move ingenious.

Twenty-Nine

Tony jerked awake. He'd dosed off. *Fool!* Stay alert! His fucking toes were killing him. He squeezed his eyes shut and refused to let the damned tears come again. His pain was nothing compared to the Adams woman's. He had no right to complain.

He was going to kill this bastard.

Where the hell was he?

He held as still as possible and listened. The soft moans were hers. Perry had spent hours during two different sessions tattooing his twisted words on Gwen Adams's back. The other sound, the sobbing, was the boy. Thank God he was still alive.

Tony had no idea of the time. So far he'd watched the night he was taken turn into the next day and the next day after that and now it was night again. He estimated he'd been in this fucking hellhole about forty-eight hours. Unable to hold back the need he'd shit and pissed himself after the son of a bitch had taken the hammer to him. The sick fuck had made Adams clean up the mess.

After hours working on his so-called masterpiece today, Perry had left long before dark and he'd been gone since.

Rocking his body, Tony rolled as far to one side as possible. He ignored the pain that engulfed his foot and shot up his leg. The wood floor was rough under his skin. He rolled to the other side. His restraints only allowed an inch or so. He raised his head and tried to see with nothing but the dim moonlight filtering in through the one window. As much as he hated being restrained facedown, having his dick protected under him was somewhat of a relief. This twisted psychopath's MO included artwork with a blade. Tony would rather have his backside tattooed from neck to ankle and his toes fucked up than have his dick touched.

How the hell are you going to get these hostages out of here?

"Ignore the pain and fear and focus," he muttered. The restraints were police-issue handcuffs. Anyone could buy the damned things on the internet or at spy shops. Gwen was secured in the same fashion, only there was a thin excuse for a mattress under her. The child had wandered into the room several times so he wasn't secured—or at least he hadn't been.

The problem with handcuffs was you needed a key or something with which to pick the lock. Not to mention the ability to reach the lock. Tony had tried to get the kid's attention several times but he wouldn't come close.

He closed his eyes and focused on trying to pull

his hands free. Maybe if he continued to sweat so profusely and drew his thumb and little finger into his palm far enough he could slip his hand free. During his training at Quantico there had been a fellow recruit who could slip out of handcuffs. Apparently, there were lots of people who could do it, which was the reason most law enforcement agencies had gone to nylon handcuffs.

Pull! He tugged until his wrists felt like they would snap apart. He'd tried every way he could think to escape. Over and over, he'd tugged and squirmed until his skin was raw from scrubbing around on the floor and his left foot and toes were screaming.

The sound of chains rattling announced Perry's return. Tony squeezed his eyes shut and held still.

The bastard entered the room, his footfalls shaking the dilapidated floor. A few seconds passed and he turned on the lamp. The silence made Tony want to explode. What was the son of a bitch doing? Staring at them? God only knew what he was planning. Tony could hear him breathing. Based on the pattern of his respiration, he was angry or aroused.

Fuck!

Perry walked across the room and crouched next to Tony. He could feel him surveying his bare backside for a moment. Tony tried not to react. The toes on his right foot instinctively curled.

"I'm quite vexed, LeDoux. I need your help."

Tony bit his lips together to prevent saying the

only thing he wanted to do was help him go straight to hell.

He leaned down and screamed into Tony's ear. "Look at me when I'm speaking to you!"

Tony snapped his eyes open. *Fuck you!*

"I've been quite clear that Detective Gentry should surrender herself to me, and she doesn't seem to get the message." Perry cocked his bald head and pursed his thin lips for a moment before going on, "She doesn't have another husband for me to kill or a child. Reenacting those painful memories with others hasn't created the shock and awe I'd hoped for. Perhaps you could make a recommendation. Or—" Perry smiled "—you could help me arrange a meeting with her."

A new rush of fury ruptured inside Tony. "Go fuck yourself."

Perry sighed. "As I told my students, such lack of originality in the words you choose is a disservice to you and to the English language. I know how intelligent you are, LeDoux, even if your professional conclusions rarely hit the mark. You were the first of your ilk to intrigue me."

Tony wouldn't piss on this bastard if his guts were on fire.

Perry's face abruptly changed, his expression hardening and menace sparking in his eyes. "Perhaps you need a little incentive to cooperate."

Fear roared through Tony. What the hell was the son of a bitch going to do now? *Fuck!*

Perry stood and moved to the table. His heart

pounding, Tony twisted his head and tried to see what he was doing. He couldn't see! Perry returned to stand between Tony and Adams, something small and shiny in his hand. *A scalpel. Shit!*

Perry stared down at the nurse. "I must say, she was the perfect canvas for another of my masterpieces." He shifted his cold, hard gaze to Tony. "This is going to hurt like a bitch, and it's on you, Agent LeDoux."

Tony gritted his teeth together until they were ready to crack. He couldn't do what Perry wanted. *Goddamn it!*

Perry knelt and traced the scalpel's edge across her buttocks and down her thigh. "Did you know that the skin of the inner thigh is some of the most sensitive flesh on the human body?"

Tony's body shook with the effort to keep his mouth shut as bright red blood bloomed along the path the bastard carved on her inner thigh. Adams's low moans turned to wails. Her body stiffened and then shuddered.

Son of a bitch. Tony hoped he got to put a bullet between his eyes.

Perry smiled as her voice grew hoarse with her screams. "Perhaps it's time for me to finish her story." He leaned forward and grabbed a handful of her hair and jerked her head back. Her eyes bulged, and fear contorted her face. Her screams dissolved into sobs.

Tony's gut clenched. The air mired in his lungs. Every nerve in his body was on fire.

Perry pressed the scalpel to her throat just above the yellow nylon noose. "I usually strangle my victims." He turned to Tony. "As you well know. Perhaps I'll slit her throat for a change of pace."

"Stop! I'll—" Tony swallowed back the bitter taste of defeat. "I'll help you."

Perry released the woman and scooted closer to Tony. "I need a name, Agent. The name of someone I can use to genuinely hurt our dear Bobbie and get her full attention."

"Her partner," Tony spit the words out. "Howard Newton."

God forgive him.

Thirty

Howard Newton pulled his tie into place and stared at his reflection. Good Lord when had he gotten so old? It seemed like just yesterday he'd dropped his daughters off at elementary school on his way to work. Now they were off living their own lives and he was just getting old.

He opened a drawer and picked through all sorts of cosmetics until he found his wife's eyebrow-tweezing mirror. He grimaced at his magnified image. Turning his head this way and that, he checked his nose and ears. Failing vision and hearing were among the many unfortunate benefits of getting old. Along with hair sprouting from places it was never intended to grow, he had what used to be charming laugh lines deepening into crevices that made shaving a hazardous endeavor.

After carefully replacing the mirror, he checked the sink for whiskers. Satisfied he'd done all he could to look presentable, he went back into the bedroom and retrieved his weapon from the bedside table. He snugged it into the holster at his waist and removed his cell from the charger and clipped it on his belt.

"Good to go," he muttered.

He turned off the bedroom light and headed for the kitchen. He and his wife had thoroughly enjoyed the house they'd bought thirty years ago. The secluded master bedroom was on the east side of the kitchen, while the kids' rooms were on the other end of the house, beyond the living room. Recently the subject of downsizing had come up. Howard wasn't sure he was ready for that just yet. This house was paid for. The taxes were cheap, and it was brick, so the upkeep was minimal. He had a landscaper who cut the grass every week. What was wrong with just spending their twilight years right here?

In the kitchen he confirmed the coffeepot was off and rinsed his cup before putting it in the dishwasher. He reached for the keys he'd left on the counter and stilled.

The rear slider leading onto the deck was open a few inches. Had his wife let the cats in or out and forgotten to close the door? She rarely forgot anything. In fact, he was the one who was more likely to forget. Only he was fairly certain he hadn't opened the door. She had been in a hurry this morning and those darn cats were always under her feet every step she made.

As if the cats had known he was trying to blame

this on one of them, the long-haired Persian raced past him and out the door. "Scat on outta here, Puff!" he called with a smile.

Damn animals. He'd always wanted a dog, but the wife and girls loved cats. There was no winning that contest.

Where was the other one? If one was left out, the other one inevitably got into trouble. "Tigger! Come on, kitty, kitty." The Siamese was far more persnickety. "Come on, boy."

A clatter in the living room made him cringe. He could just imagine one of Carlene's fancy little statues falling from the table in front of the picture window. That damned Siamese loved lounging in that window. Carlene had insisted he widen the window stool so the furry creature could watch for her to come home. With a weary sigh, he headed into the living room to assess the damage.

"You might be looking for another home, old boy, if you…" Howard's voice trailed off.

A little boy, blond hair, gray eyes, filthy as a little puppy who'd rolled in the mud stood in the middle of his living room.

Recognition shook him. "Aaron?"

The little boy's gaze shot to his. His eyes widened.

"Oh hell." Howard rushed toward the child but the boy scrambled away and cowered in the corner. "Don't be afraid. I'll…" Howard stilled, his heart doing somersaults under his sternum. If the kid was here—

He grabbed for his weapon. A strong arm looped around his throat from the left and pulled him back against a hard body. He felt a prick to his neck.

Howard struggled, twisting with all his strength. The weapon came free of its holster. A wave of unsteadiness washed over him.

Fight it! He jabbed hard with his right elbow. The bastard grunted. Howard jabbed him again, then twisted hard. He broke free and staggered forward. His finger squeezed the trigger. The blast echoed around him.

Howard couldn't be sure he'd hit the son of a bitch. He shook his head, tried to clear it. Damned drug.

Wait! The bastard was coming at him again. Howard pulled off another shot as he dropped to his knees. A scream rent the air. The child? God, he hoped not...

Howard's shoulder hit the floor next. He called out the boy's name. No response. Holding on to his weapon, he rolled onto his back and felt for his phone with his left hand. He tried to see the screen. Couldn't bring it into focus. He slid his thumb over the screen until he felt the right spot. It took two tries but he pushed the one button he knew wouldn't fail him.

"Call nine-one-one," he said, his voice faltering.

"Calling nine-one-one." The phone's reply echoed in the room.

Howard tried to get up but he couldn't manage the feat.

Where was the child?

Where was Perry?

His fingers tightened around the gun in his hand.

He prayed help would get here fast.

"Aaron?" He wasn't sure he said the boy's name out loud this time. Darkness was closing in on him.

The dirty little face came into focus.

"I'll get your...mommy..."

The lights went out.

Thirty-One

Bobbie paced the ER lobby. When she got the call, she had been preparing for her meeting with the chief while Shade reviewed the map in preparation for a new grid search. She had urged him to get started while she came here. Gwen and LeDoux were running out of time.

Her heart had hammered twice for every second of every minute during the drive across town to the hospital.

About ten minutes ago Newt's wife had been allowed back to his room.

"Bobbie, sit down, you're only working yourself up. We'll know more soon."

Her first impulse was to argue with the chief, but since the LT was seated next to him, she opted not to make a scene.

"Sorry." She dropped into a chair. Her head was pounding in time with her heart. She rubbed her forehead and wished she'd grabbed another cup of coffee or something for this damned headache.

She'd managed maybe two or three hours of sleep. Her mind kept playing over and over the bloody shirt that belonged to LeDoux. His credentials... and the idea of what Perry might be doing to him. Then there was the photo of Perry's dead mother. Bobbie was still reeling from that revelation.

The reality that the Taggart child was safe made her weak all over again. His mother was back there in an exam room with him. So far, like the Rice child, he appeared physically unharmed other than being dirty and mildly dehydrated. When the first officers on the scene arrived at Newt's home, the child had been sitting next to him on the living room floor. The syringe, still half-full of ketamine, had been hanging from Newt's neck.

Bobbie couldn't help but feel some sense of triumph when she thought of the blood on the carpet. Since neither Newt nor the child had any bleeding injuries, the blood had to be Perry's. Her partner had gotten off at least one shot that hit the target.

Perry was wounded. She wanted to jump up in the air and do a fist pump. She hoped the son of a bitch bled to death...except then Gwen and LeDoux might starve to death chained in some remote location.

Damn it all to hell.

She'd half expected the chief to interrogate her about Shade again but he hadn't. Between the Taggart reunion and worry about Newt, there had been little time for anything until now. If he asked, she intended to tell him as much of the truth about

Shade as possible. She would not allow the enigmatic man to mar Newt's record.

The doors that led back to the ER opened and Carlene came into the lobby. Bobbie pushed to her feet and hurried to meet her. "How's he doing?"

She took a breath, her eyes red from crying. "He's great. His heart rate is stable. BP is right where it should be. He'll be groggy for a few more hours, but he's good. Considering the issues with his heart, they're going to admit him and keep him overnight for observation. Just in case."

Bobbie pressed her hands to her face and struggled to hold back the tears. "That is the best news."

The chief and Owens, who had come up behind her, echoed her sentiments.

"He wants to see you, Bobbie. Room eight."

Bobbie glanced at the chief who nodded. She gave Carlene a hug and rushed back to the double doors. She showed her badge and the doors slowly opened. Holding back the urge to run, she walked to room eight. Her heart hurt when she saw Newt lying on that damned examination table looking so pale.

"Hey, partner."

Newt looked over at her. "The kid's okay? Carlene said he hadn't been hurt."

"He's fine. His mother is with him now."

Newt blew out a big breath. "That's some good news."

The trembling started deep inside Bobbie and she couldn't control it. "He could've killed you."

Her lips trembled and she tried to cover them with her hand.

He took her free hand in his and squeezed. "I'm just glad he didn't get a chance to use me to hurt you."

Bobbie swiped at the damned tears. "I have to stop him."

"*We* have to stop him," he corrected.

She nodded. "I know. We're a team." She would not let that son of a bitch take anyone else from her.

"If we're lucky he's seriously injured," Newt said. "If he goes for help, we'll get him."

"We've got people reviewing camera feeds from all over the city," Bobbie said, mostly to reassure herself. "We know he's in the Prius. The Altima was found at the Walmart over on Highland this morning." The bastard was running out of options. "We've got people out searching for his location right now. We will find him."

"They're not gonna let me out of here until tomorrow," Newt said, clearly not happy about his predicament. "I should be out there, too."

Bobbie raised an eyebrow. "Carlene tells me you've been keeping secrets."

Newt shrugged. "It's nothing. Just need a little tweaking on the ticker that's all."

She wanted to believe him. "Whatever it is, you get it fixed."

"Don't worry." He pretended to study her hand. "I'll take care of it."

"I'm counting on you," Bobbie added for good

measure. "For now, you just take it easy. You stay as long as the docs feel it's necessary."

"I need you to promise me something, girlie." His hold on her hand tightened.

"I don't know, Newt." She knew what he was going to say. "I'm not very good with promises." *Mommy keeps the monsters away.* Her husband's voice echoed through her mind. Only mommy had failed.

"Just promise me you'll stay close to backup. Don't let Perry get you cornered. He's going to be desperate now. Judging by the way he howled I'd say he's pissed. If he still wants to come after you, he'll have to do it soon. He's running out of time, Bobbie. Mark my word—he'll make a move for you next. Keep your surveillance detail and Shade close."

"Don't worry about me," Bobbie argued. "I can take care of myself."

"Bobbie." He squeezed her hand again to get her full attention. "If he gets close enough this time, he may kill you immediately just to clean up his record. Don't give him that chance."

"I won't give him that chance," she agreed. She hated lying to Newt, but he couldn't expect her to hide from what she had to do. Taking Perry into custody was not good enough. She wanted him dead.

The only way to make sure that happened was to do it herself.

"The same way you're counting on me," Newt said, "I'm counting on you."

She gave up and produced a smile for him. "I promise to be extra careful."

He nodded. "Good."

"Okay. I'm going out there and let your wife back in here. I'll tell the chief you're taking a vacation."

"You better not," he warned with a grin.

She kissed his cheek and backed toward the door, giving him a wave. "See you later today."

Smiling, he waved. "I'm holding you to it."

Before she turned away he rubbed at his chest and grimaced.

Bobbie froze. "You okay?"

The machine monitoring his heart rate suddenly screamed a warning. Newt made a gurgling sound. Bobbie yanked the door open and shouted, "We need help in here!" She rushed to his bedside and took his hand. "It's okay, Newt. It's okay. Help is coming."

The room filled with people in scrubs. Bobbie was ushered into the corridor. She heard the urgent sounds and bits of loud, hurried conversation that told the story that was going on beyond the door. None of it good. Newt had flatlined. They were trying to get his heart beating again. Long seconds… minutes ticked by. Nothing was working.

Please, please, let him be okay.

Then came the silence.

Tears poured down her cheeks.

Hospital personnel emerged one by one from

the room. The doctor shook his head. He glanced around. "Where is Mrs. Newton?"

The big double doors leading to the lobby opened and Carlene walked through as if she'd sensed something was wrong.

Bobbie turned to her, and maybe it was the devastation on her face, but Carlene stopped. She shook her head even as the doctor walked toward her. He spoke quietly. Carlene wailed and ran toward Newt's room.

Whoever was left inside the room spoke quiet reassurances. But there were no reassurances.

Newt was dead.

Perry had accomplished another goal.

Bobbie turned and walked toward the double doors as they opened. The chief and Lieutenant Owens hurried toward her.

She heard their questions but she couldn't speak. She could only shake her head. They headed for the room where Newt's wife grieved over him.

Bobbie walked through the lobby and out the ER entrance doors. There were cops holding the media at bay. They spoke to her, but she couldn't speak. She headed straight for the horde of reporters.

"Detective Gentry, how is your partner?"

Another pushed in front of the first and shouted, "Detective, is it true the Taggart child has been rescued?"

Another voice shouted, "Detective Gentry, what about Gaylon Perry? Is he still out there?"

Bobbie stared at the crowd. Cameras zeroed in

on her face. "My partner…" She couldn't make herself say the words.

The reporters stared at her as if they understood what she had to say was too painful to speak aloud. And still they wanted something.

Rage rushed through her veins. "Tell him…" Her voice failed her so she paused and started again. "Tell Gaylon Perry something for me, would you?"

Voices shouted her name as microphones were shoved in her face.

"Tell him I'm waiting for him. He knows the place. I'm ready to finish this now."

Questions were hurled at her but she didn't look back. She walked to her car. She was grateful for the officers who held back the crowd so she could escape.

As she left the parking lot, her surveillance detail right behind her, and merged into traffic her cell vibrated. She dragged it from her belt and checked the number. The lab.

"Gentry."

"Hey, Bobbie, this is Andy. I got a hit on the only other set of prints on your steering wheel—besides yours, I mean."

Numb, Bobbie wiped her eyes with her sleeve. She'd completely forgotten about having Andy run the prints. "Yeah? What'd you find?"

"They match the name Nicholas Weller."

The name sounded vaguely familiar, but right now she couldn't think clearly. Evidently Shade was an alias. "Anything else?"

"Oh yeah. Sure. I thought I'd heard the name before so I checked it out. Nicholas Weller is the son of Randolph Weller, the most…"

His words faded into the background. She didn't need Andy to tell her who Randolph Weller was— one of the most notorious serial killers on the planet. She understood what this news meant; she simply couldn't react. The damaged heart she had thought no longer capable of feelings was broken.

"Thanks, Andy. Keep this between the two of us, okay?"

"Sure thing. You know I'm always happy to help you out, Bobbie."

She ended the call and tossed the phone aside. Nick Shade was Randolph Weller's son. *Jesus Christ.* Weller had killed his wife—Shade's mother. What kind of sick shit had he seen in his life? Bobbie felt ill. No wonder he'd decided to hunt serial killers. The urge to call Newt and tell him was followed by profound sorrow.

Newt was dead.

A sob wrenched from her throat. Bobbie steeled herself. Her partner…the man she loved like a father was dead. Fury lit inside her. She was going to kill Gaylon Perry.

Today.

Bobbie drove straight to her house on Gardendale. Her cell vibrated again and again. She didn't have to look to know it would be the chief or Owens or somebody else from her team. She couldn't talk to anyone right now. She couldn't talk about Newt.

Her objective at the moment was to get rid of her

surveillance detail. ASAP. If Shade heard the news he would be trying to find her, too. She had to stay focused and she had to make this happen fast.

For that, she needed help.

She climbed out of her car and went inside. The surveillance detail would inform the chief of her whereabouts, so she didn't have much time. She did the usual check and quickly stripped off her suit and work shoes. In record time she pulled on jeans, a tee and her running shoes. She tucked her small Taser into her bra, the knife and sheath she secured to the inside of her left shin. Her Glock she settled in her waistband at the small of her back. Her ankle holster was already in place above her right sneaker.

Once she was back in her car, she drove to the end of the street and pulled over at the curb in front of Javier's place. The usual gang—his bodyguards—was on the porch. She climbed the steps and looked to the guy who generally did the talking.

"I need to see Javier."

The door opened and the man himself jerked his head for her to follow him inside.

She closed the door behind her. "I'm ready for that help you promised me."

Javier turned to face her. "I heard about your partner, *mami*."

The whirlwind of emotions that pressed against her breastbone was nearly too much to bear. "Will you help me?"

He braced his hands against the door on either

side of her and leaned in close. "Whatever you need, if it's within my power, I will help you."

Bobbie blinked back a wave of tears. "I'll drive back to my house and go inside. After a few minutes, I'll go out the back and come here." First she would call the chief and assure him she was at home and that she needed some space to deal with what happened. She would give him something to explain her message to Perry and once he was satisfied, she would move. He had far too much on his plate right now to give her any trouble. "My surveillance detail can't follow me where I'm going. I want them to believe I'm in my house. Can you take me where I need to go?"

He smiled. "It would be my pleasure."

"No bullshit, Javier."

He held his hands up. "You got it, *mami*."

Bobbie drew in a much-needed breath. "Thank you."

Before she was out the door, his voice stopped her.

"Then you will owe me, *mami*."

Bobbie hustled across the porch and down the steps. As she climbed into her Challenger, she figured that Javier would have a hell of a time collecting on her debt.

There was a good chance she'd be dead before tomorrow.

Thirty-Two

The bleeding wouldn't stop.

Gaylon screamed and banged on the steering wheel with his fists.

He'd driven past several urgent cares, but he didn't dare stop at any of them. They were required to report gunshot wounds. Then he'd remembered he had a nurse at his disposal, so he'd put on the jacket his father had left in his mother's car last winter and he'd gone into a chain pharmacy for supplies. The clerk kept looking at his hands but he'd washed them with a bottle of water before going in. The way his hands shook must have made her uncomfortable. Or maybe she'd recognized him. Women were such fucking pathetic excuses for human beings.

Since no blue lights had shown up in his rear-view mirror, he decided the worthless clerk had not recognized him.

Careful of his speed, he gritted his teeth against the pain as he drove. He kept the radio on the local news channel that had announced the cop's death.

The idea of how his death had injured Bobbie almost made getting shot worth it. Just when he'd thought his new plan to lure Bobbie had failed, he heard her voice on the radio.

Tell him I'm waiting for him. He knows the place. I'm ready to finish this now.

Indeed he knew the place. As soon as his wound was taken care of, he would go to her. His heart beat faster. He could hardly wait.

It felt like hours rather than minutes before he reached the house. He gathered the supplies he had purchased and hurried to the door. His fingers fumbled with the key and the locks. His side throbbed with pain. He could feel the blood oozing down his skin.

What if he died?

He shook his head as the lock released. He wasn't going to die. Everything was finally falling into place. He opened the door just a crack to ensure his guests remained as he'd left them. A smile tugged at his lips. All was as it should be. He was quite relieved to be rid of the children. He hated the little beasts. As they grew up they only became worse. So many times he had sat in his classroom and imagined cutting off the various limbs and heads of his students. He'd considered how exciting it would be to rape their torsos as blood gushed from the fresh wounds. Particularly the tall female ones with their beautiful long, dark hair.

LeDoux's eyes were closed. Gaylon kicked him in the side. He made a grunting sound but his eyes never opened. Perhaps he had dosed him too heavily. He would need to be sure LeDoux was fully awake later for the big finale.

It was coming very soon.

The pain in his side reminded him what needed to happen next.

He dropped the bag of supplies on the floor next to Gwen. She jerked, her eyes wide with new terror.

After peeling off his father's coat and tossing it aside, he knelt next to her. "I'm going to remove the tape from your mouth and then I'm going to release your hands. If you try to get away—" he held up the knife he kept handy at all times "—you will regret it in ways you cannot even imagine. Are we clear?"

She nodded her understanding.

"Very well." He removed the tape from her mouth.

"You're bleeding," she said, her voice rusty.

"I need you to attend to my injury." He removed the items from the bag and set them on the floor. Alcohol, sterile pads, tweezers, large sewing needles and nylon thread that were not designed for human flesh but it was the best he could do. Antibacterial ointment, gauze and tape.

He released the cuffs around her wrists. She rubbed at the red, damaged flesh and winced. She pushed up to a sitting position, and then he held still while she inspected the wound. The bullet had gone in on the front right side of his torso. His memory of anatomy eluded him at the moment, but based on the fact that he was still functioning, he felt sure no

vital organs had been damaged. Still, it was imperative the injury was attended to promptly.

He poured alcohol on a couple of sterile pads.
"Clean your hands."

When she had done so, he showed her the knife
again. "Remember to behave."

She nodded, the lead from the noose around her
neck sliding up and down between her breasts, and
quickly picked through the items he'd purchased.
Blood trickled from the wound even as she reached
with shaky hands for gauze to staunch it. "I'll need
to use alcohol to clean the wound. Can you tolerate
the pain? Maybe you need something to take the
edge off."

He grabbed her by the throat and squeezed. "Do
not patronize me, whore!" He squeezed tighter just
to watch her eyes bulge.

When she'd gagged and snorted for about five
seconds he released her.

"Now." He took a breath. "Shall we begin again?"

She nodded quickly and set to the task.

He had to give her credit; once she'd started, her
hands steadied and she worked quickly. He locked
his jaw against the pain and thought of more pleas-
ant times.

His mind took him back to that summer in France
with his friend Kevin. He had fucked and fucked
and fucked. It was that summer he'd found something far more amazing and mind-blowing than
mere sex. Feeling a woman die with his fully erect
penis deep inside her was the most incredible sen-

sation. Her body relaxed so completely, he could go deeper. Nothing touched the climax of murder. Nothing.

Too bad his old friend hadn't shared Gaylon's feelings. He'd sworn he would never tell. Ironically, Gaylon was fairly certain he never had. Still, why take the risk? A couple of years later, he'd looked his old friend up and removed the variable. He doubted anyone would ever find his body in the bottom of that old well on his father's farm.

Oh yes, there was nothing like the thrill of watching life slip away.

He could not wait to empty himself inside Bobbie Gentry as she lay dying.

Thirty-Three

11:00 a.m.

Bobbie wasn't answering her cell.

Nick was worried. He'd heard on the radio about her partner's death. He had to find her. Her emotions were already fragile. Newt's death would be the last straw.

He should have stayed close to her, but he'd needed to keep searching for Perry.

Frustration tightened his lips. He was here for Perry after all…not for Bobbie. This was exactly why he never allowed himself to become involved with the players in a case. His sole mission was to stop the serial killer.

"Damn it!"

He tried her cell again. This time it went straight to voice mail.

Speeding up, he made the turn onto Gardendale and drove to her house. According to his tracker, she was at home. Sure enough, her Challenger was in the driveway and her surveillance detail was on the street. He parked at the curb and climbed out of his vehicle. He waved to the detail before striding up to her door. He knocked. No answer. He knocked again.

A new worry crawled up his spine. He dismissed it. There was no way Bobbie would hurt herself. She wanted Gaylon Perry dead. The only way she was leaving this earth before she accomplished that goal was if someone killed her.

As he returned to his car, one of the uniforms called out to him. "Detective Gentry's partner died a little while ago. She's pretty upset. She might not be up to having company right now."

Nick shook his head. "I heard the news. It's a damn shame. I'll just check on her later."

"Yeah, she was a mess at the hospital," the driver went on.

Impatience pounding in his veins, Nick listened as the two told him how she'd thrown down the gauntlet to all those reporters outside the hospital. Dread hardened in Nick's gut as he walked toward his car.

What the hell have you done, Bobbie?

He drove around the block to the street behind her house. He parked and hustled through the rear yards until he reached the back of her house. He knocked on the back door. Still no answer. More of that foul-tasting worry churned in his gut. He tried the knob. The door opened. He eased into the dark house.

Adrenaline zinged along his nerve endings. Had

Perry already taken her? How had he slipped past her detail?

Most likely the same way you just did.

Inside was deathly quiet. He flipped on lights as he went through the house. In her bedroom, her discarded suit of the day—the one she'd been wearing when she headed to the hospital—lay on the floor. He scrubbed a hand over his jaw. The weapons she carried when running were missing. Her running shoes were gone, as well. If she'd gone for a run the detail would be following her.

Whatever means of transportation she'd used, it was clear Bobbie had left of her own volition and purposely given her detail the slip by exiting the back way.

He returned to his car and started the engine. For about two seconds he considered driving back around and giving the uniforms a heads-up, but then he changed his mind. The last thing he needed was to be detained by the cops. He would check the taxi companies. She could have crossed the property behind her and taken a cab from there.

"Where the hell are you, Bobbie?"

You know the answer.

The news resonated from the radio and he turned up the volume. Maybe something else had happened. Why hadn't she called him? According to the broadcast, the manhunt for Perry had expanded. A cop was dead; of course it had.

The voice on the radio droned on about the loss of one of the city's finest. "It's a real shame," another voice said. "I don't know about you, but I'm still reeling from the message Detective Bobbie Gentry sent to the Storyteller."

A horn blew and Nick swerved back to his side of the middle lane. He struggled to keep his attention on the road as he listened to the report.

"I don't think there's any mystery what Detective Gentry has on her mind," the first voice said. "Let's play that one more time. If one of MPD's finest wants the word out, we should give her a hand making it happen."

Nick's blood ran cold as he waited for the playback.

"Tell him I'm waiting for him," Bobbie's voice, listless and heavy with grief, filled the car. "He knows the place. I'm ready to finish this now."

"Son of a…" Nick slammed on his brakes and executed a U-turn; then he hit the gas hard. He understood exactly what she was doing and where she was going. He wished he knew how long it had been since she'd made that statement.

He could be too late.

When he reached the intersection at Fairground Road blue lights blinked in his rearview mirror.

He scrubbed a hand across his face and considered attempting to outmaneuver the vehicle. Before he could put the thought into action an MPD cruiser skidded to a stop in either direction on Fairground Road. A big black SUV moved around the cruiser in the northbound lane and pulled over next to him.

The rear passenger-side door opened and Agent

Hadden emerged. The front window on that same side powered down and Agent Mason flashed him a tight smile. "We need a few minutes of your time, Mr. Shade. Why don't you join us? We'll have someone take care of your vehicle."

"Keep your hands where I can see them," Hadden ordered.

Nick shut off the engine and got out of his car, his hands visible as the agent requested. He got into the SUV. Hadden climbed in beside him.

"Relax, Mr. Shade," Mason said with a glance in the rearview mirror. "We just have a few questions for you."

Montgomery Police Department, 11:45 a.m.

Nick had expected to be taken to an interview room but that hadn't happened. Mason had brought him to the chief of police's office and then Mason had disappeared. Nick had been sitting here alone for a good ten minutes.

The door behind him opened. He glanced over his shoulder to see Chief Peterson and Agent Mason. Peterson closed the door and took his seat behind his desk. Mason took the chair next to Nick.

"Mr. Shade, you've been spending a lot of time with Detective Gentry," Peterson said. "Can you tell us how the two of you met?"

"We met through a mutual friend. I've been doing research on the Storyteller for quite some time and Bobbie offered to help me." Keeping his tone even grew more difficult with each word.

"Detective Gentry told me you were an expert on serial killers, Mr. Shade," Mason countered.

"You could say that." His pulse rate kept building. He did not have time for this. If he could just keep his cool until they accepted his story and let him walk. *Relax.* The truth was, if Mason's security clearance was high enough he had some knowledge of who Nick was. Typically the feds stayed out of his way and he stayed out of theirs...only there was nothing typical about this case.

"I've run your name, Mr. Shade," Mason said. "You don't seem to exist outside a driver's license. Why is that, Mr. Shade?"

The constant use of his name was a pressure tactic. The agent wanted Nick to feel threatened and uncertain of what might happen next. When, in fact, the agent's body language told a whole different story. He was tense. Though he smiled, his expression was pained. His eyes were clouded with worry. But it was his overly relaxed posture that was the real tell. Agent Mason was terrified that he'd lost control of this investigation. Two people were dead. He had an agent and another hostage missing. He was feeling serious pressure to come up with some sort of break.

"I have no idea, Agent Mason. Maybe I simply haven't accomplished anything Google worthy."

"Let's cut the shit, Mr. Shade," Mason said. "Your real name is Nicholas Weller. The prints on file with the US Army confirmed your identity, and I made a few calls."

Another reason he never got this close. *You screwed up this time.*

"Your father is quite the celebrity at the bureau," Mason said. "I've been bringing Chief Peterson up to speed."

"I have nothing to do with Weller," Nick said before he could quell the defensive reaction.

"Yet you visited him just yesterday," Mason argued.

"I had a question for him." Nick forced himself to relax. Mason was desperate, it was showing.

"I know your little secret, Mr. Shade," Mason warned. "The bureau tolerates what you do, but mark my word, one wrong move and you'll be in a cell next to your daddy before you can blink an eye."

"Mason," Peterson said, "give us a minute."

The agent didn't look happy about it but he obliged. When the door closed behind him Chief Peterson's attention settled on Nick.

"Let me be clear," he said. "I don't give a damn who you are, where you came from or what you've done before today, but if you know anything about Gaylon Perry that will help us stop him I need you to share that information with me right now. If you do not and something happens to Bobbie, I will personally see to it that you regret that mistake for the rest of your life."

"Bobbie sent a message to Perry."

Peterson sighed. "You're talking about her comment to the press this morning."

"Yes."

"We have her under surveillance at Gardendale. I don't want her stepping out that door until we've taken Perry into custody. Her surveillance detail is watching her house and two roving patrols are monitoring the neighborhood. Bobbie and I spoke a short time ago. She understands my concerns and has agreed to stay put. In fact, she suggested I put eyes on the fountain since Perry will be watching for her to show up there based on the message she sent through those damned reporters."

Damn. She had made sure the chief would be focused far away from where she intended to be. Nick hated to be the one to tell him how badly he'd been fooled. "I'm afraid—"

"She's beside herself with grief," the chief cut him off. "She was in the room with Newt when he had his heart attack."

Shit. Nick needed to be out there. Now.

"Her surveillance detail let me know she wouldn't talk to you, either. She may, however, let you in before she does me. It is imperative, Mr. Shade, that we keep her locked down. At this point, she might do anything to get the son of a bitch."

They were wasting time. Nick stood. "You're too late. She's already gone."

"What do you mean? Her vehicle is in the driveway. You were just there."

"I was, and when she didn't answer her door," Shade explained, his patience at an end, "I drove around the block and went to her back door. It was unlocked and she was gone. I would be out there looking for her right now if Mason hadn't detained me."

Peterson rounded his desk. "I hope for your sake, Mr. Shade, you're not holding anything back."

"I want to find her as badly as you do."

As surprising as the revelation was…it was true.

Thirty-Four

Bobbie stared through the car window at the house that had once been her home. The place where so many happy memories were made. The place where she thought she would live the rest of her life.

The place where her life had ended. She took a big breath and reached for the door handle.

"You sure about this, *mami*?"

She turned to the man seated next to her in the Camaro. She appreciated his help, but she had to do the rest on her own.

"I expect you to stick by our deal, Javier. Do not tell anyone where you brought me and don't hang around. I want you to get the hell out of here."

He put a hand on his heart and the other in the air as if taking an oath. "On my honor, I will tell no one." He nodded to the driver and the other thug in the front seat. "My *eses* will tell no one."

Bobbie reached for the door once more.

"Hold on, *mami*."

"What?" She was out of patience.

He reached for the chain around his neck. When he lifted it over his head Bobbie recognized the Saint Christopher medal. "You should wear this." He placed the necklace over her head. "It was my mother's. She gave it to me before she died. I was just a kid living in squalor in Mexico City, but I remember her telling me that St. Christopher protected travelers. She wanted him to keep me safe in my life's journey. I think now you need it more than me."

Bobbie nodded. She didn't speak. If she dared, she might lose it and she couldn't do that right now.

She watched until Javier's car disappeared and then she turned back to her house. It was the middle of the day; most everyone in the neighborhood was at work. Bobbie unlocked the front door and walked inside, then locked it once more.

She went into the living room. The shelves on either side of the fireplace were the road maps of the life she had shared with her family. The books they had read. The movies they had watched, and the photo albums that held the images captured of those wonderful days. She crossed the room and picked up the small clay bowl Jamie had made at day camp last summer. It was lopsided and a little bumpy, but she had loved it when her son gave it to her for her birthday. It was supposed to be pink but it had turned out more of a faded rose. As much as Bobbie loved it, she couldn't bear to look at it every day. She couldn't bear to feel the incredible loss. A part of her was missing now and she would never, ever be whole again.

Placing it carefully back on the shelf, she wandered through the kitchen. The back door was still secure. He hadn't been here yet. *Good.* She wanted some time first. Memories of her husband's beautiful smile and the way he kissed her and made love to her flashed one after the other through her mind. He had been the cook. He always had dinner ready for her when she came home from a long day. It didn't matter how stressful his own day at the university had been.

There wasn't a place in this house he hadn't touched and helped to make it their home. Her heart ached. She missed him so very badly.

Slowly she climbed the stairs and went to the room they had shared. She curled up on their bed for a moment. She smoothed her hand over the inviting comforter. She thought of all the times she had fallen asleep in her husband's arms. All the times they had made love. All the precious moments they had shared.

This day…this step was for him. Loving her had cost him his life and now she intended to avenge that horrible, horrible wrong.

Finally, she went to her son's room. The moment she walked inside, her senses were overwhelmed with the memories of her sweet boy. His toys… his blanket…

"I should've taken better care of you, baby. I

am so sorry. Mommy couldn't keep this monster away."

Bobbie picked up his favorite teddy bear and hugged it, inhaling the lingering scent of her little boy.

A shift in the air or maybe the softest sound set her senses on alert. The bear fell from her hands and she moved to the door.

The sound of the back door opening echoed like a giant mallet slamming against steel.

He was here.

Bobbie reached for her Glock with her right hand. With her left, she palmed her stun gun, wrapping her fingers around it, hiding the small but effective weapon from sight. She moved soundlessly along the upstairs hall and then carefully down the staircase.

If it was Shade or someone from the department they would have called her name.

It was Perry.

She could feel him.

The entry hall and living room were empty. He was in the kitchen.

She moved swiftly through the dining room to approach from the opposite side of the kitchen. She paused at the refrigerator since it allowed for some amount of cover. No sign of him. Had he gone into the garage? The back door was closed. Braced for the unexpected, she stepped to the back door and surveyed the yard. Nothing. He had to be in the garage.

She stepped soundlessly to the door that led into the garage. It was ajar. The lights were on beyond it. Adrenaline burned through her veins.

Adopting a firing position, she elbowed the door open and stepped into the garage.

Naked save for the duct tape across her mouth and the yellow noose around her neck, Gwen stood next to James's car. Her hands were bound behind her back. A chain linked her ankles. Her body was marked and bloody from the torture Perry had already inflicted. Bobbie's soul ached for her.

When she would have taken a step toward Gwen, her eyes widened and she shook her head. A quick scan of the garage and no sign of Perry told Bobbie he was hiding. The hair on the back of Bobbie's neck prickled. She leaned her head toward the door behind her, and Gwen nodded.

Bobbie leaped away from the door and swiveled, leveling her weapon. The position put her between Perry and Gwen.

Perry pushed the door closed, revealing himself. "Hello, Detective."

Long blond hair, pink dress... The little girl hanging limp in his arms sent Bobbie's heart plummeting. The child's eyes were closed. Bobbie tried to assess if she was breathing. "Put the little girl down." She steadied her aim on the bastard.

"I searched three neighborhoods for a little boy." Perry sighed dramatically. He held a knife pressed against the child's throat. "Alas, there was only this little girl. Her mother is probably running up and down the street screaming her name now."

"Put her down now or I will shoot." Bobbie zeroed in on his head. She could make the shot.

"If you pull that trigger, I will slice her carotid artery. Do you think you and Gwen can save her?"

"This is between you and me," Bobbie snarled. "Let them go."

"The key fob is in your dead husband's car. Put Gwen in the trunk and get behind the wheel. Little Darla and I will get into the backseat. You'll drive. Agent LeDoux is counting on you as well, Detective. I'm certain you don't want him to die, either."

Heart pounding, Bobbie considered her options and made the only choice. She went to the driver's side and got the key. When she'd popped the trunk, she helped Gwen inside. Tears flowed down the nurse's cheeks and her body trembled. Before closing the lid, Bobbie put the stun gun in her hand and closed her shaking fingers around it. A knowing gaze passed between them.

She shut the lid and stared at the sadistic bastard across the room. "What're you waiting for?"

"Place your Glock, the backup piece you carry and your cell phone at your feet before you get behind the wheel."

Bobbie did as he asked.

"And the knife," he ordered.

When she'd done the same with the knife, he said, "Get in the car."

By the time she'd settled behind the wheel he

was getting into the backseat with the little girl. He held her Glock now rather than the knife.

"Where to?"

"Drive. I'll give you the directions as we go. Any wrong moves and the girl dies."

"How do I know she's not dead already?" Hand shaking in spite of her best efforts, she hit the remote for the overhead door.

"I guess you'll have to take my word for it."

Bobbie held her breath as she hit the start button. She prayed the engine wouldn't start. Maybe the battery had died. It had been eight months since it had been driven. The engine roared to life and her heart sank.

Perry's gaze collided with hers in the rearview mirror. "I never leave anything to chance, Detective."

Tamping back a blast of rage, Bobbie reached for the gearshift and her attention stumbled on a wallet-sized photo of her and Jamie. Her heart squeezed painfully. Before James even drove the car, he tucked that picture on the console. *Can't go anywhere without my babies.* His voice reverberated through her soul.

"I'd hate to soil your husband's nice car by slitting her throat right here."

Bobbie's gaze shot to the rearview mirror once more.

"Drive," the bastard ordered.

Jaw locked with fury, Bobbie backed from the garage and automatically hit the remote to close the door once more. When she'd driven out of the neighborhood, she stopped at the intersection for further directions. She had not been inside this car since before James died. His scent lingered... He'd been so thrilled when she handed him the key fob.

"Take a right."

Shaking off the memories, she made the turn onto Pike Road.

"No speeding or erratic driving," he reminded her. "We wouldn't want this sweet little girl to go home with her head missing."

Bobbie would not allow him to hurt that little girl and she would help Gwen and LeDoux escape. No matter the cost.

"People are so very predictable," Perry announced. "Even those married to a cop. I'm guessing your husband was the one who hid the spare key to your house."

Bobbie's heart banged her sternum, but she said nothing. She refused to interact with the bastard. The sound of his voice made her want to stab an ice pick into her eardrums.

"You needn't answer, Detective. I'm confident that was the case. You see—when I saw you for the first time I knew I had to have you. I came to your home when you were both at work. The spare key was under the concrete turtle on the patio."

Hurt coiled in her chest. *Make sure you put it where no one will think to look.* She'd teased James about the extra key. They'd never had one until he locked himself and Jamie out of the house. She, as usual, was working late. She and Newt had driven by to let them in. Perry was right. James had hidden the key, and she didn't even remember where. Her husband had told her, but she'd been too busy to listen.

"I've been in your home many, many times, Bobbie. You really should have taken better care of your family."

His words were like stakes driven into her heart. The bastard's scent had started to permeate the car and she wanted to vomit.

"Was this sporty car a way of making up for your absence, Detective?"

Bobbie clenched her teeth until she expected them to crack. She refused to be goaded by the son of a bitch.

"I knew it was," he taunted. "That's why I chose this one rather than your more practical car. I wanted you to remember how you failed your sweet little family."

He was right. She hadn't taken care of her family. They were dead, and she was responsible.

Her fingers trembled with the knowledge that no one had driven this car since the last time James had. She hadn't even driven her own...not since her family was taken from her. She hadn't been able to live in their home. She hadn't been able to live at all. She merely existed.

For one purpose: to kill this monster.

"I've waited too long for you, Bobbie." His voice was low, thick with desire. "All good things come to those who wait," he singsonged. "The ending to your story is going to be amazing."

She said nothing. Just drove.

He was right, though, it was going to be amazing.

Thirty-Five

Gardendale Drive, 2:00 p.m.

Forensic techs were still combing through Bobbie's house. Reporters were being held at bay at the end of the block. And the people in charge stood in the driveway having a conference about what they weren't finding.

Nick refused to waste more time.

"You're won't find any answers here."

Chief Peterson turned from his conversation with Agent Mason and Lieutenant Owens. "What do you propose we do, Mr. Shade? We have units at the Ryan Ridge house. She isn't there. We've issued a BOLO and every cop within fifty miles is searching for Bobbie."

His frank statement would have pissed Nick off, except he heard the desperation in his words and read the fear in his eyes and in his posture. Unfortunately, desperation and fear weren't going to get the job done.

"What will you do six hours from now when it's dark?" Nick asked with equal candor.

The chief opened his mouth to respond but hesitated and then reached for his cell phone. He stepped away from the huddle.

Nick held his temper and dug for more patience. He had no desire to stand around here and play this waiting game. If Bobbie wasn't with Perry already, she would be soon. She obviously left her house on foot and picked up a taxi. Every minute they wasted here was one more Perry would have to torture her—assuming he didn't go straight for the kill.

"The whole city is looking for Detective Gentry," Mason reminded Nick as if he didn't know. "What else would you suggest we do?"

"You mean besides checking the house where she lived with her family for any evidence she or Perry has been there?"

"This was Detective Gentry's last known location," Mason argued. "Starting here was proper protocol. The officers on the scene at Ryan Ridge checked the perimeter as well as the windows. The home is secure with no indication Detective Gentry has been there."

Peterson returned, ending the pointless conversation. The fear in his expression had evolved into something more like defeat. Nick's pulse reacted.

"Perry's gray Prius was found three streets away from Bobbie's Ryan Ridge home."

"We should move our efforts there," Mason announced.

Grinding his teeth to hold back a sarcastic, *You think?*, Nick followed Peterson and Mason.

Ryan Ridge, 2:50 p.m.

Nick walked through the first floor of the house. Nothing appeared to be disturbed. He climbed the stairs slowly, his senses absorbing the resignation he felt in this sad home. Rather than comb through the rooms, he went straight to the child's room. If she came upstairs, she would go there for sure.

He surveyed the toys on the floor. The bed. His gaze went back to the floor near the bed. He crossed the room and picked up the teddy bear. The last time he'd walked through this house the teddy bear had been on the bed.

"What the hell have you done, Bobbie?" He left the stuffed animal on the bed where it belonged and moved back to the staircase. He didn't need additional evidence to tell him what was abundantly clear. Bobbie had sent Perry a message and they'd rendezvoused. *Here.*

"We found something in the garage."

Nick paused halfway down the staircase and listened as the evidence tech spoke to the chief of police in the living room below.

"We found a smear of blood on the wall behind the door, on the garage side, that exits from the kitchen."

"Show me," Peterson ordered.

Nick descended the stairs. Renewed worry inched its way up his spine. They had to move quickly and still he doubted they would be in time. Her partner's death had obliterated any reason she had left. Bobbie had thrown caution to the wind and taken an enormous risk to accomplish the only thing that mattered to her anymore—killing Perry.

All Nick needed was a way to communicate with Perry. He hoped Bobbie would think to use what Nick had shown her. The bastard's mother was the one potential piece of leverage they had.

When the chief and the tech had moved back into the kitchen, Nick stepped forward. "I'd like to have a look in the garage."

The chief turned to the tech. "Have you wrapped up in there?"

"Yes, sir."

Peterson gave Nick a nod. As he took the single step down to the garage, the sensation of emptiness assaulted him. He considered where the blood had been found. Newton had insisted that he'd shot Perry so the blood could be his. Perry had a nurse at his disposal. She may have done her best to patch him up but the bleeding may have started again.

Nick stood in the empty spot next to Bobbie's forgotten Subaru. How had Perry gotten into her house with no signs of forced entry? Had the keys to the vehicle that had been sitting in the spot where Nick now stood been hanging on a hook somewhere?

Peterson joined him. "We've issued a BOLO on the BMW that belonged to James. If you have thoughts that will help us find her..."

"He was here." Nick gestured to the door leading

into the kitchen. It stood open. "He hid behind the door as she came into the garage. The blood was either on his clothes or had seeped through whatever dressing he had over the wound."

Relief filled the chief of police's face. Mason's expression remained skeptical. He argued, "You can't be sure."

Nick ignored the pompous ass. He walked slowly around the space where James Gentry's car would have been parked. There was no blood or anything else that looked out of place. He paused at the shelving unit that stood against the wall. Cans of paint that matched the interior colors in the home lined the shelves. The tip of something shiny, like metal, stuck out from under the lowest shelf. He got down on his knees and had a look. It was scarcely more than three inches off the floor but…

His gaze stalled on several objects. The first was Bobbie's cell. Nick covertly pocketed it. "We need that evidence tech back out here."

Peterson issued the command and the tech came running.

Nick moved out of his way. "There's a small handgun and what looks like a knife under there."

A few sweeps under the shelf and Nick's worst fears were confirmed. The backup piece Bobbie kept strapped to her ankle and the sheathed knife she carried lay on the floor. When a second knife— a general purpose kitchen knife—slid out, the scenario cleared in his mind.

"He was here." Nick gestured to the wall by the

door. "Waiting for her. That kitchen knife was his weapon. Now he has her Glock."

"Chief!" Another cop stuck his head through the door. "Dispatch got a call from a lady in the next subdivision whose blond-haired three-year-old is missing. It's a little girl this time."

When the chief and Mason had rushed away to follow the new lead, Nick approached one of the uniforms outside. "You can take me back to CID now."

The officer looked at Nick, and then in the direction Peterson had disappeared. "Is that what the chief said?"

Nick nodded. "There's nothing else I can do here."

"Yes, sir."

Nick didn't breathe easy until he and the officer were well away from the neighborhood. If he was lucky he'd be in his car and long gone before the chief or Mason remembered they'd left him behind.

Help me find you, Bobbie.

Thirty-Six

Though it was still hours before dark, the interior of the abandoned house was dim. Bobbie's skin started to crawl the instant she stepped inside. The final stretch of country road they had traveled was wooded. Incredibly the location was only a few miles from the city limit. This was one of the areas on Shade's list of most likely places, but he would never find them in time.

Bobbie steeled herself. As long as she killed Perry that was all that mattered.

What about the little girl? And Gwen and LeDoux?

Bobbie closed her eyes against the complication. She couldn't allow Perry to take any more lives.

Stop overanalyzing. Focus.

The little girl had roused and was curled in a ball in the corner. Her soft sobbing tore at Bobbie's heart. LeDoux was unconscious, but his torso rose and fell rhythmically. He wasn't dead; just drugged, she suspected. He was secured, face-down, to the floor. His body didn't bear the same marks that Gwen's did, but the toes of one foot had been smashed.

The bastard hadn't gotten Gwen out of the trunk yet.

Hopefully Bobbie could get close enough to Gwen for a handoff of the stun gun. Perry was wounded. Bobbie smiled to herself. Newt had gotten the son of a bitch good. He'd bled through the bandage on his side. Even his shirt was bloody. The idea that it likely hurt like hell made Bobbie very happy.

As if he'd read her thoughts, Perry gestured to her with the Glock. "Take off your clothes."

Bobbie stilled, her heart pounding.

"I said," he repeated, "take off your clothes."

Just do it. She had known this part was coming.

She took her time removing the T-shirt, then dropped it to the floor. Gritting her teeth, she reached behind her back and released the clasp of her bra. The feel of his eyes on her as she tossed it on top of the tee made her sick to her stomach.

Don't think about it.

She toed off her sneakers.

"The socks, too."

Lifting one foot and then the other, she peeled off the socks and dropped them onto the shoes. With resignation, she shucked her jeans. They landed on the pile. Drawing in a deep breath she reached for her panties and removed them.

She stood straight and steady. So what if he saw

her scarred body? It was the last thing he would see if she had her way.

"Turn around."

His voice was low, husky. He was enjoying this. *Sadistic bastard.*

Wishing she were the one with the gun, she did as he commanded, turning until her back was to him.

He gasped.

After what felt like an eternity, he tossed two pairs of metal handcuffs on the floor near her. She'd already spotted the chains secured to eyebolts in the floor.

"Do your ankles first."

He didn't have to draw her a diagram of what he wanted. The distance between the eyebolts ensured her legs would be spread. She would be secured in the same position as she had been all those months ago.

Inside, where he couldn't see, she trembled.

A few feet away were the chains and eyebolts and a stained mattress where Gwen had been secured. The bloodstains on the mattress spoke of what he'd put the poor woman through already. What he intended to put Bobbie through...*again.*

Once both she and Gwen were locked in place, there would be little hope for any of them. The worst travesty would be the little girl.

You cannot fail, Bobbie!

Mommy keeps the monsters away.

"Now secure your left hand," Perry ordered, pitching another set of cuffs on the floor.

Bobbie fumbled with the handcuffs. She had to twist her torso and reach as far as she could. On her third failed attempt Perry stamped over to the child. He jammed the muzzle into her head, making her cry harder. "Do not try my patience, Detective."

Bobbie tightened the handcuff around her left wrist and snapped it into place.

It's pretty cool being married to a superhero.

The words her husband had said to her so many times whispered through her mind. *Only I wasn't a superhero then, and I'm damned sure not now.*

Perry hurried over to her and, careful to place the gun on the floor well out of her reach, he secured her right hand.

The click reverberated in her brain as if he'd put a bullet there.

He moved away. A few seconds later she heard him go out the door. For Gwen, she supposed. He would likely force her to attend to his wound again before securing her. Bobbie had noticed the first-aid supplies. If he released Gwen to change his bandage she would have a chance to act.

If Gwen wasn't too defeated.

No. Gwen had warned Bobbie where Perry was in the garage. Her fingers had clutched at the stun gun. She was not defeated yet.

The door opened and Perry came back inside leading Gwen like a dog on a short leash. Her raw wounds made Bobbie cringe. She deeply regretted that Gwen had been forced to endure such horrendous torture. No human should have to suffer like that at the hands of another.

Perry released her. "I'm going to remove your handcuffs so you can check my wound. You may need to redo the stitches. Catching that little bitch—" he gestured to the child "—may have damaged your previous work." He pressed the barrel of the Glock to Gwen's head. "If you make a mistake, I will kill you. Do not overestimate your value. Beyond your nursing skills, you are of little use to me now. You've only lived this long so Bobbie could watch you die."

Bobbie hoped Gwen remembered to keep the small stun gun hidden from view by holding it in her closed palm where he couldn't see.

The snap that signaled the release of handcuffs had Bobbie holding her breath. If he'd spotted the stun gun he hadn't reacted.

Bobbie dared to twist her head so she could see. Perry gestured to the first-aid supplies. "Hurry."

Gwen clambered to the pile of items. Her ankles remained chained so any fast movements were out of the question. She crouched down and picked up a wad of gauze. Bobbie's heart thudded so hard she could hardly breathe as Gwen pushed upward and returned to Perry.

Since the wound was on his right side, he held his arm away from his body, but the Glock was still fairly close to Gwen's head. Bobbie held her breath as Gwen lifted his shirt with her left hand.

Her right was fisted around the gauze. Where was the stun gun?

A sizzle and pop sounded an instant before Perry screamed.

The Glock discharged, and then hit the floor.

Perry staggered backward and collapsed like a deflated air puppet.

"Where's the gun?" Bobbie cried.

Sobbing, Gwen scrambled across the floor and tore at Perry's pockets. "I have to get the key."

Bobbie craned her neck, trying to see where the Glock had landed. "You need the gun, Gwen."

Gwen cried out in relief when she held up the key. She clambered over to Bobbie. Her hands shook so hard she could hardly get the key in the tiny hole.

Bobbie smiled up at her, hoping to calm her. "Get the gun first, okay?"

Gwen stalled, her entire body shaking.

"You're doing great," Bobbie assured her. "Just get the gun and—"

The blast of the weapon exploded in the room and the top of Gwen's head flew off.

Blood and brain matter splattered Bobbie's face.

Screams filled the air.

Gwen collapsed beside Bobbie, her eyes wide with surprise or disbelief.

It wasn't until her lungs started to burn that Bobbie realized she was the one screaming. She shifted her gaze to the monster struggling to his feet, her Glock in his right hand. "I will kill you," she promised.

He towered over Bobbie, the weapon hanging at his side. "Look what you made me do, Detective."

He got down on all fours, his hands and knees on either side of her. "Now I'm going to have to hurry, just in case someone heard that shot. You'll have to help me, Bobbie." He leaned down and licked blood from her face. "Who's going to die next? The child or the agent? You pick."

She tried to pull free of her restraints, fury screaming from her throat. She couldn't stop it.

He laughed, leaned close again. "Is that all you can do, Bobbie?"

With every ounce of strength and anger she possessed, she head-butted him.

Perry drew away and howled in pain.

"Let me loose and I'll show you what I can do, motherfucker."

He glared at her, blood dripping from his nose. He reached for his fly and made a ravenous sound. "You know just what to do to make me want you, Bobbie. I can't wait to be inside you again."

Fear exploded in her chest.

"No!"

Bobbie swiveled her head to look at the man chained facedown to the floor a few feet away. She'd thought LeDoux was unconscious.

"Always picking on women, aren't you, Perry?" LeDoux taunted. "Not man enough to take on someone your own size, is that it?"

Bobbie shook her head, but it was too late. Perry was already moving away from her and toward LeDoux. He straddled him and ripped his jeans open. Bobbie looked away and tugged harder at her restraints.

"I haven't mixed things up like this in decades," Perry mocked, "but I'm quite certain it's like riding a bicycle."

Perry groaned in satisfaction and LeDoux made a sound…not a scream, more a whimper of defeat. Bobbie squeezed her eyes shut and bit her lips together to hold back her own screams.

"Mmm," Perry crowed, "you are so tight, Agent LeDoux. And so hot."

LeDoux moaned in agony. The sound of the bastard thrusting had Bobbie squeezing her eyes shut more tightly. Memories of all those weeks he had tortured her…raped her…swam in her head. The smell of him, the sound of his breathing and the *smack, smack* of skin as he pounded into her…

"Later, when I've finished my work with the lovely detective," Perry said, "I'm going to sever your balls and cock from your body, Agent LeDoux, and shove them down your throat. It'll be interesting to see what comes first—choking to death or bleeding out."

Bobbie had to do something. Determination burned through the fear and uncertainty. The photo Nick had shown her bloomed into vivid focus in her mind.

She forced her eyes open and turned just in time

to see the sick piece of shit fastening his trousers. His side was bleeding worse now. *Die, you son of a bitch.*

"Now." He straddled Gwen's body and removed the noose from her neck, allowing her head to drop back to the floor like a loose, fractured bowling ball. "Since time is of the essence, we should begin, Detective."

Squashing the agony and fear rising inside her, Bobbie produced a smile. "Poor Gaylon, you have no idea what's happened." She shook her head. "He took her, and now she's going to be very upset with you."

"You should be well aware, Detective, that mind games don't work with me." Perry crouched next to her and traced the fingertips of his left hand from her throat to her navel, pausing a moment at her breasts.

As hard as she tried not to react, her body trembled.

Perry smiled. "Let's not waste any more time." He yanked the Saint Christopher charm from her neck and dragged the bloodstained noose over her head.

Bobbie's heart thundered. "You don't care that he took her? He told me he's going to cut her into little pieces and mail her to you in prison."

Gaylon tightened the noose around her neck to the point she could scarcely breathe. "Very well, Bobbie. I'll play your little game. Who did he take?"

"Your mother, of course. Loved the red dress you picked for her to be buried in. It covered all those hideous scars so well."

Thirty-Seven

Gardendale Drive, 4:15 p.m.

Nick slowed as he passed Bobbie's house. The crime scene tape on her door made his gut clench.

She'd left from here and somehow gone to the Ryan Ridge house. Perry had taken her from there. Her cell phone vibrated with another incoming call. He dragged it from his pocket and checked the screen. She had dozens of missed calls from the members of her team and the chief.

"Why didn't you wait for me, Bobbie?"

Before coming here Nick had questioned the clerk at the convenience store down the road from the Ryan Ridge house. Cops were crawling all over the subdivisions in the neighborhood, questioning residents and looking for anything at all that would point them in the right direction.

They weren't going to find what they needed.

Nick's gaze shifted to the far end of the street. Quintero lorded over this neighborhood; nothing happened here without his knowledge. He had no doubt seen Bobbie leave.

Nick eased off the brake and headed in that direction. Anticipation had his pulse racing. He parked at the house he and Bobbie had visited after LeDoux's shirt and badge had been discovered at her door. He emerged and walked across the yard. The usual crew lounged on the porch.

The biggest of the five said, "He's waiting for you."

Not entirely surprised, Nick walked to the door and went inside without the formality of a pat down. Then again, since he wasn't wearing a jacket it was fairly obvious that he wasn't armed.

Quintero sat on the sofa, one of his men seated on either side of him. What looked like a porn flick played on a wall-mounted television. Quintero raised the remote and muted the sound.

"We need privacy," he announced.

The room cleared.

Quintero settled his attention on Nick. "Before I trust you, *amigo*, I will know your connection to Detective Gentry."

Nick's anticipation sharpened. "If—" he emphasized the word "—you waste whatever time we have left before that son of a bitch kills Bobbie, I will see that you regret it."

One side of Quintero's mouth lifted in a half smile. "Your threats mean nothing to me. I ask a simple question. If time is wasted, it is on you."

Nick decided the truth would serve him better. "I

hunt serial killers. I'm here for Perry. Bobbie and I have been working together to find him."

Quintero looked impressed. "You kill the motherfuckers?"

"I stop them."

Quintero nodded. "Like a vampire hunter."

"You could say that."

Quintero stood. "Bobbie came to me." He shrugged. "I guess you were not around."

The jab shouldn't have bothered him, but it did.

"She said the po-po were watching her and she needed a favor." He grinned. "I've been trying for months to get me some of that so I figured here was my chance."

Rage washed over Nick before he could check the reaction. The bastard eyeing him noticed.

"I see how it is. You got a thing for her, too, don't you, hunter?"

Nick ignored the question. "What kind of favor did she want?"

"She needed a ride to her other house."

"You dropped her off there?"

"That's what she asked me to do." Quintero folded his arms over his chest in a classic defensive maneuver.

He was lying. It was far more than the folding over of the arms. It was the quick glance away rather than hold Nick's gaze. It was the ever so subtle shift of his weight as if he were bracing for battle.

"Did you come straight back here after dropping her off?"

Quintero held his gaze for a long moment. "I did." He shrugged. "But two of my *eses* stayed behind. Funny thing is, our detective didn't stay too long before she left in a BMW. It must have been in the garage."

Blood roaring in his ears, Nick asked, "Was she alone?"

Quintero shook his head. "There was someone in the backseat, but that someone stayed hunkered down like he didn't want to be seen."

"Did your people follow her?"

Quintero nodded.

"Take me there," Nick demanded. "Now."

"I can do that," Quintero agreed. "If you ask nicely."

Rage roared through Nick. He held it back, his fingers curling into fists with the effort. "Trust me, Quintero—this is me being nice."

"Aiight then."

Nick followed Quintero and two of his men to the Camaro waiting at the curb. As he loaded into the front passenger seat, Nick reached for Bobbie's phone. He pulled up the number for Sergeant Holt.

He hesitated only a second. Bobbie was going to need all the backup he could bring.

If she was still alive.

Thirty-Eight

LeDoux lay so damned still, his eyes closed. But he was alive and so was she. Bobbie's heart squeezed with pain when she thought of Gwen. She lay on the floor next to her. And the poor little girl. She had gone quiet, too exhausted and terrified even to sob any longer. Her little chest rose and fell with shuddering breaths.

Perry paced the floor. She had given him Shade's number and told him to call if he didn't believe her. Evidently afraid it was a setup, he hadn't done so. He just kept pacing.

Perry abruptly walked out the door, slamming it behind him.

Bobbie's heart shuddered. She winced as she scanned the floor around Gwen's body. Where was that key? Then she saw it lying near Gwen's feet.

"Little girl!" Bobbie whispered as loudly as she dared. She couldn't hear Perry so she had no idea what he was doing outside or when he would walk back in.

The child didn't move, but she heard Bobbie. The rhythm of her breathing changed.

"Please help me," Bobbie urged. "There's a key on the floor, and I need you to get it for me."

The little girl raised her head and peered across the room.

"Hurry," Bobbie urged. If Perry suddenly came back inside to find the little girl helping her, he would kill the child the way he had Gwen. Fear expanded in Bobbie's chest. What else could she do?

The child got up and walked tentatively over to Bobbie.

They were all dead anyway. Bobbie took a breath. "See that key on the floor next to her feet?"

The child looked at the floor where the key lay. She blinked once, twice.

"Can you pick it up and unlock this thing on my hand?" She moved her right hand to show her what she meant.

The little girl bent down, her pink dress falling into the blood, and picked up the key.

"There's a little hole. Come closer and you can see it."

While the little girl moved closer, Bobbie listened for Perry. "Now stick that key into the hole."

Sweat beaded on Bobbie's forehead. Her heart slammed mercilessly against her rib cage. *Please, please, don't let me get this baby hurt.*

The key fell out of the hole and hit the floor.

Bobbie's heart lunged into her throat.

The little girl's eyes widened, and she looked to Bobbie.

There was still no sound outside.

"Try again," Bobbie urged softly.

She picked up the key and put it in the hole.

"Can you turn it?"

The little girl's lips pressed together as she struggled to do as Bobbie asked. *Hurry!*

The cuff around Bobbie's right wrist popped open.

The key hit the floor again. Bobbie snatched it up and released her left hand. "Go back and stay in the corner," she urged the little girl. "Be very quiet."

Eyes still wide with fear, the child nodded.

Bobbie had just released her right ankle when the little girl tripped over Gwen's body.

Bobbie reached for the final cuff.

The door swung open and Perry stormed back in.

His gaze lit first on the child and then on Bobbie.

She dropped the key and dove for the gun he'd left on the floor.

Perry threw himself atop her.

Bobbie's fingers closed around the Glock.

Perry rolled her onto her back, twisting her left leg, which was still chained to the floor. Bobbie ignored the pain and squeezed the trigger.

The bullet whizzed past his right ear. Perry flinched and grabbed her right arm, forcing the barrel away from his head.

Bobbie rammed her right knee into his groin.

His eyes bulged and his mouth gaped, but he didn't let go of her arm.

She rammed harder with her knee. This time he dodged the move and forced the muzzle against her forehead.

"I will still fuck you after you're dead," Perry warned.

Fear coursed like thick, dark oil through her veins.

"Don't let him win, Bobbie."

LeDoux's hoarse words were like gasoline poured on a fire. Strength from some place deep inside her rushed into her arms and she strained to move the weapon away from her face and toward Perry.

"Not if I fuck you first," she growled.

Bobbie squeezed the trigger.

The bullet bored through Perry's shoulder. He howled in pain.

The little girl screamed.

Bobbie shoved him off her and scrambled as far away as she could. Shaking so hard she could scarcely hold the Glock, she fumbled for the key with her free hand. "You move," she warned, "and I'll blow your head off."

Hunched over and clutching his shoulder, he glowered at her. "Look at the brave detective," he jeered. "Trying to make up for letting her family down."

Bobbie released her left ankle and struggled to her feet. Pain shot up her leg. She winced. "Shut up."

Perry laughed, his face twisted with his own agony. "You couldn't protect them—could you, Bobbie?"

Bobbie wiped the blood from her face with her forearm, fury expanding in her chest. "Something else your mother and I had in common. She couldn't protect you either, could she? Maybe she didn't want to. Is that why you've spent all this time raping and murdering women who reminded you of her?"

"If he touched my mother," Perry threatened, "I will—"

"Nothing," Bobbie promised. She smiled. "Because you're going to be in hell where you belong."

"Gentry, let me loose!" LeDoux shouted. "Now, goddamn it!"

Bobbie didn't dare take her eyes off Perry. "Give me a minute." She considered her options for getting the little girl to safety. Alone outside she could get lost in the woods. "Hey, little girl!"

Like a rabid dog, Perry's head whipped around toward the child.

The little girl lifted her gaze to Bobbie's, her entire body shaking.

"I want you to turn around toward the wall and close your eyes," Bobbie told her, her aim never leaving Perry. "Whatever you do, don't look."

The little girl did as she was told. Whatever happened next, Bobbie didn't want the child to see. She'd seen too much already.

Perry grinned at Bobbie even as blood oozed from the wound in his shoulder, soaking the T-shirt he wore. "What're you going to do, Bobbie?" His body shuddered. "Blow my head off?" he mocked.

"Won't you go to prison for killing an unarmed man?"

Keeping the barrel steady on Perry, she eased toward LeDoux. All she had to do was release one hand and he could do the rest.

"Don't move," she reminded Perry.

"Whatever you say, Detective." He watched her, that disgusting grin seemingly frozen on his lips.

It took three attempts but she managed to get one of LeDoux's hands free. He grabbed the key and did the rest while Bobbie moved to where her clothes lay in a pile near Gwen's body. Her heart ached for the poor woman. Bobbie clenched her jaw. She would make him pay.

LeDoux groaned as he stood.

"Can you walk?" His foot was swollen and turning nasty colors.

"Yeah."

"Get your clothes on and take the little girl outside."

LeDoux cried out as he dragged on his jeans.

"I need medical attention," Perry demanded. "My cell phone is in my pocket. You have a duty to call for assistance."

Bobbie ignored him. She grabbed her jeans and worked at getting them on one-handed.

"Let me have the gun." LeDoux moved up beside her.

"Take the girl outside," Bobbie countered as she slipped the rope off her neck, and then pulled the tee she'd been wearing over her head. "Do it now,

LeDoux." She stuck one arm through a sleeve, passed the Glock to the other hand to finish.

LeDoux stared at Perry, saying nothing. His nostrils flared with the rage expanding inside him.

"Take the girl outside," Bobbie repeated, her pulse hammering in her ears. She did not want LeDoux to challenge her on this. Perry could not walk away from this place. Whatever the cost, she would not let that happen.

Finally LeDoux nodded. Bobbie sagged with relief.

"I need medical attention," Perry repeated.

LeDoux paused midway across the room. Bobbie held her breath. When he started walking again, she dared to breathe.

Perry shot to his feet and reached for LeDoux with his uninjured arm.

Bobbie fired.

Perry fell against LeDoux.

The little girl screamed.

LeDoux shoved the bastard to the floor. Bobbie rushed to where he lay. Blood bloomed and spread quickly around his waist.

For a long minute she and LeDoux only stood there, staring down at Perry.

Hardly able to breathe with the emotions rushing through her body, Bobbie lifted her gaze to LeDoux. "Thank you for stopping him from raping me… again."

He nodded before meeting her gaze. "Never tell.

For me," he urged, his gaze saying more than his words. "Never tell."

She nodded in understanding. "Go. Take the girl outside."

Before LeDoux could do as she asked the door burst inward.

Bobbie swung her aim in that direction.

Shade.

She lowered her weapon.

Shade looked from her to the dying man on the floor, and then to Gwen's body.

Holt and Bauer pushed in around him.

The urge to collapse was nearly overwhelming. Bobbie shook it off. "Wait outside," she said, looking from one to the next, her gaze landing lastly on Shade. "All of you."

No one moved. Time seemed to suddenly stand still as they all considered the situation.

LeDoux was the first to act. He crossed the room, picked up the little girl and walked out.

"Are you sure this is what you want to do, Bobbie?" Shade's voice was low and gentle.

Bobbie couldn't answer. Emotion had crowded so tightly into her chest and throat that she couldn't have spoken if her life depended on it.

"Help...me." The words gurgled out of Perry.

The weight of silence pushed the air from the room.

Bobbie's gaze swung to Holt's.

When no one moved, the sergeant looked from Bauer to Shade. "We'll wait outside."

Bauer gave Bobbie a nod and filed out the door behind Holt. Shade held Bobbie's gaze a moment longer before he followed.

When the door closed her body started to tremble and she dropped to her knees.

Perry's gaze shifted to her. A pool of the blackest crimson had formed beneath him now. It wouldn't be long.

Clutching the Glock with both hands, she waited without saying a word until his eyes ceased to blink and his chest no longer rose and fell.

There was nothing to say.

Her story was finished. The monster was dead, and she was still alive.

Thirty-Nine

"Yes," Ted agreed as he unfastened his seat belt. "Your team did an outstanding job, Dorey."

"Are you still at the office? I was thinking we might celebrate."

Ted stared at the building in front of him. "I have something to do first. I'll call you when I'm finished here."

"Bobbie's okay, isn't she? I dropped by to see her this afternoon and she seemed to be doing all right. We talked about her continuing the counseling and she understands it would be for the best."

"I believe she will finally be able to begin to heal now." Ted prayed the little girl, Darla, would in time be able to forget the horrors she had witnessed, as well. Thank God she was unharmed physically. LeDoux had been treated for his injuries and released. He had been all too ready to return to Virginia.

Gaylon Perry was dead, and that was damned good news. Despite her cooperative attitude, Ted had insisted Bobbie take some more time off work. She wasn't happy about it but she hadn't protested as much as he'd expected.

"I'll see you around eight." Ted ended the call before Dorey could ask anything else.

He tossed the cell onto the passenger seat and sat a while longer. More than half an hour had elapsed since he'd pulled into the parking lot. The truth was, visiting his wife had grown harder and harder. He closed his eyes. But it was wrong to pretend she no longer existed. With all that was going on he hadn't visited her on Sunday. He needed to make up for that missed visit.

But it hurt so much to walk into her room and know that she likely would not recognize him. She rarely even spoke anymore. She was in the final stage now. There was no way to know how much time she had left. Whether or not she recognized him, he owed it to her after nearly forty years of marriage to show up.

"Stop being a coward," he growled as he climbed out of the car.

The woman inside this facility—the woman who had shared most of his life with him—deserved better.

Ted squared his shoulders and entered the building. He smiled and chatted with the receptionist as he signed in. Then he took the elevator to the second floor and greeted the folks at the nurses' station. When he arrived at his wife's room, she was seated in her wheelchair looking out the window over the parklike grounds that spread across several acres behind the facility.

She was secured in the chair, preventing her from falling and injuring herself. Each room was monitored via audio as well as video around the clock by the nurses' station.

Ted leaned down and pressed a kiss to her cheek. As usual, she didn't respond. Not even a flinch.

He pulled up a chair and sat beside her, pretending to enjoy the view. Then, as he did each time he visited, he told her the story of their life together.

Forty

Tricia rubbed her naked and swollen belly. Lynette sat on the sofa pretending to be caught up in the book she held. She and Tricia had barely spoken for three days now.

Had they made a mistake? Was it not possible for them to enjoy a life together? It seemed unthinkable to Lynette that they could have shared such a wonderful relationship for three years and suddenly now that they were expecting a child everything was wrong.

"I know you're not really reading that book," Tricia announced as she adjusted her position in her favorite chair. "You're just using it so you don't have to talk to me."

Lynette tossed the paperback aside. "What do you want to talk about, Tricia? The way you hate my job or the idea that you're going to be stuck taking care of the baby all the time?"

Tricia glared at her. She had the most beautiful green eyes, and when she was angry, like now, they grew as dark as emeralds. "Aren't they one and the same?"

Lynette shook her head. "Here we go again."

Tricia struggled up from her chair and came over to the sofa, surprising Lynette. She sat down next to her and took Lynette's face in her hands. "Don't you understand that I'm frustrated and angry not because you love your job but because I'm terrified it's going to take you from me." She put Lynette's hand on her belly. "From us."

The tension melted from Lynette and she leaned down and pressed a kiss to her wife's belly. "I've told you again and again." She lifted her gaze to Tricia. "I'm very good at my job. I'm not going to get myself killed and leave you. You have my word on that."

"This coming from the cop who just this week was shot at by a deranged old man?"

Lynette pulled Tricia into her arms. "You're right. I can't promise you I won't be in the line of fire. I guess I can't even promise you that I won't get hurt on the job. There are a lot of crazies out there. But—" she held Tricia close when she would have pulled away "—I can promise you that I will do all within my power to make sure I come home to you and this baby at the end of every shift."

Tricia drew back and searched her face, her eyes. "We need you."

Lynette smiled. "I need you. Both of you."

Tricia kissed her so tenderly that Lynette lost her breath.

Lynette stood and held out her hand. Tricia put her hand in Lynette's and got to her feet. They walked hand in hand to their bedroom.

Taking their time, they undressed each other. Lynette kissed every part of her lover's body. She was so grateful for this woman. So grateful for this child. Never in her life had she felt so blessed, so complete. She would not allow anything or anyone to come between them.

Tricia lay down on the bed, and Lynette joined her.

"We will always be together like this," Lynette promised.

"A family," Tricia confirmed.

"The best family," Lynette agreed.

Then they lost themselves to the sweet pleasure of making love.

Forty-One

Asher picked up the clean cloth and wiped down his Glock once more.

Cleaned and lubricated, he placed the weapon on the towel he had spread across the table. He lit a cigarette, drawing in a deep lungful and then slowly exhaling.

Feeling restless, he got up and walked to the window. His loft wasn't anything to brag about. One big room with a decent-sized bathroom. But the view was killer. The big-ass front window overlooked the Court Square. In fact, he'd been the one to first spot the body Perry had left by the fountain. Then he'd been pissed as hell when that dick LeDoux had chosen Gentry over him for his task force.

Asher went to the counter and reached into the cabinet over the sink for the pint of JD he'd stashed there. He opened the bottle and downed as much as he could swallow before choking. He gagged, then wiped his mouth. For ten seconds he just stood there with his eyes closed, waiting for the alcohol to hit his bloodstream.

If he drank the whole damned thing, it wouldn't be enough.

He went back to the table and sat down. He stared at the framed photo that sat in the center of the table.

"I miss you so much, Leyla. Why did you have to die on me?"

He'd found her in the tub, the water cold, a half-empty bottle of wine on the floor along with the entirely empty bottle of sleeping pills.

Because he'd been a womanizing ass before he met Leyla, everyone assumed he'd screwed up and done something to hurt her that made her take her life. Not true. She'd found out she had stage-four ovarian cancer, and the doctor had told her the only possible chance of extending her life was to remove her ovaries and undergo chemo. Even then she wasn't likely to live long.

They were planning their wedding, and she'd already stopped taking her birth control pills because they wanted to have a baby as soon as possible.

Her letter said she'd decided to die her way to save her family and him the agony of her slow, painful death from cancer. She'd told him how much she loved him, and then she'd closed with *fuck cancer*.

She'd left a similar letter for her parents and sister.

He downed another mouthful of bourbon.

No matter how much he drank, the pain never really went away. He'd been so damned mad the other day when he'd confronted that old man. For a split second Asher had hoped the old guy would whip around and put that last slug in him. Asher doubted the distraught man would have had the balls to shoot anyone. He'd just wanted to have his say in a way where someone would pay attention.

Asher stared at his Glock. He'd stuck that thing in his mouth a hundred times and he still didn't have the balls.

"Sorry," he said to Leyla. He was too big a coward to be as courageous as she had been. Instead, he folded the towel and sat the Glock on top of it. He fished his cell from his pocket and scrolled through his contacts. He tapped the name of the woman who'd hit on him in that bar the other night. When she answered, he said, "Hey, this is Asher."

She went through the whole spiel of how glad she was he'd called because she'd thought he wasn't going to.

He licked his lips and forced them into a smile. "Well, I've had a hell of a week, and I'm a little drunk. I thought maybe you might pick me up, and we can get to know each other a little better."

"Text me your addy, and I'll be right there," she promised.

"All right. I'll do that now." He ended the call and sent her his address.

Asher downed another swig of JD.

He'd drink a little more and he'd fuck this girl's brains out, and maybe he could forget for a little while how much he hated himself.

Forty-Two

Oakwood Cemetery,
Friday, September 2, 10:00 a.m.

I was dead once.

In every way that mattered. The Storyteller took all that mattered from her. What was the point of living…of breathing?

Come back, Detective Gentry.

But a voice Bobbie still didn't recognize had called her back. She had decided the vague memory she couldn't quite grasp all these months was a dream or one of those near-death experiences. Maybe she would never know what or who had brought her back from that coma where she'd hidden from the desolate life that refused to end…the broken heart that refused to stop beating.

Bobbie placed the small teddy bear on Jamie's grave. Beside him, she'd arranged dahlias on his father's. James had loved dahlias. He said they reminded him of the honeymoon they'd spent in Mexico. She dragged a few fallen leaves away from their headstones. James's parents had owned a family plot in this cemetery for more than a century. She and James never talked about where they should be buried, but this had seemed like the right thing to do.

It was the one step she'd taken that had pleased his parents.

The cemetery was a famous one with lots of big old trees and lovely burial monuments. There were visitors nearly all the time. James would appreciate that part. He'd loved the constant flow of people in the university library where he'd worked since he was a student himself. *There's always someone looking for a good book*, he would say.

"I miss you so much." Tears welled in her eyes. How could she possibly go on without them? Without Newt?

From the day she'd left the hospital for good she had been certain she wouldn't survive the showdown with the Storyteller. She hadn't wanted to survive. Yet here she was. Not once in the past forty or so hours had she felt the urge to do anything about it. Before, she had known without doubt that she wanted to die. How could she possibly live without her husband and her child?

Now, rather than the suffocating certainty that she couldn't go on without them, she felt a growing desire to get through the day—one day at a time.

For me.

Her fingers stilled on the cool grass blanketing the ground. A tiny part of her was ashamed of the selfish feeling, but in her heart she knew the people she had loved with every part of her being would want her to go on. They would want her to keep living. They would want her to be happy.

"I will always love you." She pushed the hair from her face and tucked it behind her ears. "I think I'll be okay now."

In truth, she probably owed her survival to Nick Shade. When she'd told Perry about his mother, he'd lost his ability to stay focused. He'd gone off the rails for a few minutes. That momentary lapse had given her a chance to gain the upper hand.

The bastard was in hell now where he belonged. The FBI was on top of his father. He was going down for his crimes, as well. Tomorrow Gwen would be buried. Bobbie's heart ached for the woman who had helped her so much. She planned to make a significant donation to Tara Evans's ongoing leukemia treatments in Gwen's name. It was the least she could do for the devastated family of Carl Evans. Between James's insurance policy and the trust he'd inherited when he turned twenty-five, she could afford to help. James would agree with her decision.

LeDoux and his team had left yesterday. Bobbie would keep his secret, but she wished she could make him see what a mistake that decision was.

He'd have to learn the hard way just as she had.

Today, she would be attending Newt's funeral. The fresh ache in her heart was sharp and crushing. Her team and the chief would be at her side. Something else she'd realized in the past forty hours, she owed it to Newt to pull her life back together. He'd lost his protecting her. She owed him for that sacrifice. Taking the easy way out would be a truly selfish act. In a couple of weeks she would go back to work and be the kind of cop her father was…that Newt was. She would make her uncle Teddy proud.

Bobbie stood. It was time for her to move on. She felt certain it wouldn't be easy some days, but she was prepared for the challenge. Determined to start right now, she squared her shoulders, lifted her chin and walked forward. At the gate she hesitated. She wasn't sure what the future held and, frankly, it was more than a little unsettling.

"I've been looking for you, Detective Gentry."

Shade's voice had her lifting her hand to block the sun so she could see him moving toward her. Her pulse reacted. She hadn't told him she knew his real name or that she was aware who his father was. Mere details. Details that were completely irrelevant to who this man truly was.

"I thought you were gone." The feelings he elicited, desire, need, hope—the ones Perry had stolen from her—welled inside her now.

"I wanted to find you first. To say goodbye."

His words, *find, Detective Gentry*, echoed through her soul. "Wait." She searched his eyes. "It was you." Emotion stole her breath for a moment. "All this time I remembered hearing this voice, but I could never grasp where the words had come from. It was you," she repeated. "When you visited me in the hospital, you made a promise."

Come back, Detective Gentry. I will find him.

She swiped at a tear that managed to slip past her determination not to cry in front of this mysterious man. "Your promise brought me back when I was—" she took a breath "—done with living."

He reached out and traced another tear that managed to escape. The warmth of his touch shimmered through her. "We did it together."

She nodded. He was right. They had. "So what now?" She summoned a smile. "I suppose you're off to catch the next serial killer on your list."

"It's what I do."

For one long moment she could only stare at him. There were so many things she wanted to ask…to say. *No.* He didn't owe her any answers and anything she said right now would likely come out far too needy and emotional.

"What about you?" he asked, breaking the awkward moment. "It's time to take your life back."

"That's the plan." She shrugged. "I'm thinking of getting a dog." She had decided during her run last night to approach the woman down the street about taking D-Boy off her hands.

"Good plan, Detective."

"Yeah."

More of those tense seconds ticked off with them both standing there in the morning sun not knowing exactly what to do or to say next.

"I guess this is goodbye then," she said, her

heart pounding. She extended her hand for a so-long shake.

His fingers curled around hers, and she realized at that instant she couldn't let this end that way. She threw her arms around his neck and hugged him with all her might. "Thank you." He smelled like the sun and the breeze, and she wanted to stay right here in his strong arms for far longer than either of them was prepared to allow.

She drew back first. "Be safe, Nick Shade."

"You, too, Detective." He cupped her face and traced her cheek with his thumb. "You, too."

Bobbie watched him walk away.

When he was gone, she lifted her face to the sun and let go of the darkness.

* * * * *

Watch for the next SHADES OF DEATH,
*A DEEPER GRAVE, coming soon from
Debra Webb and MIRA Books.
Did you miss the shocking prequel?
Be sure to order your copy of
THE BLACKEST CRIMSON
wherever ebooks are sold!*